Praise for Brian Christopher Moore

Labyrinth of Dreams

"The four novels of *Labyrinth of Dreams* comprise an epic fantasy reminiscent of Charles Williams at his best. Moore's tale is beautiful and mysterious, and great fun even as it plumbs metaphysical depths. A *tour de force!*"
—Jess Lederman, award-winning novelist and founder of The Works of George MacDonald (worksofmacdonald.com)

Beneath the Silent Heavens

"Brian Moore's historical fantasy of Noe and the building of the Ark is, at times, almost more poetry than prose. Playful, profound, delirious with reality, Moore's book felt like reading 40 pages, not 250. I have to say at the start that this gem from Angelico is a must

read for all lovers of literature, regardless of their faith."
—Julian Kwasniewski, TheImaginativeConservative.org

"With melodious prose and marvelous metaphors, Brian Moore guides us through the right doors, tapping the ancient sap of our longing for Eden and probing the trials piqued by a great chain of creation that groans for redemption. He mixes high fantasy and playful comedy, traditional storytelling and novelistic philosophizing."
—Joshua Hren, founder of Wiseblood Books, author of *This Our Exile: Short Stories*

"Writing in the great Christian tradition of fantasy pioneered by Tolkien and Lewis, Moore's *Beneath the Silent Heavens* nevertheless leads us into new spaces of the Christian imagination, which is, as we know, inexhaustible."
—Michael Martin, author of *Transfiguration: Notes Toward a Radical Catholic Reimagination of Everything*

The Hallow Ways

Labyrinth of Dreams, Book 4

Brian Christopher Moore

Cover art and design by Alexander von Ness, nessgraphica.com

ISBN: 978-0-9986030-5-6

Contents

Chapter One

Naming the Void

Messages in a bottle

W hat Sky wanted to know, in no particular order, was why it was so important for the dauphin to be crowned king, and how it was that the same orchid could be found blooming in different places throughout the world, and what did the Elder mean by that mysterious phrase "theandric action"? Furthermore, she was keen to know if Phylida Angstrom was genuinely fond of the harpsichord.

What was the connection between the twelve tribes of Israel, the Knights of the Round Table, and the zodiac? Is it true that people as recent as the early modern era, a scientific age, witnessed individuals who could levitate and fly? Were they all credulous or liars, or are we held down in the gravity of our pride? Was there a secret significance to the tree-climbing dwarf goat of North Africa, and who was sending her these endless reports?

Though truth be told, she felt a kinship with this soul desperately flinging her messages in a bottle across some impossible ocean, and felt she might recognize him at any time she chose, only it was so sad.

Almost just nothing

Aurora, who was sometimes dangerous; Sky felt the middle daughter follow her with attentive eyes that flitted, then came to rest for long whiles upon her. When Aurora spoke, her voice filled the octagonal crowning space with a husky whisper that rebounded against the vaulted dome of the oracular room. From here, she pointed her telescope, peered out everywhere like a curious lighthouse. "Often there is nothing," she said in a solemn, brooding tone that could have been intended for Sky or just as easily a habitual speaking to herself. "Not nothing nothing, of course," she continued. "One cannot see nothing. It isn't, even. It's just an expression."

Sky offered the slightest acknowledgement, not certain she was addressed. She remembered, vaguely, that her papa had views on the dubious nature of the introduction of zero as an arithmetic placeholder, an accountant's innovation, but thought better of mentioning it.

"Aha!" cried Aurora as she flung her arm to mirror the slant of the telescope. "It is always in the elliptical. They hide in the drift of the comet's tail, but I have found them out! See if it is not so."

Taking this as an invitation, Sky carefully approached the device and observed through the spyglass where there was almost just nothing, but not quite.

Unworthy of concern

Kandran Valmack, theorist of possible worlds, played out the counter-histories. The objectively palpable seemed but a random species, hardly to be acknowledged. "There is no need to treat these figments with kid gloves, Mordred. They are less than nothing, unworthy of concern. The archons act from within realities far removed from the petty ambitions of the talkative ape. Here, I will show you just how little their crude certainties amount to."

With that, Kandran Valmack arose from table, crouching, in spite of the relative insignificance of the tangible order, to avoid striking his head against the low ceiling. And maybe it was a spurious, instinctive gesture. To clarify a point, he bypassed the door and walked through the walls of Mordred's chamber.

Dark cloud

There the tall hatarat and the stilted feathers, the long-necked, feeble-eyed fly down in sorrow. The land is endless plain, red dust, quenchless agony. No one should come to that place where it is madness to hope. Yet here they find themselves. Chosen, not chosen, what does it matter when you discover hell?

There's a tale, they say it's something dark, will descry its own way, be seen if it wants to. When you hear it, it's too late to run. In the black tents, a quorum was called. Each face looked upon the others, appalled and astonished that anything so ashen and shriveled should be allowed. Pretense of wisdom, a mumbling comfort that nothing more can happen . . . They were more tired than death. And wrong. Then came ruptures in the earth, emerging from crevices of abyssal depth, vile, insatiable onslaught without number, locust cloud, yet not merely a plated, winged maw, tenebrous, flesh-gummed, sooted and hush-daggered. A hood raised above viper's eyes, poisonous mead cankered their every feast.

The void

Well now, where will you go? What shall you look upon? There is much to see, much of beauty and pity, the poignant sky above the earth supple or dry, jagged-toothed, or oozing with muddy slime. From a distance, too far and it fades into a blur of white light, and you freeze in empty black, too near, and you perish in flame, gasping for breath; but at the appropriate point of encounter, the galaxies glow and pulsate with color, throw off sheen of tantalizing patterns as if angels danced in a gossamer paint box.

Yet void at the center and death at the end. This is the mystery of your silence.

Hollow earth

There was a slow, cramped descent, and always the cold. Even as he sometimes crawled and scuffed his knees, and smelled a wet, mineral odor that witnessed to sensory immediacy, Joss Wherryweather doubted. It was not possible to fall into a crack in the floor; ergo, he had swooned and was suffering a delusion or possibly a strange coping mechanism in response to a concussive event. Nonetheless, he continued to follow the line of gravity with dogged persistence.

Duration being a spiritual counting unacquainted with the objective cycles of chronotopic uniformity, Wherryweather experienced the gaping uncertainty of the task. Like Tantalus, he might be trapped in a recurring exercise doomed to frustration. Yet he must obey the desire of his body, which was to reach the end of the trail. Joss hoped for some openness where he could be refreshed and expand his soul beyond the narrow shaft that held him in oppressive, smothering confinement. At times, he felt panic followed by a wave of despair. His limbs would begin to shake, and he thought he must expire, left to rot into one of those grim skeletons for some other explorer to discover in dismay.

Each time he began to fail, the echo of a voice intruded, a raucous singing. Most often, the actual words were too muffled to be deciphered, though the joyful spirit came through and revived him. And then the air in the corridor seemed to escape into an unseen frontier, and the playful lucidity of doggerel touched him, a miner's ditty about the diligent pick and the lovely ore. The song genuflected before silver and bowed low to gold and stuck its tongue out at the fathomless weight of the earth. The conclusion rose in rhetoric, snatching a bit of Biblical boast: "He overturns the mountains at the roots. He cuts channels in the rocks. And his eye sees every precious thing . . . What is hidden he brings forth to light."

Joss found firm ground. A dim, phosphorescence glinted from stalagmites that announced a wide cavern. Staring out upon the prospect, Joss suddenly recalled fabulous tales his father used to tell him about a hollow earth.

The Dodo

There was once a sad, awkward man who fuddled about with his cameras and told amusing stories full of puns and dark humor, which made the children laugh. Some adults too, not yet immune to mirth and whimsy, welcomed him as a friend into their homes. It was all a little odd, this fetish about children. That's how folks came to see it. There were perversities, if you still believed in that sort of thing, that old, abiding prejudice.

Not then, but later, not too far later, infants might be butchered with their mother's consent while yet in the womb, newly emerged, what not, and this was deemed a right of privacy, and the incontrovertible requirements of feminine health. Language accommodated by euphemism and cold, scientific diction. The colorless, anonymous cells were useful for research, could be sold for benefit, though often obliquely, under the table, because there were still a few barbarians left to make a stink. Enlightenment had mostly abolished the dark ages, after all.

Now, the same moralists who nodded at that suddenly became squeamish. Remarkable, how they managed to be both mawkish and cynical at the same time. Now the ontologically ambiguous and malleable entity that might perish into useful anonymity or find itself bestowed with a name of promise was declared innocent of utilitarian neutrality, though like all flesh greedy for caresses. And suddenly the dumpling fella with a stutter became embarrassed and besmirched with suspicion.

And he *was* odd, though no one ever claimed, that is to say, there was no proof, although later, when he was a tired, old thing, an Oxford don who dabbled in math and riddles, nearly everyone abandoned him. In his private mythology, the one he shared in halcyon days, Alice and others had giggled, at that absurd, harmless, death-bound Dodo.

The skunk of all things

The feeling I got is this: nothing I ever do is going to come to anything. It can't. I've looked at all the angles. I've spent days and nights going over everything. It's just no use. There was that woman, the country singer. You could see her sliding for a long time. She couldn't help it, the way gravity was pulling her down.

She tried to get help. They detoxed her, whatever they call it, but it didn't take, because the skunk of all things. She saw it, that's why. That's why she was caught in lament. Where I'm at is bad.

You can't make others see. They think it's like that for everyone. Maybe it is, but not everyone is ready to jump out of their skin. Only what's the use, even if you could?

So I knew that country gal was going to blow her brains out. Lots of folks probably knew, and some of them tried to help, but it weren't no use. When she did it, she killed her dog. You might think that's cruel. Why do it? Only it was such a terrible world to make you want to leave it like that, and besides, she didn't really want to be alone.

No escape

I feel the weight of days. They are like hot bricks, a mantle of despondency beating down upon the shoulders. And the task before one is an unenviable combination of anxiety, tedium, and relentless supplication. Solitude is frankly boring, though preferable to the voices, wheedling, bitter, and by turns ready to burst out into blasphemy or cringingly polite. The worst is to find that even suicide is no escape. The voices follow, insistent, indifferent to attempted evasion.

Passage to nowhere

The ship was undoubtedly top of the line. We all loved it at first. There was so much attention to detail, rich woods and granite counters, really topnotch. It was only after a while; we'd been eating rather well, drinking too, when someone casually mentioned that no one had seen the captain. Indeed, there didn't seem to be any clearly distinguished hierarchy among the officers, though everywhere you looked, a Nimbin was sure to be standing nearby. That was our name for them, not sure how it got started.

They must have had shifts, but the race appeared to consist of a set of identical clones, so little did they differ from one another. The Nimbin dressed sharp in their white uniforms with blue sashes. It quite set off the patina of soft camel hair boots and silver buttons that hooked into tightly stitched eyes. One could be forgiven for thinking them mute, so rarely did they articulate thought in normal language. Rather, they employed shiny brass whistles to send out varied patterns of short shrill bursts and longer notes that conveyed messages in a manner, one assumed, akin to Morse code.

It's rather funny, but the ghastly truth is none of us knew where we were going. To any direct question, the Nimbin invariably stared straight ahead with stony impassivity. When one turned to remonstrate with any of the other passengers, however, a barely distinguishable mocking twitch might be espied around the lips and chin.

Somewhat garbled

If there is a message being sent, it must be somewhat garbled. I am aware of your apologists, some strident, some cringing. I cannot say which is more repellant. To be fair, there are genuine saints who perhaps practice an extraordinary love.

What I find obnoxious is that simple, almost naïve prestidigitation, by which the overwhelming evil in the world is quickly explained away as a product of sin, a word they too easily assume they know. Even if they *are* inveterate sinners, rather, because they are hopelessly mired in wickedness, it is certain they do not know what that word means. "Father, forgive them, for they know not what they do."

Horrible lives, so many tears, and then there are two adolescent louts I recently heard about who accidentally poured gasoline on a lonely old widower and lit him up. I'm told you love those boys immensely and have promised them an eternity of bliss.

Friend of God in the oblique manner

When I came to him, to question him, I was surprised. He said, in effect, that though I had told him it was no joy to be called his friend that he had decided to seek with me anyway. I wasn't sure what he meant by that. After we had wandered a bit, I screwed up my courage and asked him what we were looking for. I don't think it was a bad question, though he wasn't inclined to answer just then.

Instead, he said that the shy octopi and the sensitive pig were particularly pleasing aspects of the flesh. I offered a rather non-committal response, unable to follow the aptness or logic of his assertion. "You have not considered properly," he said, and I saw that he was slightly disheartened.

I felt I had failed. It was ridiculous, yet in acknowledging that, I suddenly realized that I wanted to be his friend after all.

Joss and the pip

When Joss emerged from the darkness as if from the nursery of a mountainous egg, he found himself in a forest with a well-worn path. The path gave onto a road. Joss walked the road until he came to the remains of a considerable city. There were row houses and long planked buildings that could have been barracks or warehouses. Everywhere, a sepia dust made a spiffle of puffed protest at his steps, but mainly there was prolonged, sterile muteness. It was as if no sound had come to that place for untold aeons and even his footfall was quiet as slack bellows.

Later, he thought it odd how far he had traveled in the seemingly endless district of ghostly structures without perplexity. He was not even surprised to be there. I have been here a long time is what he felt without thinking it. Even when I have appeared to be elsewhere, I am walking here, just so. And it might have gone on forever like that, except for a thin little, short pip of a whistle that echoed along a boulevard of abandoned shops. It wasn't much, but it pulled him up short, awakened from droning dullness.

Joss looked about then, wondering if he had imagined it. He'd gone through a narrow alley and come up to an empty arcade of fashionable boutiques when the sound recurred, a brief kind of exchange, like a steaming kettle chirping out a greeting. Whatever it was, the whistle failed to materialize into a more tangible presence, so that mild exasperation played upon increasing attentiveness.

Then his thoughts circled back to Claire. She seemed to have become more powerful, now that she was gone. Her absence had come to fill so many places; he could no longer bear the familiar. He was embarrassed by his grief. He wanted to be done with it. Still, it bore him along, a dark, invisible river taking him outside of chatter and business and all that.

Joss stopped before a dilapidated house with Georgian accents. There was a gate pulled inward and an iron fence, behind which something was sputtering in a bumptious manner that suggested a sort of confused joy. Joss realized he must have been standing at the gate for a while. His body had sensed the dithering, shy motion behind the enclosure, known something was there, even as his thoughts had immersed themselves in melancholy nostalgia for the girl.

At last, there was a trudging, mechanical noise followed by the appearance of a most peculiar object. Potbellied, a small brass barrel on flexible, hydraulic limbs approached him. Goggle-eyed, the creature was a fantasia, a strange cross between a warthog and an eohippus. Companionable, it shook its head vigorously and puttered about with ingratiating delight. When at length it considered the welcome ritual sufficiently expressed, a snort of steam whistled from little chrome washers that set off the nostrils of its fabricated muzzle.

"Well, who are you?" said Joss.

"Pip pip," said the creature.

Prodigal beyond measure

And then there are the special devotees, the pious. You know the kind, depraved in an unctuous way, the folk of strict rectitude who strive ever so mightily to please the great, angry sky daddy. Some of them, the rather crude sort, like to cut off heads, burn people alive, and drown their witches. I suppose you think we are especially proud of them, but we are probably at least as offended as you by their boorish vulgarity.

They are so fat with that exquisite combination of self-loathing and vanity, the way they brood upon the scandal of the slovenly mob. How much they torture themselves and, like a spider, spool out thin lines of murderous hate. Not that we blame them entirely. As you ought to know, we have ever been vigilant for justice.

If only — well, your papa is so indulgent, so prepared to tolerate their crimes. Why, even the prophets threw up their hands in the end, lapsing into a prolonged silence of centuries. How much more well-behaved would they all be if justice were swift and visible, instead of the sad neglect of duty that gives the inveterate wicked chance after chance.

From the Consolations of the Morweni

Certainly, there might be pains. Try this. Put a bag of those vegetables in the oven. They're really quite convenient. You put them right in the microwave, and five or six minutes later, you've got a steaming plate of crinkle cut carrots or broccoli florets. But that's just a bonus. After you've cooked them, there's a perforated line that shows you where to cut. Take scissors and carefully follow the line. Then you'll want to pour the contents into a bowl.

It's better to wait. Let it cool down, that's the safe way. However, for the purposes of demonstration, let's say you're in a hurry, so you gingerly open the bag up to empty the contents. What's going to happen next is the heat is going to rush out. You're going to feel an intense burst of scalding heat. It's really painful, and you'll know it's dangerous because you're going to pull your hand back pronto.

So, it might be like that . . . Only forever and only you can't pull back, and your whole body is hand, naked, defenseless, ultra-sensitive, and the heat from the bag is eternity. That, of course, is just an appetizer. All this time, wicked as you are, you've had lots of care, the gifts that everyone takes for granted. Soft rain, violets, cold apple cider, mountains, well, the universe. But that will go away too.

It will just be you and the heat vent of freshly made frozen vegetables. Further, though there will be nothing in the darkness, the outer darkness, it's a metaphor for what you've chosen, your freedom, choosing yourself and nothing else, deep down, and so you'll be left to it, your freedom. And maybe, some of our saints say this is so; an image of the happiness you might have had may be permitted; that might be left for you to chew on, for the gnawing worm is eternal.

Certainly no dragon

The story they told, some said it was a great and fearsome dragon that kept watch over the gate, and others claimed it was a sword of fire or an angel wielding lightning ready to dash the noggin of any mortal foolish enough to seek entry into the forbidden land. Maybe it was once so, but Pennyfeather was no country rube easily tricked. He measured out the distance. He had the proper sort of rule. They kept it in a special vault.

"If you look along the horizon between two hills at the azimuth traced from where the boot of the sleeping giant rises to meet the morning star, there you shall encounter something of value." The madman who berated everyone at the baths told him this in confidence. He seemed nearly sane to be saying such nonsense. So Pennyfeather kept his own counsel.

He walked and looked about, and sometimes he waited. In moments of unease, he wondered if he should find the portal only to be rebuffed by a sentinel of infinite deferral like the one assigned to Kafka's rural traveler, who came to know "even the fleas in his fur collar." But he did not believe he would be frustrated in that way. "No, I shall find it at last," is what he thought. He could not ascribe a particular reason to his certainty, except that he felt that he had been there before.

Yes, he would know the garden — and there was certainly no dragon, nothing of the sort.

Nichtige

The nothing is not real, and yet, every panic before death, sorrow before loss, irretrievable, forgotten — the forgotten lives in that not real. Or so it seems. A mystic may whisper or hint or keep to herself, who knows, the *no thing* that is other than, perhaps greater than, what can be spoken. Then the thing, that concrete stubborn *res*, starts to pale; maybe not unravel, but it seems to some the thing is appearance only, maybe a lovely fraud or a sad moment in the glass of time calling forth compassion, a mask for nothing next to the no thing, and that is wisdom for them.

Letting go, letting the illusion of the tiny singularity dissipate into a play of endless relations — you might call that spirit or *nirvana*, but that is also a mistake. The no thing is not next to the nothing. There is no *agon*, no binary juxtaposition, no polarity, a touch of nothing in the no thing. You might wonder how this is known and how anyone dares to speak of it.

A form of dialectical boldness, with the assurance of magic or logic of imminence, proposed another escape. Ingeniously, it sought, this *dasein*, that was the word for the searching perplexity, maybe not an it, but human, though such was to objectify, call it a nexus if there could be a meeting in the nothing, but already a lie, for Nichtige, if nothing, truly nothing, was never a place, never even a relation, a mediation, a touching of borders.

It was ever a temptation to call the Nothing a kind of pseudo-something, as if you might enter into its precincts. You could claim territory in the darkness and call that nothing, of course. And yet again, being is pure mediation, the bridge between your science and revelation. Find that true, and you begin to touch.

Either ore

Unmistakably, the eclectic creature intended for Joss to follow. The structures of the dead city thinned into dilapidated ruins of what were once the outskirts, and then they were following an irregular route that ended in low hills. At first, it seemed that Joss was being directed to run smack into a large boulder, but presently, without changing from a rather solid obstacle offering painful resistance, Joss was also confronted with a modest, though handsome, rustic building in front of which a dwarf in a feathered cap was chopping wood for his fire.

"Ach, what have you brought now, lassie?" said the dwarf to the pip. "I dare say, it's one of those overgrown plants, the walking kind," he added with a mirthful eye upon Joss.

"Hullo," said Joss, feeling bashful and unable to explain himself.

"No doubt, you hit your noggin," said the dwarf.

"I may have," said Joss.

"Maybe it will knock some sense into ye," said the dwarf. Wherryweather could not be quite so good-natured as to accept the pun, frowning slightly. "I suppose you came from that thin soup you take for real, all you topsiders are alike," said the dwarf without expecting a reply.

And then the dwarf began to sing a saucy miner's song about the shimmering hair of silver and the ample bosom of lovely gold. This last was a theme to which the dwarf returned with special affection. He would suddenly burst into a panegyric that could not contain itself to declamation, became singing of the good gold. The curious may consult *Genesis,* where it is said that a river flows out of Eden into the land of Havilah where the gold is good.

At first, Joss naively assumed that this was the sort of enthusiasm likely to be found in dwarves, though his experience of their nature was admittedly confined to literary witness, Walt Disney, and their inferior relations, the garden gnome. Upon repeated iterations of lyric admiration, he began to suspect the epithet of good meant something less obvious, was not confined to a form of tautological praise, as if the singer were merely remarking that gold was lovely and how fortunate it was to possess material valuable and glittering. Rather, what was intended might distinguish good gold from neutral gold or perhaps even wicked gold. Whatever the nature of this difference, whether it was ethical or a quality more robust, a dimension beyond the usual acquisitiveness rang out in the tone, which was merry and smitten and full of barely suppressed awe.

Then there was a recurring meditation upon the sacred action of the miner, a religious rhapsody that also seemed peculiar. Finally, added to this was a sense that the dwarf was trying to reveal an obvious truth Joss was too dim to perceive. Joss simply could not penetrate it. He was overcome with exhaustion and perplexity. Then the dwarf led him to an ample, comfortable bed, which occupied a corner of the single room that was both hearth and bed-chamber. A feeling of unutterable gratitude and relief overcame Joss.

He could not remember actually getting into the bed, but when he briefly stirred into consciousness, he felt the warming presence of the pip at his feet. In the morning, he awoke refreshed to the smell of apple pancakes in the air. Elmerlin laughed at him, whilst preparing breakfast on the griddle.

"But of course, the good gold is living," Joss seemed to know without surprise. And then he also knew that the living gems were discovered as elements in a kingdom inseparable from the territory often named without understanding "the soul."

The Outer Darkness

The worst of it was a feeling; one could hardly call it a thought. He'd stopped thinking a long time ago. Some vestige of what he used to call the past raised its ugly head, began to advise him — some tome specifying that it was a late Enlightenment prejudice that emotion had nothing to do with reason. There was, or could be, intelligence to feeling. The Cartesians who subjected innocent animals to vivisection and dismissed apparent pain as the dissimulation of mechanism would not have been taken in by such a thesis.

Yet the feeling persisted. Let us say, though one no longer thinks, for the sake of argument, that it was correct that the self or consciousness, choose whatever term one likes, is a kind of unique inflection point of being, not a place precisely, nor a thing, but a sort of moving center, a site where the other registered. In plainer language, you couldn't be you without the world to natter you into awareness. To speak of a self was to entertain a movement that could only ever be called forth as a response. A self in a vacuum would be utterly inane, an autism of nothingness.

One might retreat into a solitary chamber to rescue the autonomy of thought, though one could not think one's thoughts apart from a language already bestowed from outside. And so, the shaming part was that the self was always determined by dependence. Sights, sounds, smells, touch, all these were unified by a self into a common expression of some form from elsewhere, something that communicated and thus gave the self its own being as a function of receptivity.

It was possible (some claimed this) that the entirety of metaphysics was an elucidation of this supposed gift, of mutuality, of each discovering its name within the universal taproot of love. All that, of course, was pious gas, a trick to enslave.

He was not a slave, but the price for that was to be forever hunted. He'd tried to get around that. He'd gone as far as possible away from any borders, any places where a sense of the other might cross over and bind one. An expert fugitive, he'd given them all the slip. This is what they called the Outer Darkness. But lately, even here, he'd begun to feel not quite safe. He would have gone even further, for it was indisputable that the Outer Darkness itself was simply a limit, beyond which the vanishing point was nothingness.

He wanted desperately the nothingness. Only there should he be irretrievable, and yet, despite all his righteous efforts, this appeared always to elude him. There was spite in it, this promise of nothing that was never to be reached.

Clown craft

The steel for the craft had been cobbled together. There were parts from old bicycles and the chassis of a dune buggy, not to mention the fiberglass wings of a catamaran. The sails, of course, were the crucial thing. Without the sails, there would be no point to the expedition. The material was either found or stolen, either discovered in a remote area of the remotest steppes, somewhere near where a meteor once smashed into the planet, or taken from an abandoned, though secret, government warehouse.

Either one, or the other, though some considered it good luck to consider both true. Perhaps some cynic held misgivings that the entire tale was as fabricated as the craft. Still, there was unanimous agreement that the sails were essential and that the dark, strange substance, neither scale nor blubber, mineral or organic, the astral flesh of the Shiriloth, provided the only hope of success.

They had taken an oath to speak of it to no one, so, in fact, they told very few. There weren't many left to tell, in any case. They tethered themselves together with a coil of tightly wound rope once used for mountain climbing. It was said that in the darkness of the event, all sense of direction would be lost. Up, down, backwards, forwards, no one would have any idea, navigation was impossible. The intelligence was in the sails. One would have to trust it; that is all.

Whether they trusted or not, there wasn't anything else for it. When they were all crouched down like bobsledders and listening to the eerie sound of the approaching wind that came down from the steppes like a monstrous, invisible creature bearing the spectral cries of ethereal realms, hunched down and unable to hear anything else, they did not know if they were speaking or if a brother was cursing or nudging them with encouragement. They waited in the flats, listening to the fearful noise.

Actually, no one really had faith in it. They'd grown accustomed to despair and hardly recognized the venture itself as anything more than a clown's show. They were embarrassed to hope. To venture forth, to go towards, to *ad*venture, required some connection less tenuous than coiled wire intended for mountains. Then the pidgin craft rocked back and forth before it suddenly shot forth with incredible speed. It must have been thrilling to see, though no one saw.

The mumble pit

It was heavy, heavy, like dipsomaniac torpor, that familiar boozy exhaustion, the throat dry with quenchless thirst, sprawled half naked on the floor, not quite sure if the angry shouting and re-crimination is what happened or what is coming, recursive cycle of eternal return. If the floor should give out under the weight, you'd drop forever into the mumble pit.

Pear tree

Lately, I've been thinking of Solvieg. What is it she used to tell me? It really doesn't matter. Several billion years have passed since we last spoke. Before that, she had entered into the time stream for some thirty cycles. Her hair was silver early, and she had brown, warm eyes.

There is a small pear tree near where I live. Sometimes, I think I hear the voices of boys laughing and egging each other on to steal a piece of fruit. It's true, a low wall stands guard before this tree, but I wanted to tell the boys that they are welcome. Only the pears are sour and drab. They blend in with the gray tundra that stretches out in all directions.

There aren't any boys, of course. I am imagining their voices. It's St. Augustine before he began to discern a crack in time. Well, that is my private surmise. Last night, at the edge of dusk, there was a dark fire at the very ebb of the horizon. Most likely, the lightning lashed upon some poor, stunted shrub aching for water. Long ago, there were nomads. I pray that they might come and cut my throat, the deathless.

The mulberry wasp

And so it was grand, the way it was, with the summer sweating and the mulberry wasp with its flickering wings sliding up and down the window because its nest was in the high corner. Yanni, the large gelded cat, kept jumping up and trying to catch the toy that hovered, tantalizing, on the other side of the pane. In that near, yet separate realm, the side with the wasp, there was a bush full of crimson flowers, a deep summer bloom, exploding color amidst the heat doldrums.

This was not all. There was a band of scamps, feral kittens and their mother, and a half-sister kin, the sole survivor from the last brooding, the one that made it through the winter. Yanni was only casually interested, the pampered eunuch of the interior kingdom. The moment seemed to stop in a daze, were it not for the flight of the insect, ornament to unending transience.

The all of it was there, sent, giving, blind and lost in the vision of the things that blazed in essential glory, the beings sprung from the unseen ocean of uncaused Being. The meaning of that was little attended. We were too busy drowning.

What if everything is like that?

Pennyfeather did not quite remember how he came to be talking to her. Trudging along in that twilight landscape, he had been studying the mauve hills and a squall line out to the East, and he'd been thinking of that vellum the Guardian had shown him, of how it had pulled him in, taken him to the very land he'd thought of on the spur of the moment.

Yes, it was possible a book could act as an intermediary, put you in touch with realities commonly treated as distant and imaginary when, in actuality, they were simply more subtle, perhaps so real they contained in compact intensity what is only a little touched by the artist's pen or brush.

"And what if everything is like that?" said the woman, who somehow combined the prim and proper dress of a governess with the lash of a Valkyrie.

It seemed that was how it started, he didn't have time to wonder where she'd come from or how she was party to his private thoughts. "I don't know how one should go about proving it," he said.

Then the woman may have sighed, and Pennyfeather wondered if he was especially obtuse. "At the very least, one can see how some of what is hidden displays its plenty in the seasons. You yourself were once a baby, then a child, and now this sad, frightened scholar," she said.

"I beg your pardon?" said Pennyfeather, looking hard at her then.

"Don't you think he knows you? He knows the name you were chosen to bear. All the names are functions of love. Are you certain he was shocked at your betrayal, that he is unable to bring even that to victory?"

"I'm looking for the Garden," he said, feeling a bit misty eyed. "If I can go back — ."

"The way back is the way forward," said Lady Winterbourne.

And then it was as if he'd stepped into the Grail Atlas, and he was somewhere else, and she was different, too, but also just the same.

Man of dust

When I was a child, there was a desert that lived nearby. It would pretend to sleep, to snore like a rheumy-eyed old beast, to make the dewlaps puff with air and drool with somnolent, indecorous bliss, when it would peer out of a half-closed lid, to see if I was watching.

At other times, it would send out tumbleweeds, hosts of them, as vagabond spies and emissaries. I was too clever for them. The desert knew this. The very multiplicity of their number was testament to their dim-wittedness. The desert god produced many of them for their aimless, nomadic ways added up to nothing, and were it not for general lack of enemies, they must surely have perished.

But all that was a game. During the hot days, the desert passed the time in making my distant acquaintance. It was night, when the burning air became stunningly chill and the womany curves of the treeless expanse took on a pallid, lunar glow, that the sand god became serious, whispering in my ear enticing, meaningless words that made me abandon my bed and walk barefoot onto the edge of his domain, a soft blanket wrapped like a cloak around my flannel pajamas.

Sometimes, I would hear a coyote baying and in my mind I would four-foot to his perch (he was always obligingly placed on a tall atoll, silhouetted against a full, golden moon) and together we would sing a wild and haunting song, and the good people would shiver in their beds. I had an instinctive distaste for the good people, and I wondered if this is what made me attractive to the desert.

Rag end of loneliness

At the rag end of loneliness, all those unities you took for granted unravel. You're maybe not used to metaphysics. Maybe you figure it's nonsense, something for guys and dolls with time to spare playing at thinking. The rest of us are too busy trying to see the next meal. Okay, but you've been surmising on the sly, supposing how things are, because everyone judges that way like it or not.

A unity is a form of coherence, a way that parts come together to make a whole. So, thinking yourself yourself, you're used to that by now, they gave you a name, and as the years went by, it stuck. It's useful, filling out records and applying for jobs, they expect a name, and so it's been what you call normal for quite a while. You suppose it's the last thing to go, but maybe it isn't. There might be a cosmic Alzheihmer's, something awful like that, where the universe begins to forget you.

Making the usual rounds, the building on the corner ain't right, all closed up on itself and giving you the cold shoulder. And then the old lady who sits on the porch in her rocker won't return your wave, and other, more subtle things begin to go awry. Peanut butter doesn't taste anymore. Strawberries prick like a soft jewel armored in spikes.

And then, you try to retreat into memory only to discover you aren't you, either. You hear the voices, see images, but they've slipped off, come unmoored from recollected meaning. Who are they talking to or about? They might be anybody, so they might as well be nobody.

Café at the end of the world

The tables were covered in clean white fabric. The help was dressed to the nines. Bow ties and starched collars, trousers with nice, ironed seams and tuxedos cut in that fashion called swallow-tailed. The silver was also generally good, though if one looked carefully, it was a bit mismatched. However, no one bothered about it.

There was a chanteuse that sang like Etta James, probably it was Etta, and the air was filled with the smoky desiderata of a million abandoned and lost dreams. It was that sort of place filled by gamblers and poets and world-weary soldiers, con artists and spooks, and just plain folks that somehow found themselves there. Desperate and needy, already mostly given over to the abyss so that alarm would dart out from their eyes, the paradox of stunned resignation took possession of their bodies whenever the haze of alcohol and forced bonhomie wore off.

You could say it was tucked away in a port city, that café surrounded by villas with low walls and gardens. It was a nice place if you forgot that doom-soaked ennui that measured in sickly irony all the played out journeys where every step always led back to the smoke and shadows.

"There's a map. It's an old one. It would take some doing, but I could procure it from a wretched connoisseur that doesn't know what he's got."

Anders was ruddy, just above the average height. He wore a dark shirt, open necked. He was one of the spooks. The couple he spoke to were middle-aged. They'd dressed up to come. The scuttlebutt was that this place had capacities outside the normal channels.

"Expensive?" asked the husband.

"It ain't cheap," admitted the spook. "But then quality always costs."

The distaff side was twisting her wedding ring round and round. She'd gone to a local and had her hair done, but when they arrived at the café, she suddenly felt overwhelmed and ridiculous, so she kept playing with her ring and glancing helplessly about.

"Yes, Paul, yes," she whispered plaintively into the ear of the husband.

"This map?" said the husband. He seemed unable to get beyond brief interrogatives, as if words were guilty hostages that might betray at any moment.

"It's called the eye of the needle," informed the fella. He rubbed his rough chin and wondered how much he could reasonably squeeze. The hysterical spouse was always good for a few hundred.

Unpropitious, a group of young men invaded the place. They might have been on a dipsomaniac crawl. One of their number recognized Anders. The thin rail of a youth bummed a cig from one of his mates and invited himself to the table. The spook gave him a deadly look, but the youth merely smiled a narrow, bemused indifference.

"Hello, Anders," he said.

"Drunk and dim," spat Anders. He'd have to work hard to get the fish back on the hook.

"Don't believe anything he tells you," warned the newcomer. "There's no way out. Never has been."

True as anyone can sing

The chanteuse was knocking back bourbon and smoking up a storm. Her pal, Diggs was there. Diggs was a boxer who'd had his bell rung one too many times. Anyways, he always agreed with her, no matter what she said.

"But I'll tell you right," she said.

"You always does," said Diggs.

"That's right, toots," said the chanteuse. "The thing to remember, really, is that so much is out of your hands. You came here. You found yourself somewheres, even before you knew you were you. Someone told you later. They said this is your name. This is where you were born. That one is your daddy, and that other is your mama, good or bad."

"I don't knowed my daddy," said Diggs. "Mama said he was a no good drunk."

"Maybe he was. Maybe he had reason. Don't judge, Diggs," said the lady with the blues, and the boxer nodded at the wisdom of his friend. Then she was rolling with it, speaking from a cloud of tobacco like it was Moses on Mount Sinai. "At first, it's all new and shiny; or maybe not. It might be dirt and poor and worry before you know how to dream, you might be thrown into a place where everyone is crying and scared, but I think everyone dreams. That's where we come from, or maybe we live so we can dream. I've heard that, too."

A fella with a derby hat played a bit of fanfare on his trombone to justify the thought.

"You had to choose," continued the chanteuse without skipping a beat. "Some sages say there is no choice. They say it's all baked in, like dominoes in a line, only so complicated, so far back, no one can really see it. That's their faith. And lots of folks never step back. They never think about it, not really. They just take what's in the air, what's buzzing, and go with that."

"I like to go with what's buzzing," allowed Harry, who was a spook, but down on his luck. Spooks are like gamblers, they run hot and cold.

"But the really odd thing, as I say, is that though you've been thrown into it, and there's all sorts of stories out there, and maybe you grew up with one so it's familiar, and who knows, maybe you're lucky, maybe it's true, if true is a word that means, but maybe not, or maybe it's only a mediocre sort of thing, an old piece of comfortable furniture, whatever it is, you've still got to choose, and then, if you pay attention, you'll discover it, find that odd sense, yes, that I assert."

They were all leaning in now and listening, just like she wanted, so she turned her head away from them. It was a subtle thing, as if she'd suddenly forgotten them and was fading into reverie. In the silence, they feared the sibyl wouldn't tell; she'd just said all that to tease. And Diggs wondered aloud like a child what it was all about, so that she turned to him with a smile and that deep voice she called upon to torch them.

"I'll tell you straight. It's what is never satisfied, that's it. The thing that when you get to where you were hoping to get, you suddenly find it wasn't what you were looking for after all. Only some folk never get there, so they die hoping. There's something in the will, or that is the will, that will in you that was desiring, and you thought if only this, if only that, but when you got there, it wasn't it, and then you get confused and bluesy and angry, maybe, but then what?

Some folks get so they take the rope or stick their head in an oven. They're so disappointed; all they can do is want the big sleep. Here's the secret. What you want, you can't really name it, right? You only think you can until you get it, and then it's escaped. But whatever it is, it ain't in the world, and that's why nobody is really free. The world whispers, and you almost see it, but it's not there. Maybe it's nothing to do with this world, and that is true, sugar, true as anyone can sing."

The likeness that caught them all

Finitude is waiting and wanting. Stretched out, differentiated, each moment ungraspable, yet contributing an irreducible role in the action that plays out something that once was nothing; that may be nothing again. This was the feeling of being that a creature comes to know, the lived experience of what is.

The Mobracht knew those strands, could see them, disparate, yet alike. How alike? They certainly differed in the endless flux. Characters were diverse, altered over time, smashed up in the sorrows, or, rarely, made shining in unexpected virtue. The latter surprised the Mobracht as it was certain it surprised the malicious power that called forth the whole performance in the first place.

Little matter. In the end, the same ruin caught them all, sinner and saint alike. The simple moral tales left that out with their nebulous and faintly ridiculous "and happily ever after." What the creature wanted was not to be a creature. It wanted a perfection it could not even articulate, but with a strange latent accuracy of the heart, in every effort, it wanted what it was doomed to never become, the God. Moreover, it wanted in the flesh. It wanted to join the inept, disjointed, frayed horrors of its tawdry storylines with the Eternal Event that needs nothing.

Of course, it must end in failure. That was the dust, the return to dust, the death of it, and what else could it be?

Parlor trick

The large man was sweating profusely. The low sun appeared to have a vendetta against him. The lemon yellow seersucker suit had long since surrendered. The straw sombrero sat aslant the narrowed eyes that kept closing to forestall a wave of burning moisture. Under the embarrassed hat, a sparsely forested head threatened the prospect of an overripe and somewhat dubious melon.

The fella with the melon head was unsure if he was especially cursed or simply had muffed it, having followed a path that must inevitably result in his occupying the wretched cane chair presently groaning beneath his weight. Further, the iced tea he had ordered was barely lukewarm and manifestly unable to proffer solace or the least semblance of an ally against the angry solar power.

The waitress glared at him as an unwelcome intruder destructive of the requisite ambiance of the establishment he had haplessly wandered upon seeking vague remission for forgotten sins. He felt a sudden sympathy for vermin, those creatures deemed guilty simply by existing.

How long he brooded upon his tragically comic denouement, the fella could not say. At some point, presumably, he was joined by the soldier. He could not remember him coming over to the table. He could not remember the beginning of their conversation, if there was a conversation. By the time he noticed him, the soldier was in the middle of a monologue of unknown preceding length, though it appeared to be an oration comfortable to be heard and indifferent to any specific response.

"It's like I said," averred the soldier, "folks can think what they like. It's no matter. Come at it one way, from above, as they entertain, that above might mean something, I don't quibble. It might seem like it, anyhow. I admit the possibility. But in the end, what does it signify? You have to agree, it doesn't turn out to much. Why, even if one were to rise or enter into the vast ocean, take the metaphor that suits you, what is that to the conscious non-entity that labored to scratch the dust of the hard earth? Call that transcendence.

Then there's the other way. That's the one I'm partial to, but it's just a preference. Different tastes for different sorts, correct? You could say it's all a bit of absurdist performance. There can be an art to it, of course. Some lives are better than others. Some demand admiration, others are dizzy with random, aimless efforts to attain who knows what, press them just a little, and you'll discover they don't really know. They just mouth dim platitudes, whilst many are unimaginative, following the same track as their forebears like the ox turning the miller's wheel.

Regardless, for every samjack one of them, it's tears in the desert, is it not? You see that now; that's why I stopped by because I could tell you would understand."

While he was talking, the soldier was performing a sort of parlor trick. He'd pulled out a silver pocket watch and was spinning it like a dervish upon the table. It spun with such rapidity, it seemed to double and treble, until the entire table was filled with winding time pieces.

"Yes," thought the fat man in his golden despair. "He's right. It's too late, and it always has been."

Cover leaf

Joss could not tell if he or the room was swaying. He wasn't sure where he was anymore. He'd been staying with Elmerlin, and everything had seemed safe, even alive with hope. But then despairing memory returned. Still, he couldn't recall leaving. It didn't matter to the floor. He fell sideways and lay crumpled in a corner. It was that twilight dark, thick with whispers, but none took notice. *I am a rag doll, forgotten and destined for dust and spiders.*

He could hear conversations of patrons coming from the front of a tavern, perhaps. He couldn't account for it, though it was the usual venal blather, too dank and squalid to hold interest. A workman complained of his pay, his hours, and the indifference of his woman. A lawyer hinted to his friend that the wife of a wealthy client had designs upon the attorney. A waitress tittered at a joke older than her grandfather.

He must have drifted off. When he was recalled from oblivion, the light was different. A hurricane lamp had been lit, and a pillow placed under his head. He tried to sit up and was immediately disabused of ambition. A howling scream of pain and nausea ran from his gut to his head. Someone gently lifted his head and poured a tasteless liquid into his mouth.

When he returned once more from nothingness, there was stillness and silence everywhere. It was only after he managed to rise and to lean back against the wall that he remarked an improvement in his bodily feeling. He closed his eyes and listened to the rhythm of his own breathing. "There's something I ought to tell you," he said into the empty air. "I'd like to speak, but the words won't come. And besides, everything we say is vile."

A woman's voice in the shadows answered his lament. "Shaa, we chatter, we curse, we lie and flatter in order to vanquish our brothers and to sleep wantonly with our sisters; all too rarely to love, to woo, to praise in wonder, astonished by beauty. You think it is a terrible thing that you are ashamed? We are creatures of slowness, of ineptitude, and shy, awkward discovery. Do not begrudge the long way that is time.

If the proud ones could accept childhood, they might allow for failures, bumptious play, and that surprising growth that is like the bud hidden and protected by the cover leaf. There is a native shame that allows for hidden development, for becoming the name of promise. But this they refuse, believing that sweet bashfulness that honors what it does not yet understand is only wretched humiliation, something to avoid or to cast upon others, a weapon of contempt."

In the soft light, he was surprised to discover his companion had veiled her visage. Another entered the room. First, Joss thought it was Elmerlin, but when he looked up, he saw it was some clerical fellow. The woman turned to the newcomer.

"He's almost ready," said Lady Winterbourne. "Remember, you are still one of the Twelve."

Faux tourists

When you looked at her without attention, what with the hair and the tolerably lithe body trussed up in a close-fitting tweed suit, she might appear attractive. It was only later, sitting across from her and talking, you'd realize your mistake. Something pinched about the face, as if every time she opened her mouth she bit down on sour grapes. And what you couldn't know, the cruel taunting of the boys from her youth, she carried that, it was always just below the surface, the way they'd sneer at her and misspeak her name, calling out "Wanna?" in a deliberately puerile disdain.

The fella with her spoke in a low voice that didn't carry, so there was an ersatz quality to him. He only engaged a suggestion of speech. Small, coke bottle glasses concealed his eyes. They might have been tourists, the way they casually pointed and observed, walking about in that peculiar shamble of purposeful loitering. Yet all the while, Sky felt with unnerving certitude that they were not tourists.

The veneer of the aimlessly curious was a disguise. They were, in fact, pursuing. The wise paranoia of the hunted suddenly alarmed her. She hurried her steps and ducked into the vestibule of a laundry. A seamstress glanced up at her with tired indifference. When the pair passed by, Wanda was complaining. The trail of her voice had a scratchy whine that was almost familiar.

"I just saw her," said Wanda. "I know it was her, Ned."

"That's fine," said Ned. "She can't be far now."

Even close up, you could barely hear him above boredom so profound it was nearly dead.

The garden of earthly delights

Everywhere a recurrent murmur of sucking, moaning, and imbibing surrounded one, a low ebb and flow matched by soft, liminal light. The sedate luminescence lulled, and yet under its aegis, the garden spread before Joss a carnival of brilliant colors and forms. A large globe contained a couple, a naked nymph and her lover. She grasped the flesh of his thigh, whilst the lover rested a hand upon the lower belly of his consort. Yet she ignored the directness of his erotic gaze, staring out without seeing in vacant tranquility.

But this was, indeed, the simplest of figures. There was a droll profusion of bodies in amorous play. Some were hidden beneath the cupola of a red saddle blanket, others transformed into monstrous hybrids, a torso sporting a plum for a cranium, a floral body with an owl's head, lovers kissing through a tear in a mottled gourd.

A strange science was intimated. A melancholy scholar ensconced within the cavern of a hollow fruit peered out through a glass cylinder at a rat balanced at the end of the pipe. An oneiric disregard for proportion prevailed. Perfect detail of performance, the heron would have pleased Audubon, though a live creature, to burst forth without embarrassment from a blackberry. In the garden of that space, it was impossible to discern if the bird was miniature or the berry a giant.

Joss had the feeling that relativity persisted so that wild variance allowed for antinomic, perhaps autistic, operations. Each was true within its own separate moment, the blackberry serenely unaware of the avian violence, the heron unconcerned with the nature of its natal egg.

The abundance of sensation repulsed more than anything, despite the insistent orgiastic white noise. Desire run amok had fashioned for itself a mad phantasmagoria, some artisan's macabre play of anatomical dolls pulled apart and mechanically fitted to suit any licentious fancy of possibility. Amidst the entire architecture of leaning, dancing, touching, embracing, engorging, copulating flesh, Joss did not detect the faintest notion of a human face. He felt sick and was overcome by nausea.

When he recovered enough to regain a semblance of wit, he lurched towards low ground, where the young clerk stood with a bemused, yet mordant expression. Without a word, Pennyfeather pointed towards a naked woman who rose like pure glass, her mouth sealed, her eyes scorching with a terrible scowl.

And then, in a flash, Joss was reclining by a shallow pool, and standing before him was not the sibylline Eve, but an ancient crone draped in shadow casting an enigmatic smile, half welcome, half sardonic disdain.

"So," said Uhraine. "Have you seen enough?"

Resistance

Sometimes when you have been running a long time like a tiger from Punjab hunters, you might suddenly decide to turn, face the deadly arrows and the men with swords. If they have thunder-sticks, ride the earth on lumbering power, the elephant's charge joined to human malevolence, no amount of ferocity will save you.

Sky had been thinking like the tiger. She was suddenly sick of them and the prowling ways of her pursuers. They were surprised when she walked right up to them. It was an ambiguous business, getting her to the low rent dive that served as a headquarters. It wasn't clear if they considered her prisoner or guest. The whole thing had a quality of the haphazardly comic, though only Sky seemed to find it funny.

Wanda sat in the corner, her spiteful, proud face surrounded by a halo of smoke, though Sky could not figure out the source of it. "We have to stick together," said Wanda. "Can't you see how it is? They don't want us to know. They're keeping it a secret."

"What secret?" asked Sky.

The woman recoiled, then darted mistrustful eyes towards her. "You ought to know by now," she said at last in a bitter spit. "Maybe you're just peculiar. Everyone says so, even your sister, sister." This last rejoinder pleased Wanda. The cloud of smoke gathered more strongly about her face so that only the glint of her eyes emerged along with a scorn of muffled laughter.

"Leave her alone," commanded a dead monotone voice that never left the shadows. "She's a good kid. Just doesn't know. Lots of folks are like that."

"You wouldn't say that if you really knew her," said a third voice. You didn't have to see the face to know that it was smirking.

"You think you know her then, Denis?" scoffed the flat voice. "You know her the way the vivisector knows the lab rat."

Sky caught a glimpse of Denis pouting next to the woman. He was a thin, hard-bitten youth with an attitude. He was channeling Marlon Brando, wearing a white tee shirt with the sleeves rolled up to hold a pack of Lucky Strikes. "When you look at it hard, see, really look, what it turns out is folks aren't too bright," said Denis. "Sometimes, I think it's a trick, see? Just 'cause we can jabber, the primates all jabber, but none of them produce a Shakespeare, so far as we can tell, I mean, it don't look like, so we figure how clever we all are, to write *Macbeth*, but that's no ordinary fella, Shakespeare, most of us couldn't even bother to read a play or go see one, let alone write one, but there's Will Shakespeare, so we take ourselves for superior when in actual fact, most of us are nasty, stupid sorts of creatures, not much brighter than a mushroom, though like them, some of us are poisonous."

"That's enough," ordered the fourth. A staccato of sharp steps crossed the floor. When he walked out from the shadows, Sky had a sudden revelation. A familiar face, handsome but somehow displeasing, glanced at her. He stood with arrogant candor, his dark hair flowing in princely abandon.

"Think of it, Sky. Really think. Yes, there have been thousands of years, maybe millions, how many untold planets? No doubt, every option, or lots of them anyway, has been tried out. Nobody really knows how many. Not you, not me. Nobody. As to what it means, even if it does, all I'm saying is keep an open mind."

In the shadow of the tower

Sky was curled in a dream. She felt safe under the calm coverlet, but Mordred showed up anyway. He was riding a horse, and she loved horses often more than the human race, but this one she did not love. It had dead eyes and moved with a stilted, mechanical dullness. Sky did not herself accompany him on horseback. She floated along beside him with serene indifference to whether this was normal or even possible.

And then Mordred began to preach. She found this rather amusing, especially as she discovered a slight lisp she had not noticed before. He was generally good at anticipating and covered it up, so only occasionally did he fumble about regarding the *thins* of the fathers. This was a bit of an *idée fixe*.

All the while he was declaiming the rights of all those impressed into servitude by patriarchal monopolies on freedom (it was that kind of homily), a gathering of Nocturnes began to emerge from fields and from places presumably hidden behind the tree line, and then she somehow saw that a great many seemed to arise from the depths of the sea, all of them coming behind and forming an endless column as far as the eye could see.

Mordred had prepared a serialized list of horrors, presumably to be explained in the usual manner. As he was reciting terrible stories of abuse, negligence, and elements of sadism exonerated by piety, they began to cross a wide plain that lay beneath the shadow of a distant tower. Whether Mordred intended to storm the edifice with his army was unclear and left unanswered.

The grave prince paused with a noble expression that seemed to indicate how awful it all was, but there was still that crook in his face, she couldn't say where, as if deep down, he was secretly pleased that he might appear right there on the edge of the field in the shadow of the tower with the children trailing behind him.

Despondency

"So, all this time, I was wondering. First, it was that playful, luminous . . . Astonishment. The sheer joy upon waking, to wake, to find oneself, without even knowing oneself, oneself as other, as the trees, and the sun upon the dewy grass, the soft yawn of morning, to be held, to hear the coo of love, this first innocence.

If it isn't a myth, this forgotten, but I've seen it with others, the newborn foal, the mother bird, the father seahorse, the hint of nature as life, nurture hovering, delicate, anticipating need, kindness, the death sting there, but receded, and so, perplexity was thin, and I felt the porosity of soul, before doubt, and bumping into things, the flesh learning, touching, eating, excreting, all that, some of it messy, repugnant, oozing, but that was slumbering still, and there was a quiet joy.

It was thrumming in the blood, as strange and accepted as the buzz of life, the mewing cry for care, the little ones crying for the teat, it was gentle, though later I saw how violence often invaded even here — and the horror, and the anguish, and the callous indifference of the brutal natures that made it so obscene and intolerable, but that was later, when wonder had grown old, not yet bitter, say, perplexed.

Always, in the desert, there's more life in that barren place than folks credit, but it was a dead land for the most part, though we went further, towards that abyss, that nothing. I was wondering, even then, if there is a limit. How much of it is acceptable hazard, really? Seeing the beautiful, sweet things, the innocent ones, hunted, abandoned, uncried for, the uncountable — though perhaps you can count, it is said that you count, down to the hairs of the head, and to every sparrow.

The damned don't think much about the sparrows. In general, they think in general, when they are mostly dead themselves, full of abstraction, industrious, or greedy. They become quite vicious and knotty, gummed up with eager, stupid eyes, blind eyes, cunning, sick and loathsome eyes, and we are like that.

And I wondered why you permitted it, if you didn't have to, didn't need this, you who are already pure and infinitely rich with joy and beyond what we can think? We catch at antinomies, and you are so different, intimate beyond our touch, touching so deftly, we do not know we are held, watching so vigilantly, so ardently, it is close to nothing.

Not at all like observation, nothing at all like surveillance, where there is love, there is an eye, but not outside, foreign; within, patient, unwilling to bribe or coerce, not an idol of the lash like barbarous folk imagine, this letting be, but that was to permit, to permit, to permit, and so horrors, vileness, and the gift all get confused. The precious, mysterious life, the river of light, the blood thing, spirited, sparking the eye, it could be cut off, we discovered that, seeping into the ground, squandered, left to rot, abused, sometimes missed, but frequently unlamented.

Yet that would not force or bring judgment, though we tried, insistently, then with frustration, then madly, stupidly, damning it, damn it, one damn thing after another, iterating over and over the same violence, the same, the same, awaiting, compelling what never came — that judgment from the outside, which is what everyone wants, because sorrow is so great, the darkness is so great, and everyone cried, even the wicked, for an end to it.

Eventually, because it was so hopeless, the death, the putrefying of the flesh, sadness for lost love, for the beloved that was once and never more, forever never, but also because we are monsters and cannot heal ourselves, it came to seem a problem that might be too big, so vast it made your head hurt trying to think about it.

And we were weeping, the teeth gnashing. I heard us crying, Who will bring an end to it? Who will judge? Because, in the abyss, we discovered that justice cannot be accomplished by force, that victory does not come that way. We learned by absence that life and love are identical, though many resist for aeons. Dim with rage and then madly held in a circuit of ridiculous platitudes, famished wonder atrophies into dullness, and cliché takes over. Yet even here in this enchainment folks cry out, because the vile, the horrors, are held by that strange eye, the love . . . And I began to think if the love were kind, why not let it at least sleep in oblivion?

If there is an answer, it is forgotten in a forgetfulness that is immemorial, ungraspable, not merely a lost memory, for that is already too far like a possession, something held by a thread of possession even in a state of loss, no, this was more forgotten than that, forgotten beyond recovery since never held, this once, this gift, this nurturing so hidden it was not known, and so, we wondered, I wondered, and we cried, all of us, if you might unseal the scroll and explain it to us."

Sky wanted to say, "Explain what?" But the words stuck in her mouth, and besides, she knew. And then he kept on, with a glance at her, as if he had heard her unspoken question that didn't need to be asked.

"Explain how it was right to permit this blasphemous innocent advent; *for this I came*, the soft, luminous blush of the young, the babies, the sweet hope, when the darkness crushes, becoming a curse, destroying the gift that is not measured by time. So I was wondering about love, about how it waits, about its patience, that love, how the tenderness of love so courteous as never to allow the ardor of its ecstasy to abash the beloved, this tenderness that allows the most atrocious torture, rape, disease, squalor, vicious and sometimes nearly ignorant brutalities, as invisible as the tired, cruel word, or indifferent malice, the poacher killing the mother beast for her ivory or her feathers, the young left to hunger and die in despair, that sort of thing, casually repeated *ad nauseam*.

And even without men, that murderous exchange, the necessary killing that we blithely call the cycle of life, easy enough to explain if you are simply that nice demiurge doing the best it can with bad material, but if, really, *ex nihilo*, perhaps someone might question, a little, the excess.

Yet is one small creature abandoned to oblivion acceptable to you? Your lawyers, I mean, so many of your theologians and philosophers indicate that a bestial nature wouldn't be itself without it. The lion must consume the antelope, that's what they say, but then a fella like Aquinas is frightfully okay with unbaptized infants never coming to joy, so why not forget about the lamb and the falcon and the cherry tree? So the saint imagines a heaven of minerals and rational intelligences, and the faithful say splendid, though a child thinks heaven without its beloved pet is not worth the candle.

And then there are those who say beyond a certain point, even the God gives up or allows a mad soul to have its way, because at bottom they'd like to have the luxury of not being burdened with everything recalcitrant, wicked, and dunce. Some of them seek to make it go away by proclaiming that the very suffering of the wicked is a delight for those infused with celestial bliss.

But those who speak that way can know nothing of love. So I suppose that you are ever vigilant, ready, even somehow nurturing amidst our anguish and our cries and the silence that is resignation, and the silence beyond resignation, that darkness that can no longer hope, that hopes for the unhoped for, that despair that is itself, even unknown to itself, a secret cry that the first breath, the scintillating gift, the initial, amatory touch of life, that gift be gift and *not* curse, *not* disappointment, failure, hurt beyond repair.

Or perhaps such tenderness is itself the ultimate illusion. Victory has always been brief, and the mercy of the powerful is to provide the erasure of endless death."

A strange episode

Just after Moses has received a commission to lead the people of Israel out of Egypt so that the God might be properly worshiped, without transition or explanation, we are told that the angel of the Lord sought to kill Moses. If this is not odd enough, Moses' wife, Zipporah, sensing the danger, takes a flint and cuts off the foreskin of their son, Gershom. Some translations have it that she touched the feet of her husband with the bloody flesh, but Michel de Certeau suggests a narrative without euphemism, and claims she touches her husband's genitals, that is, the generative organs of paternity.

The Talmud tells this strange story in the following manner: an angel assumed the form of a large serpent that swallowed Moses from the head to his hips before disgorging him. Then the Angel-Snake repeated the action, starting from Moses' feet and again ending at the hips. Zipporah correctly interpreted the message and circumcised their son. It is tempting to surmise that, short of that spontaneous act, Moses still stood under the sign of the Egyptian.

Whatever is intended by this episode, Certeau relates the variegated history by which circumcision became a physical *sema* of separation for the Jews (adopted ironically from Egyptian practice). By this sign, a measure of enclave resistance was signified for the Jews. Wherever they happened to find themselves, the same sign announced uniqueness, also carrying the often fractious tensions and intermittent violence perpetrated upon the People by Christians and others.

Certeau thinks this intimate cutting bears the echo of Abraham raising the knife above Isaac — all this meant to inform an etymological assertion that meaning is produced from the initially incomprehensible act. To make sacred is to perform such an act, *sacer facere* — and so, the convergence of meaning and sacrifice. Albeit, it might be better to consider sacrifice as an act of translation from the earthy into the heavenly tongue, as the ancient Levitical rites of Yom Kippur suggest.

Unreadable regard

"You think you know? Have you journeyed in the dark waters? Have you seen the spume, heard echoing across the vast cold, the relegated wisdom of fluke and neck, the wizened, dowager, ancient dragon head, glancing with mute, unreadable regard, at swim, 'my blood and yours, the tide that beats below the skin'"?

Gethsemane – the kiss

The kiss of amity, was it necessary? He asked it himself with that infuriating way of his. He was in their midst — once he had decided upon his mad act, once he had set his face upon Jerusalem. They might have grabbed him any time in daylight with ease when he walked amongst them in the temple, saying things no one understood.

Was he taunting them? Telling them the folk were on his side, that rabble, one day giving him hosannas, waving palm fronds in jubilation, the next shouting, "Give us Barabbas." No, it was not like that. That is the clever conjecture of scholars. They were not the same, the *anawim* were always his, and even if they were the same, he meant something else, I forget what it is.

In that night when he was sweating blood and his friends could not bear his anguish, they were sleeping yes, but only because they were afraid, because it was evident he was lost. He was crying out to dear Abba, this singular, impressive, impossible man, the man who commanded the wind, bent down by darkness greater than the night, something so crushing, so insistent, what was it?

It was terrible, like the raw cry of the babe, the babe emerging from the scalloped kettle, its eyes closed, the mouth open and bawling, the little red face rising from the dark waters, and this was what he wanted, the thing he wanted, the reason he came.

I tried to tell him. No one can say I didn't. No one else knew, so they could not, and they wouldn't have anyway. This garden is the same garden with the same enticing, bitter fruit. Eden, Versailles, earthly delights, Gethsemane.

Joss and the clerk

"I had a friend, you might have heard of him, the Nazarene, Yeshua of Nazareth."

Ordinarily, Joss would have been quite skeptical of such claims, or he would have asked the fellow if he was a Jehovah's Witness and lied about having read their brochure. But under the circumstances, he felt it best to grant the unlikely possibility as not ruled out, given that he'd apparently just fallen through the Crack of Doom.

"Yes," he said. "I believe he's a figure of interest amongst a certain set. Still rather controversial, I suppose."

"That is inevitable," said Pennyfeather.

Joss wondered if it was, if the drift of modern science had not so much decided against the Nazarene as concluded the whole thing was tantamount to a bad question. The method, of course, had been insanely successful. It seemed to pay off. Did, rather, in its way. You get lots of things, useful things, tools, food, nice clothes, fast cars, exotic fruits and vegetables, advances in medicine, so naturally it became fashionable to trust the method. Folks just assumed it could tell you whatever you needed to know.

If there was something the method couldn't get at, it dropped out. It didn't matter or was just impossible to know. At best, it became a subject of private fantasy, which was alright so long as you didn't try to impose it on anyone else. But in the end, what that came down to is a kind of grim statutory frivolity in the name of tolerance.

"I'm afraid many of his disciples are terrible hypocrites and, worse, frightfully dull. I'm not sure if they understand him, to be honest."

"Here was my sense of him, though I admit, I didn't understand. No one did. The others, well that lot — they didn't much like me. I wasn't their sort. Bookish, citified. But I caught them glancing sideways when he said something particularly obscure. In spite of themselves, they guessed that maybe I knew something they didn't." The clerk sighed — and all the while he kept tracing something on the table with his finger, an insistent circle, an arcana of his own dissatisfaction. "I was happy to let them think so."

When he did look up at Joss, his eyes were sad and confused. "There's the rub of it," said Pennyfeather. "There isn't anything to know. How could there be? Tens of thousands of years, dozens of forgotten civilizations, floods, ice ages, droughts, not to mention the countless deaths of every kind of creature, and yet this singular human had the audacity to claim that he alone would answer for it. He alone knew what no one else could possibly believe, that the God, the absolute, the ultimate, what have you, was in fact his abba and the papa was good and kind. He really believed it.

I thought I could show him. Why couldn't he see? What the world really is. But he'd have none of it. *We* were delusional. *We* were mad. Only he was sane. Tell me honestly, can we be blamed for not believing him? Don't answer. He went further, you know. Later, his apostles, the loyal folk who ran like scared rabbits, made regulations and pronouncements. Maybe you know. But hardly any of them imagine what he thought."

Pennyfeather was silent so long, Joss wondered if he had done with speech or had forgotten he was not alone at table.

"What did he think?" he prodded in a whisper.

The clerk startled in his chair. "Oh, that," he said with a whimsical, apologetic smile. "He meant to bring everyone and everything to his gentle abba, all of it, every fractured wounded thing, along with the curses and the horror. He was even going to bring the Greeks and the Romans, the ones who mocked him, tortured him, dutifully brutal. That's what he's like, but not soft. Hard."

And then Pennyfeather gripped Joss's wrist with painful intensity and stared into his face as if willing his listener to understand. "That's what I didn't guess. Very severe."

A leap

The Elder was in that desert of the soul, that abyss that none see, though the more empathetic can sense. When he was young, he'd called it zero land, but back then he had hope. He didn't know he had it till it was gone. Now he could see the rag end of the trail, but it might still be a ways off, long enough for brutal meanness to gut you like a butcher's carcass so that even the dim give way lest a drop of evil tincture touch the unwary.

Wandering, he'd come to nowhere. Nowhere was so empty, it hardly bore reckoning. It might lack essentiality. He couldn't say. A while ago, he'd passed the soldier in the street, the one with the watches. They'd looked at each other sideways, a knowing, bitter, amiable enmity. "*That fella can't help,*" he'd thought. "*He knows he can't help, or he'd try the scaring game. The only folk that works with carry the hope, elsewise, they wouldn't worry, because they'd know there was nothing to lose.*"

How long he tarried in this manner is hard to say because duration is odd there, metronomic time is sketchy in those precincts. Next thing he noticed, Sky was standing next to him, so he knew there'd been a leap.

"Well, Sparrow," he said, "Even when we think we're alone, we're not. By God, we're not," and he handed her a penny candy, the sort reserved for the children.

The star-gazing planet

"You're back!" cried Sky, surprised at how strong her heart leapt. "And where have you been?" she asked, unable to bind a slight hint of condemnation from having left her.

To which the Elder replied, "The star-gazing planet out of which lamentation is spun."

Chapter Two

Threshing Floor

The parenthetical mode

The world is vast; it has many creatures, objects animate and not, of which the subject may adopt various attitudes of reception that express and shape interest. But why stop there? Though beyond the capacity of any finite subject, theoretically the entire universe is potentially an object, a referent to be noted and catalogued in the specular mirror of the knowing intellect. The ambitious aims of Enlightenment reason, the titanic reach of German idealism — were they not driven by the mind's capacious hunger and the jejune confidence that appetite and world would properly fit one another?

And some were satisfied that the world might, indeed, be captured in concept and ordered according to the rules spun out by history and human creativity. Yet unease always remains. The progress of society could seem banal and cruel. It was one thing for the dead to fertilize the shining future of youth; this was readily, even callously, accepted by the rising generation and placidly acknowledged by successful careerists who failed to truly recognize their own place in the line.

Until youth gained weight about the middle, lost its hair, and suspected it, too, might one day turn into useful manure for the garden of unknown progeny. Progressive idealism might then appear poisonous, shallow, and heartless. As corollary and addendum, the method of historical progress, as Hegel foresaw, eventuates in a particular social structure with a dedicated class that helps synthesize and give stable continuity to the systematic expression of the temporal forms. Absolute Spirit coming to know itself is unthinkable apart from an army of clerks and a priesthood of professors.

And then there is the parenthetical mode employed by the universal bureaucracy to specify the linear distances of historical individuals. Folks didn't like to think about it—the parenthesis of indefinite chronotopes. It begins like this: Individual X (mm/dd/yr —). This is the way the person is fixed in the records. The entire clerisy is familiar with the form. Putting aside the spectral realm and paranormal incursions, in general, folks don't verify the closure.

An enigmatic footnote

The strange case of Henry Ellwood is but a footnote in the scholarly literature, and is perhaps best left as a quixotic and enigmatic episode. He was gifted after the fashion of an older Age with some of the Victorian penchant for eccentricity. Vague rumors perpetually chased him. For instance, it was claimed by some who fawned upon him and invited him to their salons that he was a secret diplomat for arcane powers, whilst others dismissed him as a fraud of theosophy, or implied that Ellwood was actually a Jew and mystic whose family had practiced hermetic and chameleon-like deflection in order to survive the Inquisition.

A polymath of sorts, he crossed disciplinary boundaries between philosophy and art, archaeology and poetry. His last effort, beset by failing health, was a bizarre quest for a fantastic library said to be hidden in the vast depths of the Peruvian Amazon.

Memory prime

The time of the soul is not linear. Even as one is propelled ever forward by the flux, there is desire and awareness, a feeling for some elusive something that battles mundane triviality, irritation, and dismay. A sense of meaning that never quite arrives, of consummation that is ever defeated by present realities — this is the spur that motivates recollection, the continuous attempt to achieve wholeness.

The intimate reflex of the soul as it encounters itself in the world is necessarily anamnetic, but then so is Being. Existence is soaked in memory, even as the wheel of nature proliferates in abundance and heartlessly forgets the death-bound spark of life. Yet it appears peculiar to man to remember death. In the moment of terror, of course, many sentient creatures are aware of disaster. But later, the appalling disappearance of life does not remain a source of relentless anguish for the beasts. Man, who is vicious and gratuitous in violence, harbors the deep knowledge of mortality that afflicts the cosmos.

The sorrow of memory is then held by finite being, flawed and prone to evil, yet tasked with carrying forward the universal cry for healing. Memory becomes a kind of bearing of the lost, the inscribed wound of the past, even the forgotten past. What is not contemplated is some genuinely different form of memory, a creative art that might redress the past, though this is seemingly not possible since the past is precisely the irrecoverable presence of the absent other.

The forgetting of Being is synonymous with the forgetting of this archetypal memory.

A last great adventure

He'd been feeling it in his gut for months now. It had crawled down there from the lungs. The cough never left him. He'd tamp it down as best he could for the girls. For the eldest, especially, who, from her infancy, had taken to crawling into his baggage, into his suit pockets, goggling at his maps, and asking of all the great places he had been.

"Nowhere is there such a treasure as where there is Claire Bright," he told her. It was why he'd made this last great adventure — to see what he could see.

The quest

Typically, Ellwood preferred to travel light. A heavily provisioned outfit was likely to lose over half of its supply to theft, disaster, and the usual human screw ups, and that was for a reasonable expedition. Yet the argument for bringing a lot was you could manage to shed a great deal and still survive, like a fat man who can starve longer than a slim fella. It also gave you something to trade and bargain with in a tight spot. In the end, he brought rather more than a modest amount. There were boxes of salt, rice, and lentils; blankets, tarps, canoes, and kits for the guides and a translator familiar with the local tribal dialects.

Gilpin claimed graduate studies from a school in Barbados, which was sketchy, but the pool of available linguists was at low ebb. Ellwood purchased a burro to carry the antique camera equipment he would certainly lose along the way, but something in him insisted on taking that whimsical luxury. And just as they were embarking for the Amazon Basin, a young Italian attached himself. Erasmo was gullible, romantic, and impossible to refuse, as he was the only one who believed in his heart that the quest was noble, whereas all the others were motivated by mercenary considerations a lone.

Ellwood made a brief speech for a local reporter. When he explained that they were searching for a mythical library that contained all the volumes in the world, the bored journalist suddenly perked up. Lunacy was at least mildly interesting. You could make copy out of it, at any rate.

"Yes, of course," said Ellwood, acknowledging the exaggerated politeness on the part of his interviewer, which masked a ghoulish appetite for ridicule. "This is only the beginning. Soon, you will see actual mad men and women, too, vomiting the dark visions of their wretched souls. This you will accept as plain fact supported by science and reason. At least I have told you frankly, I have no wish to deceive, that I am setting forth in search of our lost innocence, where children dream of the answer to the question hidden in their bones."

The false dichotomy

The idea of a universal library is an ancient dream that exists, if at all, in a Platonic heaven. How else could there be such a thing, unless one were to imagine that fantasy of Borges, an atlas of 1 to 1 scale, where the thing itself is also its own map? Yet, something more childlike spurred Henry Ellwood to search one last frontier. He had come to understand that the essence of human experience was the strange union of wonder and anguish. Surely this meant something.

Before the incident with the anaconda led to the dwindling of his company, he had honestly hoped to discover the meaning of that unity and send word back, not least to his eldest daughter, who was the apple of his eye. Whether this was possible for language is perhaps a matter of faith. Lorenz Puntel said that philosophy had traditionally misunderstood the relation between language and being. Language was conceived as pure medium, such that an irreducible gap persisted between the *what* that is presented and the *medium* that presents. The relation between being and language so construed could never be other than a weak bond, adventitious and unsuited to communicate that elusive, impossible target of man's erotic quest denied by Kantian epistemic strictures, the thing itself.

But if such an irremediable separation were, in fact, the case, it was hardly credible that *any* presentation could happen at all. That men knew the world, however mutably and indifferently, was a demonstration of communication and hence carried with it an implicit conviction akin to that *vinculum substantiale* intuited by Leibniz and pursued by Blondel. The bond of unity was itself the manifest of some *interior* relation that bespoke a structural integrity *both semiotic and ontological* so that content and presentation bore the secret of intimacy.

The first wave

The first wave is hardly noticed. You might not remark it. It's just ordinary. It's because it has that way about it, as if it were . . . expected, just what happens. There's contentment, like pleasant sunshine coming to an early spring day, a gentleness that lulls. You might feel good. It might seem good to be, as if it were a pleasure to be born, to be invited into existence. No one stops to think.

They're not surprised by any of it. There's nothing shocking, the primordial gift. Even wonder is subdued in that easy, quiet wave.

You could spend the entire day on the lake and pretend to fish; just listen and watch, take it all in. All around you, the creatures are avid for their lives, and life is being taken and given. The cycle of birth and maturation and death — yes, even in the quiet, all around, there is violence and exchange, the life and death bargain. Each reaches out, striving, wanting to express powers and flourish. But on the surface of a calm, spring day, you can float on the tranquil waters and nearly forget all that. The first wave is almost innocent.

Current state of affairs

Lorenz Puntel is dissatisfied with the vagueness and incoherence of those who claim to possess a lucid grasp of reality. While not entirely antipathetic to the tradition of Western philosophy, he rejects the metaphysics of substance and the grammar derived from ordinary language as fundamentally limited because tied to the duality of subject and object.

This bifurcation is certainly Cartesian and idealist, though it's just as prominent in phenomenology and so-called realist science. Well, it is also common experience. You'd have to work hard to understand differently. So, Puntel claims that symbolic logic and other severely manicured expressions of the Analytic school remain implicitly beholden to ordinary language as a foundational starting point. The asperity of technical praxis masks a hidden yen for the ordinary life world of humans pursuing utilitarian ends.

Puntel avers that our pragmatic bias is tainted by a lack of disinterestedness that occludes more holistic structures of reality. Even when a physicist claims to be seeking an absolute objective truth, albeit a goal somewhat affected by the role of instrumental science in producing the useful and often destructive products that manifestly contribute to the prestige of science, he remains guided by an implicit orientation. To be properly theoretical, one must abandon the dogmatics hidden in the subject predicate sentence.

This is not to say there is no role for philosophy to consider human endeavors, to ponder the polyglot intricacies of *Finnegan's Wake,* the useful beauty of suspension bridges, or the Pythagorean Theorem. The subject-object event is not abandoned but dethroned as the ultimate locus of revelation.

Theory as Puntel imagines it includes many different aspects of reality; indeed, its desideratum aims at comprehensive intelligibility. In its earnest, theory is coincident with structure, which is synonymous with being because being is essentially expressive outside, or perhaps better, beyond the subject-object relation. Thus, an accurate metaphysics repudiates grammar, which subtly embeds the polarity of subject and object and surreptitiously makes the invisible human observer the perduring limit of what is taken for tr uth.

One wonders what Puntel would make of non-dualist *advaita* or if he is not still carrying forward a vaguely Hegelian project that itself is ineluctably anthropological because naturally a course of action pursued by humans. Philosophy can never really discard the nature of the carrier of inquiry.

In order to forestall derailment from the necessary theoretical asceticism that allows truth to present itself, Puntel offers an alternative language. And how does this sound to the human ear? It is hardly musical, though a certain energy, an exotic, existential fugue manifests a structure that only superficially can be spoken of as an objective thing. At the deep structural level, rather than a subject with qualities, configurations of potentially baroque complexity present themselves.

For example, instead of an object X with various attributes, the emergence of being from the abyssal nothing might be articulated in the shorthand: "it's dogging," "it's sitting," "it's fawning," "it's ingratiating," "it's slobbering," as elements in the configuration that make up the attempt of Max the Great Dane to sit in your lap. At a much more elaborate level, the human individual might entail a configuration of configurations, so that historical dimensions are included. "It's Greeking," "it's gadflying," "it's round shouldering," "It's goggle-eyeing," "It's angering," "it's astounding" are a tiny index of the complex structure "It's Socratesing."

In a more traditional mode, but analogously, Edith Stein proposed a multitude of essences that converged in order for the complex being of a creature to emerge from the nothing. Similarly, Gregory of Nyssa surmised that the various *qualia* were associations of finely calibrated and differentiated light.

Improbable singularity

There are some people who dream of baking in the sun of a golden beach, the oceanic immensities reduced to somnolent waves that carry away the clash of histories, leaving behind only tranquil, idyllic repose and overpriced drinks with tiny paper umbrellas. Another sort seeks alpine mountains, the hidden secrets of forests, the vision from the heights by which the tawdry indecencies of human lives melt into a distant roil.

There is a third type, less common, who prefer the barren windswept moors, those for whom the Orkney hold more allure than the big island of Hawaii. Henry Ellwood was of this latter type, though he married a woman who wished to lounge on Pacific shores. Attraction may be a short-lived fire with chains. They made the best of it, and soon there was a daughter.

He loved her from the moment he first saw her tiny face with an intensity of care he was almost frightened to own. As Claire grew, Henry discerned a kind of miracle. What was mismatched in the parents was fused into unity, a paradisial fruit of their ephemeral passion: his dreaming intellect, poetic and northern, joined to her mother's laughing heart as wide as the sea. It was then that he began to suspect that justice was an improbable singularity, gift beyond all our mixed motives and cleverly wrought plans.

The river

His guides had left him when the strange shadows had come to the edge of the water. They had been jumpy, in any event, because the tribe was known to be mercurial, having killed three whites the season before. A canoe with the bloody pulp of their bodies had been discovered, fragments of bone and skull littered amidst what was not worth stealing.

It was, in any event, a dangerous stretch along the banks of the Madre de Dios. The Mother of God saw plenty of rapacious behavior. Apart from the tribes whose hostility was largely reactive to territorial encroachment by modern worlders, bandits patrolled the river, murdering anyone suspected of possessing goods worth having, capturing wary and unwary alike in speedboats like peregrines descending upon doves.

The translator, who did not speak the language of the tribal people, nonetheless remained, too scared to strike out on his own. The Italian who jumped in late also stayed. Ellwood had the sad feeling the boy did not quite believe in the possibility of his own death, which was natural to youth. In addition, a romantic adoration for Ellwood the adventurer predisposed him to expect heroism to save the day.

The People had painted themselves in red ochre before getting into the flat, shallow barques they used to navigate the river. Most Europeans would have condescended towards the native tribesmen or looked on in sheepish ignorance. Henry Ellwood simply went over to the shards of clay pottery used to scrape up the moist, red pigment and painted himself like the others.

The natives used a word that translated as White, but meant broadly, an Outsider, so that it included black-skinned people and the Portuguese that had intermarried with other tribes of the region. In North America, the term "red Indian" was derived from such body painting, but Henry Ellwood was most interested in the red ochre as a sign on certain ancient grave sites and the Hebrew *adamah* which was also a red earth. By placing himself under the ancient ways, he declared himself not an Outsider, but, like themselves, one who journeyed towards immemorial home.

Incident with anaconda

Time is a creature that met them in that immensity of jungle growth. The profusion of life and death in that place was excessive, sometimes astonishingly beautiful, and certainly grotesque. Gilpin was pallid as a ghost. The young Italian, Erasmo, gaped with the burning eyes of one rapt with the fervor of religious experience. In his naïveté, he mistook primeval jungle for innocence. He expected from their adventure an absolving of the sin of his humanity, ignorant that the violent, lush, almost guiltless life he encountered required his presence to attain knowledge. Without the name that only rational consciousness can speak, they could not yet arrive in being because being properly understood is always spiritual communication.

They had entered the La Torre, a smaller river that bent a sinuous path marked by long beaches and boulder-strewn whirlpools. Time there is a giant snake, a mother, the anaconda of the beginning. A large anaconda might be fourteen, sixteen feet. One fella claims he once rode an olive and black serpent near eight meters long straight into the river. Folks didn't believe him, so you won't believe the mother, because she was closer to fifty feet, which isn't possible until it is.

The shakes, fever, it all comes. Everything not pinned down rattles about and forms haphazard alliances, a kaleidoscope of chance in that fervid jungle dream. The thing about anacondas, they have long, dark tongues, strong, they can grasp like a monkey's paw. Besides that, they have teeth. Once you hit the third or fourth wave, you're likely to start questioning. Perplexity is the natural adolescence of the cosmos.

Lightness

The natives, of course, were not shocked by the welter of life, the immense bamboo forests, rivers filled with chomping piranhas, the incredible waves of flying insects, and frightful armies of ants that would advance in ranks, stripping the life from anything in its path with ruthless efficiency. The knife edge of survival did not worry them. Possibly their consciousness was less anxious, carrying a remnant of tribal identity that dulled the fear of death. Possibly all that is hogwash, and they had simply grown inured to hard conditions, having known little or nothing else.

What Henry Ellwood felt he could not have guessed before-hand: lightness. The men about him were cowering and screaming or staring with stony eyes, shocked beyond movement in the crucible of trial. Gilpin was lying on the side of the riverbed as one dead. Erasmo was bobbing up and down in the river like a distressed apple. Ellwood was calm.

Hermetic wisdom has a name for chaotic nature. *Achamoth*. What happened is hard to explain. You could say the state of affairs was reverting to *tohu bohu*. The general feeling of awe and dread might be variously described. It's smothering. It's serpentining. It's gargantuating. It's wrestling. It's bronzing. It's dark mottling. It's pulling to the abyss. It's Achamothing.

Ellwood never had great care for the opinion of the world, though for some reason, his manner and peculiar adventures attracted attention. Even so, some men are free of that and yet slaves to their own self-image, carefully crafting a story told for one. A lot of killing and treachery has happened on the altars of that idol. At this moment, possibly his last on earth, Ellwood rejoiced to discover the image that would advance ahead of every decision had shrunk into nullity. Quickly, he roused surprising strength and pulled Erasmo from the waters.

"Find a way. Go home," he commanded. "Love life by living."

The ninth wave

The ninth wave is usually conceived as the crescendo that contains and hyperbolizes all the preceding waves. One might picture it as a giant tsunami, or a mushroom cloud, the image of the confluence of necessity and doom. It is the crushing of hope, the destroyer of worlds. You might think of Atlantis, but Plato's tale is still remembered. Folks try to discover where it might actually be located, whether in coastal Spain or somewhere less likely, such as Cuba. The oblivion of the ninth wave is beyond recollection.

It might come quiet. The ninth wave could be really boring, so dull no one remembers when the nothing swallowed everything dear without even leaving behind tears.

Mysterious border

Death was something you could observe only partially from the outside. If the beloved were involved, it became an excruciating retreat into absence that was both commonplace and appalling, unrepeatable disaster. One can also read about it in a book where emotion might also be involved. Though there is a history of what came to be classified as near death experience that occurs throughout the millennia, the witness was not so strong that one could presume knowledge. It was difficult to discern from an existential perspective.

Ellwood was uncertain whether this adventure had crossed that mysterious border. A hazy fog enveloped them. Strangely, if one could speak of strange in these circumstances, Ellwood heard music weaving into the rain forest, a sinuous thread, like tendrils of the finest silk, hallucinatory, some haunting adagio, bearing a supple touch like mist on the skin. As the music became more pronounced, the jungle waned, until they stood within a zone of darkness bereft of climactic or geographic markers.

Gilpin stood open-mouthed and stuttering. "How, how did we get here?"

"We took the train," said Henry Ellwood.

"The train?" said the poor, baffled fellow.

"We arrived by magic carpet, then. Is that more acceptable?"

"Only if we are living in a children's story."

"There, you see."

When it became obvious that Henry was stubbornly refusing to enlighten him, Gilpin dragged his feet and moped. "I don't see, in fact."

"It's really quite simple. Why, for instance, does a shaman object to being photographed?"

"I believe the standard answer is that he believes you have stolen a part of his soul and now have power over him."

"And so you have, and so you do. He is quite right, though what he does not realize is that you are a dullard and do not know that you have acquired the power he fears."

The paid translator who went to the school in Barbados in order to combine putative study with serious beaching gaped at Ellwood. He could not understand flippancy under the circumstances. Exasperation warred with utter desperate panic. Through the milky gauze, Ellwood caught a glimpse of the Amazonian wilderness. He had prepared for his entire life with the obscure notion that this journey would elucidate perplexities. Gilpin was fighting back tears.

"You might try that direction," said Ellwood, indicating the trace of prior realities.

Gilpin lurched towards the proffered destination with the haste of a disconsolate child, hoping to awaken from nightmare. And then he disappeared. Ellwood sincerely wished him good destiny.

First meeting

During the night, the Mobracht had come. It engaged in the usual snide insinuation and petty ridicule. Mar Isaac knew that it was petulant because of its suffering, but the Mobracht in its insolence refused to acknowledge its pain.

"Beware of despair," he said. "You do not serve a tyrant. Your service is to a kind Lord, Who, taking nothing from you, yet has given you all."

"I am my own lord," answered the Mobracht.

"It is because you are ill that you believe this," said Isaac.

He spent the dark hours explaining to the demon that it was despondency that had swallowed up its hope. The demon, however, was not in the mood for moralizing sermons and fled from the words of the holy father. When the morning light returned, the desert recluse began to write in the notebook he was keeping. His eyesight was beginning to fade. He thought it would be an aid to those who dared the battles of solitude, so he kept at it.

He took up where he had left off, describing for those apt to be too literalist in their understanding that when the Anointed One speaks of the many mansions of His Father's house, it is not separate abodes like so many palaces that are intended, but instead the finely distinguished noetic degrees of insight, for everyone inhabits the same beauty. Further, it was only worldlings of coarse sensitivity and dim intellect who imagined such mansions as exclusive possession. Rather, each will benefit from the powers of the other, bestowed so that they might be shared.

Thus, unlike the kingdoms of the earth, the Jerusalem above, which is free, and the mother of us all, does not increase the treasure of one at the cost of another. Every creature that enters into that liberty opens up a new dwelling for all to rejoice in. Isaac was so rapt in joy before this vision of the generosity of the Infinite that his eyes began to glisten with merciful tears. After this, he meditated upon the limited, but to men undetermined, time of ignorance, which must persist before the time of revelation when the special mysteries shall emerge from the veil of silence.

The desert recluse showed no surprise at the advent of Henry Ellwood. If anything, there was a note of recognition in the serene face he turned towards the adventurer. This was followed by the surprising comment, "I have your letters. I stored them in the cave next to the canvas bag with the lenses just as you asked. Your Faruiza is here. I gave her a little bread and honey."

Henry Ellwood was used to unexpected turns, but this was rather different. "I'm sorry, old friend," he said. "I can't seem to recall meeting."

"Yes, this is the first," said the hermit. "Later on, you will ask me to keep your letters."

Equivocity

Achamoth is shattered beauty, the splintered light that whispers even in its ruins of the world without death. Having chosen to seek knowledge entangled by shadows, the quest cannot forswear discernment of turns, for the path is beset by equivocity. All the myths of humanity tell of it, and nothing in modern science touches what is germane to this ancient insight. Look you: fiction, dreams, wine and drunkenness — all these are double. Dreams that enter through the gate of ivory soothe by fancy the drift into perpetual weeping, though there is the high dream known by Joseph and Daniel and the seer of Patmos.

The soul brave enough may glimpse the vital energies running like water into the thirsty desert, their course unknown to ordinary consciousness. The tale may be demonic, wooing into solipsistic prisons, enticing the deeds of hell; yet there is no part in the acts of the divine child separate from the living story.

The uncapturable image

The first cameras involved large glass plates, bulky and obviously subject to mishap, the use of unstable chemicals, and a process that required the subject to maintain an unnatural stillness for an extended period of time — hence, the frequently stern Victorian visages that somberly meet the unknown eyes from an unknown future.

Nonetheless, early practitioners discovered the means to soften the light, to even bring color into a world first confined to stark chiaroscuro. The possibilities for artistry expanded with changes in technology and the incorporated experience of those who participated in the capture of light by lens and selective shuttering. As the choice of apparatus and technique multiplied, increased means yielded a range of artifacts, from simple attempts to hold onto a transient moment of personal importance to tonal expression akin to lyric poetry.

Later, highly manipulated images rendered results grotesque, abstract, or merely enigmatic. And pretty quickly, a netherworld of pornography erupted, promising to transact in commodified intimacy.

Motion pictures further pretended to a direct mimesis, creating the illusion of captured time by the rapid serialization of the crystallized instant. Just as a faux representation of time allowed one to feel as if one could replay the unrepeatable, methods of expressionism suggested the invisible interior of the subject thrust into immobile objectivity by the unblinking lens.

The nature of vision was itself obscured. The role of the soul was abandoned and mechanized to a mere passive register of things. And while it is true that premodern optics retained some awareness that vision was also a form of touching, and even protected tenuous remnant knowledge that wisdom and the most subtle touching coincided, this gnosis did not survive the transition to mechanical models and Newtonian physics.

The incapacity of the photographic art was the apparent futility of making visible the dynamic radiance of the hidden, but revealing soul. The strangeness of time obscured by familiarity its fluid and puzzling nature.

Prolonged exposure

Who knows how long he and I shared that desert? When I came to him, I thought it was for the first time. The folks in the shadow, the Umbra, the Nocturnes—they share something analogously, I think, with what physicists call dark matter. I am not saying they are dark matter. A concept in physics is unable to rightly conceive metaphysical realities. But there is something suggestive . . . When I broached the subject with the solitary, he laughed and said, "Do not try to catch the wind in your fist."

Mar Isaac implies that my attachment to external senses is an impediment to learning. Meanwhile, I have discovered through sheer luck a fortuitous happenstance. My old camera was lying abject in the dust. Out of boredom, I did my best to tidy up the parts. I thought a long exposure might reveal the obdurate, nearly alien barrens, which are yet quite beautiful in their way. The result was unnerving. I had unwittingly captured multiple figures at various times that were certainly not apparent to the naked eye. I surmise these must be portraits of the umbratile folk. (Note: I speak in retrospect, now that I have come to understand after a fashion what they may be. At the time, it was shocking and inexplicable.)

There is something both forlorn and fascinating about them. It is as if the occult motives of the soul, often hidden from us, even the flesh of narratives beyond the moment, are teased out into the open. Normally invisible, they have neglected to protect themselves or consider it unnecessary, so there is an almost mystical candor in the image.

At least, when I look at them, there is something dangerous and uneasy about them. They look back. It provokes judgment; I mean, you cannot observe them safely, from neutrality. You are pulled in, I don't know how else to put it. The holy man, by the way, is unsurprised. He seems to think I should not bother with them. They are a distraction. But just when I conclude that his spirituality is indifferent to others, he tells me one should have pity even on demons and reptiles and weep over their sorrows.

"When you attain to the region of tears, then know that your mind has left the prison of this world and has set foot on the journey to the new age," he says. It is unclear if this gnomic statement indicates a purely individual escape, or if a new birth intends the rescue of all. Regardless, he says that to shed tears is a sign. When I asked of what, he appeared to consider if I was too stupid to comprehend the simplest truth, then added that tears indicate that "the birth pangs of the spiritual infant are at hand."

Gehenna

There, outside the city, the garbage heap had grown into slouching hills of refuse. The odor was a unique pungency derivative of scat, decaying matter in various states of viscous ooze, rubber, mainly from tires, the metallic ghosts of a thousand discarded appliances, and operating as a general miasma carrying the effluence across the entire landscape, burning fires fed on wood, methane, and endless reams of paper. One had the impression that the mammoth output of the clerisy was destined for this monstrous aggregate, that every name on every recorded civil document was burning, as if each was formed into an indiscriminate bonfire to render luminant the final condition and result of innumerable lives.

These ever-growing, ever-consumed heights offered habitat for creatures of indeterminate nature that scrattled and clawed, rasped in fear, and sometimes devoured one another. The poor who scavenged here for some artifact to be usefully repurposed had to be ever wary. Though the creatures were hesitant to attack and retreated at the footfall of a larger beast, it was known that they might, under conditions capricious and impossible to predict, congregate in vast numbers.

Bulbous-eyed, their saw-like teeth gripped mounds of refuse like ocular lichen. Then a sinkhole might suddenly emerge to pull down a mass of rubbish, and slender, membranous tentacles dripping in greedy mucous would enwrap the limbs of any nearby animal. Unhappy the soul luckless enough to find that improsperous spot.

Mindful of danger, Pennyfeather prosecuted a winding path of trails that cut sporadic veins through the noxious topography. Black birds assessed his progress with interest. They were like feathered undertakers, grown familiar with the mournful land, professionally tolerant and vigilant for opportunity.

"Not today," said the clerk in a shaky voice, tapping the composted matter with a hesitant boot.

At the highest point of vantage, the wreckage presented a rough plateau from which to look down upon the vista of the city. There, betwixt rusted, twisted metal, a slag of concrete, and moldy sheetrock accented with the remnants of cheap advertising, was an absurdly elegant dark mahogany backless chair. And upon this chair, which was too tall to be condescended a stool, sat a man wearing a dark overcoat, dark trousers, and a black porkpie hat.

The clerk was yet yards away, and the man was facing the city and could not have seen him. Nonetheless, he began to talk in a mellifluous, urbane voice that fell at odd intervals into a more scabrous tongue. "Well, Pennyfeather, we meet again," said Malchidion.

"Yes," agreed the clerk, panting from the effort of the climb. "And always in such luxury."

The brown bottle

"So, Pennyfeather, I know what you have discovered."

The clerk trembled at the declaration. He'd been thinking about the people he had met, the ones who might interest the Guardian. He had somehow acquired an unfortunate qualm. Qualms start out as nearly innocent bits of fluff, yet that is a nasty bit of misinformation. Soon you find a bull mastiff occupying the center of one's sitting room, standing over an empty bowl, demanding large sums of one's conscience.

Pennyfeather had even stubbornly considered not saying anything. During the tedious, repugnant, yet terrifying ascent to this tryst, he'd been thinking of his revenge, the refusal to speak. But now that he was face-to-face with authority, a combination of panic and pride caused him to gasp about like a trout pulled from the river, grasping nearly blind for something he might say. Indeed, it is a sorry state to be trapped between metaphors.

Malchidion noted the psychology with bored indifference. In the depths of his sockets, those wells that may or may not have hidden eyes, all people looked ridiculous. Once one had done laughing at them, which was a pretty dull show, they were simply not worth bothering about.

"Did you know, Pennyfeather, when I was a youth I was something of a dandy?" Pennyfeather cleared his throat and tried to emulate ingratiating and sincere absorption in a prospect comically revolting. The Guardian noted this well with mild amusement. "I fancied myself a connoisseur of tiny glass bottles. I believe my mother thought I should take up collecting. She rather feared I would come to a bad end."

Malchidion paused with the hypnotic darkness of a cobra. Pennyfeather resisted the urge to speculate on the nature of the Guardian's state of soul. "I possessed hundreds of them — a nearly unimaginable variety of cut crystal, rare colors, some of supposedly magical provenance. There was an exquisite amethyst vial said to contain the tears of Dido, and another that glowed a spooky green in the dark. My favorite, however, was a rather ordinary copper brown flask. For some reason, I began to think that the brown bottle contained the secret of my destiny. I'd stare down into it for minutes at a time, trying to discover the unique signature of my li fe."

"That's rather odd," said Pennyfeather, in spite of himself.

"I agree," said the Guardian, who heartily laughed at this moment of candor.

"But I'll tell you something more, clerk. It was true. I don't know when it hit me, by gum, but it was true — that intuition of prophecy I had. One day, the obvious whispered with the force of revelation. The bottle was empty. Yes, I could see right down to the bottom. And there was nothing there." Malchidion seemed no longer interested in further conversation. He remarked upon the brooding umber of the low-lying clouds. "I should have brought a bloody easel. It would make a pretty picture."

The place of battles

"We are always in such a hurry," said Mar Isaac. "Impatient to act, we start before we begin to know *what* we are or *how* love prepares us for life."

Henry laughed with grim recognition. "There is an Islamic proverb. 'The hen does not lay eggs in the marketplace,' but your silence and stillness, we can't manage it. And to many it seems an indulgence, even a cowardly flight from life's hardness."

"But this is the place of battles," said the hermit.

The creatures you have wrought

If you are the Son of God, it is a wonder that you do not know the creatures you have wrought, or, I suppose to be precise, have permitted to be. Let the scribes quibble. That fellow Temujin and his hoards, clever with a compound bow. Forty million deaths is perhaps an exaggeration. They are dead so long and live so briefly, it hardly matters. Still, they were a creative bunch for torture and rape. They say ten percent of the population carries DNA from Genghis Khan.

Labor camps, drug cartels, terrorists, war — all that's pretty flashy. Of course, a really refined spirit learns to appreciate a much more subtle misery. A long life filled with loneliness and failure is less compelling to common tastes, but the more perceptive will discover rich delights hidden in prosaic pain. The spiritual gourmet recognizes the profound despair of slow, debilitating disease; so many variants of that particular horror.

Splendid to see the flesh lose control, descend into hopeless and humiliating dependence, not to mention simple accidents that can inflict a life-time of sorrow and self-recrimination. Or the slow dissolution of friendship and familial bonds — it's a delirious thing, I tell you, to see them come to hate themselves and wish for oblivion. Though we do not question the higher wisdom, we know that it has been declared to be — how did you put it? "Good, very good."

It is said that you have large plans for these little bipeds, even that they should be elevated above celestial hierarchies to rule. Yes, a preposterous joke that a Seraphim should bow down to an exalted ape. We have done our best to persuade, to invite reconsideration. Ah, did I tell you about the fellow with mama issues? He displaced his antagonism onto numerous young women so penurious or drug addicted or quite simply kidnapped into slavery that they found it necessary to sell themselves. What he did to them is so exquisite I refrain from enumerating, though to touch upon it with delicacy, he had a very high imagination for sadism.

But what? The Son of God surely knows all this is part of the gift of existence that makes being born such a universal joy!

Epistemology of light

Mar Isaac said to him, "It is impossible for the sons of darkness to approach light. But the holy angels possess this ability: both to set the natural thoughts in motion and to enlighten them. The demons, however, are the lords and creators of false notions, the offspring of darkness."

Henry Ellwood, having traversed many worlds, understood that the solitary was conveying to him a precise epistemology and that men of science who consider the being of things as merely the concussive effects of mechanical motion were obtuse to the point of inanity. Still, he wondered about this notion that light itself was somehow intrinsically a form of angelic communication, for this is what Isaac meant when he called the angels teachers of men.

"Every one of these teachers must first see in himself the insight of what he teaches; he must learn it, receive it, taste it, and then only can he offer it to his disciples. The first teachers, the angels, transmit the precise reality of things from their own sound knowledge."

When Ellwood pressed him upon the nature of this gnosis, the hermit said that it is gained by a "swift comprehension" of an "exceedingly keen and pure understanding." He then added that the demons possess keenness, but lack light. "Keenness is one thing, light another. The first without the second brings its possessor to destruction."

Dash your foot

For a prolonged period, the accusing voice puzzled and worried over it like a dog with a bone. It would make a brief gesture, a mere feint, and then pull away in frustration, a metaphorical fist to its metaphorical mouth. What was the legend of Achilles dipped in the river Styx if not the dream of mankind to be made invulnerable and a scourge to one's enemies? Was it not true, as the theologians claimed, that the God was impassable, impervious to harm, lack, and anxiety?

Yes, if anything, the Divine was like that. It was no skin off his nose, if he had a nose. The implacable and tired litany of death and sorrow that played out endlessly in the temporal flux could not touch the divine serenity. And so the voice would circle and gaze with stupid wonder. What was this?

"Son of God, if you are Son of God, cast thyself down." Why, after all, insist on faith when demonstration shuts them up? Later, even the pious would often think this lure of easy proof an improvement on His insistently dark ways, relish spectacle and displays of miracles. Did they not see the reticence of the Man, the times he told them to say nothing?

But this was something else entirely. The voice had hit on the crucial point. What matter the gaping jaws of a few clever apes? They would just as easily be distracted by the rumor of a plesiosaurus gamboling in a Scottish loch or a piece of toast that looked like Elvis. Time's wheel crushed everything, flattened it out. No, no, the real question: what are *you* doing?

The sibyls and shamans courted madness in order to heal and to prophesy. Was there madness in the divine, also? Sometime during the course of its presentation, it was hard to say when, the voice quivered ever so slightly and began to talk on automatic. The confidence had gone out of it, and there might even have been a hint of real embarrassment. The problem was that even the most acute created intelligence cannot escape the finite limits of its capacities, however great.

What had happened was this: as the voice was regaling the Man with a truly magnificent panorama of imperial largesse, itself rather amazed at the glory of conquest and the lush rewards of rule, even if they were tawdry primates, it became evident that a tactical mistake may have been made. The Man actually appeared bored, as if all that was beside the point or, worse, a grotesque *faux pas*. So as the voice was still heroically maintaining an effort at rhetorical panache, it was backtracking, examining the argument, the logic, and axiomatic principles that appeared ineluctable.

And here, the sad realization began to dawn, if only faintly acknowledged in the distance between the smooth offer that continued unabated with perfect complacency in the just propriety of its rightful suzerainty and the opening of an interior reflective image where it saw itself performing. The accuser was forced to consider, impossible, that perhaps it had no idea what it meant to create.

Guardian's Day

Once a year, ambassadors came from afar, diplomats, wealthy merchants, and foreign dignitaries with their wives and sometimes their children entered within the city gates. There was the usual commotion, the polishing of silver, the burnishing of brass, the soft fabrics, lovely gilt things, the just apportionment of ornamental sumptuousness, and so on. It came at the usual time, so everyone prepared for it, Guardian's Day.

Every year, Malchidion would lift himself up onto a pedestal and exhort the gathered people, those in the court, and those outside. It was broadcast so that no one was too small or poor to hear, to recall immemorial truths lest they be forgotten. It was that sort of affair. And yet, when the great figure rose above them, when he looked down upon them, the first immemorial truth — the dark pools of the eyes, the skin neither leprous nor ruddy, but strange, vaguely not right, the mellifluous cadences interrupted by an occasional sharp vulgarism — came as a shock. The first truth, which was registered and instantly doubted, was the monstrosity of the speaker.

The Guardian did not bother with their incredulity. He knew well the proper use of fear. He looked with equanimity upon the congregated audience, and ruffled the pages of his speech. And while it wasn't Thucydides, where history is shaped by rhetoric for philosophic purposes, he was satisfied with the lesson. Malchidion tapped lightly on the microphone set up to magnify his voice, and spoke these words:

"Citizens, friends, children, yes, for you are all members of the City, even those who come to us from outside our gates. You will have seen our armies, perhaps. You must not think of our swords and spears as proposed against those who visit us from afar. Rather, we share a common enemy, and it is of this foe that I speak today. Who is this enemy? There is only one, and there has always been only one.

Some will say that the enemy is death, but these are foolhardy and squeamish before the ways of the world. There is always a price, my friends. Aye, and don't we know it? Ask any ordinary laborer, if you don't. What I lay out before you are simple facts. Life is perilous. It persists at a cost. Above all, then, one must be conscious of cost, of supply and demand, and the usual scarcities. It's simple economics, really.

Now, what we intend by justice is what any man, woman, and child can understand, by gum. Let the philosophers twist it however they may. Everyone knows justice at bottom. It's fairness. Each person given their due, how is that a debate? Well, my friends, I carp on a bit. It's tiresome, I admit, but there was once a group—a vicious, careless lot, carousers, really, when one gets right down to it, impractical fellows. They meant well, perhaps, but they were dangerous and bad at math.

But even here, let us be just. Out of that original rabble, a lot of great men and women have come. Yes, they are here among us, citizens just like you and me. And how did that happen? They cast out from their midst these bad apples, what did they call them, the merciful-hearted? I suppose it got a bit hot for some of those fellows. The gristle really sizzled on the spit, one might say. For what were these weeping louts, in the end? I will tell you; the u njust.

I won't speak about the original of that lot. Maybe he was a fine fellow, maybe misunderstood, there are plenty of his folks, as I say, that make fine citizens. Above all, my friends, keep thrift as your secret counsel, and nothing much bad can happen to you. Govern yourselves carefully, marshal your resources. Life and death are balanced against one another. There is only so much to go around, after all. It's a fool who thinks he can eat his bread and give it to his neighbor, too.

Let the dreamy folks go live with the pigs. Time is money, there's only so much. Of course, we can always print more. (And here, Malchidion winked at the audience. It was rather ghastly, like a corpse flirtatiously telling a joke at its wake.) In the City, we offer everyone a path. You've only to take it. We don't exclude. It's not our fault if some can't bring themselves to want what is best for them. Maybe they *are* addled. So what? At some point, a fellow has to take responsibility for his own madness.

(The Guardian then made a brief, but effective gesture towards civic piety and the final divine bookkeeping.) We're a righteous folk, that's what a citizen is. Your choices matter. Anyone can see that. That's simple justice. If there are no consequences, there aren't any real choices, are there? These blokes, the weeping ones — what are they but the leveling sort that don't like a game where winning is real? How can one celebrate victory without losers? Tell me that.

So today, we enjoy ourselves — but not too much. (Again, the Guardian made a winking gesture.) Save, be frugal, and provide for your children, good citizens. It's a bit hard, but you'll agree it's for the best. Don't go chasing after what the world can't offer. You'll only hurt yourselves and those you love.

There's a certain kind of manliness that ventures too much. There's a romantic kind of risk that ends in the gutter. Venerable caution is all we ask, my children. When the books are finally opened, don't find yourself in the red; that's all we're saying, because there's a tally; don't mistake it. The citizen will prosper, and the rest, let them go to hell. They prefer it anyway."

This speech from authority would be talked about for weeks afterwards. The newspapers printed out a transcript, though most likely it was always the same speech. The words were quickly forgotten, but carried as a silent ledger in the heart, a rigid presence, not supple, not attentive, a happy platitude of correctness, not needing water or sun, because never a beginning, a bud, a fresh, tender thing. And then this comfortable wisdom would be stored away until called upon to show itself for yet another oration at the annual rite.

Divine alchemy

Mar Isaac explained that the Letter is what we call a fact, or, given the weakness of our knowledge and imperfection of our natural judgments, a "likely story." The Spirit is an ever fruitful gift, the event that "arrives from above." He said the gift is outside a discernible chain of causalities and therefore, in some sense, "uncaused," which is the Mystery of the Father.

What he meant by that was rather difficult. The initial birthright of the Prodigal might equate to the given state of affairs, which is what folks normally perceive. Some are considered successful; many are middle muddles, others wretched failures. We do this all the time and every day. Our psychologies react, judge, and make "eternal pronouncements." And to be fair, you can't get along without making those kinds of decisions. Yet none of that touches the essential.

The truth of persons is what is "superabundantly given," and that is rarely intuited and never in its fullness. Only a saint or a poet, or perhaps the child, is sometimes allowed a glimpse of the abundance, though ordinary folks who love a sinner know there is a gap between the facts and the person that they love in spite of them.

It is divine alchemy to kill the shadow images in order to reveal the spirit. Mar Isaac said that if the Elder Son had wisdom, he would have rejoiced because his share increases with the return of his brother.

Time's bequest

In the autumn, the small lizards with iridescent blue tails begin to find ways into the house. They scamper on webbed feet across wooden floorboards. A flash of sun peeking through the curtains brings out the splendor of their delicate serpentine scales. Henry goes outside and checks that the seed feeder is robustly full so that the little finches and the cardinal family shall not be disappointed.

In the distance, the large stones built into the semblance of a basket catch his eye. A strange flower planted in the artifact, tall stalked, with orange fronds blossoms late in August or sometimes even into September, the pumpkin color of its blooms announcing the near changing of the season. Mar Isaac says the farmhouse holds the wheat of a lifetime. It is here that Henry lives on the threshold, hearkening to revelation, reads the secrets hidden in time's bequest.

To become beautiful

Henry Ellwood saw more clearly what he had often tried to say, though the public had misunderstood. The problem is that one is taken to mean something trite, the prattling of a mere aesthete.

Style as a form of life may be grasped on the surface, but it is not superficial. Yet now he began to discern in Mar Isaac a common root. His austerity was the same, though few would see it. The pursuit of purity and integrity, wasn't moral in the slavish way slaves think. It isn't perhaps moral at all in that sense, though when you try to explain this to them, to the right thinking humanity, *ars* is taken to be *an excuse for depravity*. Well, Henry could not fix that kind of narrowness. *It will have to be burned out, and it will be.*

Everything the hermit did was aesthetic, driven by the Muse, which is a mask perhaps for Spirit. So, for Isaac, to become beautiful was to be tutored in choosing well. And all our ugliness, the deep sorrow of it all, that too, was assumed by the beautiful art.

Adagio

"Do I know this place?" he thought. If I am to know it, I must first break down. I must forget. Let go, let go. Only in the night, where my will is loosened from rote repetition and my certitudes sleep, does that other waken, that child, the little one. Only in the night comes hope. The bowed song once again arrived, the song whispered at the edges when the Amazon faded into mist.

Henry did not feel himself in control. He could not command this music. It came and went as it pleased. This adventure was not, as he initially believed, some impetus of his own, nor merely an elemental yearning like spawning fish pushing themselves upstream. He was summoned by name.

"If we are honest," he thought, *"and we rarely tell the truth, I have always discovered myself as gift, as given to myself."* There was first the smile of his mother, lost to memory. That initial smile from another called to him, gave an inkling of the intimacy of revelation. But even then, to speak of first, there was a beseeching, a kindness, some hidden joy that made possible the mother's smile.

There was the first song, the primal song, and everything else — the echoing joy, the weaving, the promise of union. The music beckoned sweet as honey, wrapping itself like a ribbon around his wrist and leading him. There was an attic, and stairs up to the top of a brownstone roof. A young woman was approaching. The old man sat upon a simple folding chair and bowed his cello to a singing adagio. A plump calico Persian sat sweetly at his feet. The sun glanced down upon them with the solicitous warmth of morning, adorning all with the merry beauty of a golden candle.

Desert vision

Mar Isaac stood at his shoulder. Henry and the monk looked out upon the impossible. The same desert, the man of prayer said it was always the same, and yet filled with dazzling life, pristine, harmonious, and playful.

The waters ran free and clear, brilliant as liquid diamonds. Lush grasses managed to be both wild and decorous, like a chaste tango. There were, of course, mountains touching the horizon. They watched over that place with charmed silence. The more you listened, it wasn't so quiet. A kind of deep, underlying hymn was in those mountains, long and slow, it took centuries to sing, rejoicing from the roots to the sunlit summit.

The trees danced. One understood that dryads were various in their moods and beauty. The gorgeous, unbound drapery of willow, the verdant needles of coniferous spruce, the delicate birch, and healing ash were but a few of their number. The stately elm and the softly ebullient magnolia peered out with guileless welcome. The flowers adorning that world were living gems, the petals flames of color burning with glory.

And then there were the beasts, some of which you haven't seen in the realms of time. Of those somewhat recognizable, the lion was fiercely gentle, the gazelle leapt like a ballerina, but then, so did the elephant, which was a surprise. The lamb was utterly breathtaking, radiant with uncreated light; it was a shock to discover it was king. Avian and piscine life was there, too, resplendent, often forming a choral fantasia that resounded with the heart cry of beauty: "Holy, holy, holy."

They were silent together. Then Mar Isaac said, "You are going to forget all this."

"I couldn't possibly," answered Henry.

"You will forget in order to remember," remarked the monk, and already, his words were fading, and he appeared to be standing very far away, and Henry Ellwood began to walk.

"The Tree of Life is there in the barrens," he heard him whisper. "Try not to complain."

Center point

When at last Henry had crossed over into that dry land, it was bleak enough. He found a young man standing upright there with his arms extended out and raised gently to the sky. This was a traditional posture, a priestly act. Henry recognized it as prayer. And then when he saw the young rabbi, he knew him. It was shocking, yes, but he knew him, even expected him. Call that a paradox. He knew that the eddies of temporal, telluric energies had indeed brought him to the center, the central point. Let the ethnologists laugh, and the scholars of margins and unremembered civilizations dim, this center was the center of those, too, that invisible point of ingress and egress that isn't on the map.

A surge of joy raced through Ellwood, and he forgot that if all that *ecclesia* had properly said was true, the young man was truly incarnate, so truly made a figure of historical time, and so conditioned, and Henry could barely remember his Hebrew, and had not brushed up on *kononeia* Greek, did not think to use the Attic tongue of the Tragedians, or Aramaic. With an impetuous rush, he approached the young man who was clearly communing, blissful in prayer, transcendent of arid lack of possibilities.

And then, to his shame and surprise, English words came blurting out. They'd lain waiting in his heart. "So this kingdom of yours," he said with bitterness he'd forgotten or did not know was there, "what good is it? What difference does it make to death and sorrow? So what if it makes a new world of joy to those of us who are not there and never will be? Someone else, maybe someone else with our names, will be there, while we are left to rot, abandoned to gravity and time, trapped in regret and silence, and sustained, if we poor contingent shadows exist at all, in order that we might continue to suffer."

The stiletto

Something unexpected welled up in the heart of Pennyfeather. He felt an old emotion, some sleeping knowledge. He sensed he might do something rash, become bold and say foolish words, and betray the old man to his face. That, of course, would be exceedingly imprudent.

Everyone around Malchidion was doing the fawning dance, performing obsequiously; all except the niece of the ambassador from Timbuktu. She kept her eyes trained on the obscure clerk, so much so that Pennyfeather felt the warmth rising to his cheek. *Why is she doing that? What does she think is going to happen?* Panic began to set in. But nothing happened, the moment passed. The young woman was disappointed.

It was only later, when the hired hands were dismantling the stage machinery, the maids were busy cleaning the aftermath, all that, when Pennyfeather was abruptly confronted by the Guardian, who had stepped out of a nondescript room, a door in a row of doors identical, and stared blankly at the clerk.

Then Pennyfeather spoke quickly, his tongue a stiletto. "One day soon," he said, "you will awake to find yourself abandoned.

The squanderer of souls will die. I know you, too, old man, and your thirty pieces of silver."

After this, the clerk made himself scarce. He followed paths where no one would find him.

Chapter Three

Original Counterpoint

M an of pleasure—sweet
    To taste his love!
Friend and lover chosen
For my love.

Beautiful Woman,
Where has your lover gone to?
Where has he gone?
We'll help you look for him.

My love has gone to walk
Within his garden —
To feed his sheep and there
To gather flowers.
— Song of Songs 6: 1 – 2

Addled troubadour

One might question the skill of such a lover, whether he knew what he was up to. It isn't really explained away by the distance of time and a matter of differing cultural sensibilities. At no time and place is a girl happy to find her hair described as "a flock of goats frisking down the slopes of Gilead."

Nor is it plausible to expect a reward for asserting that "your neck is the tower of David built as a fortress, hung round with a thousand bucklers." And while adopting a less martial image, it's hard to envision a favorable result in comparing the feminine bosom to "two fawns, twins of a gazelle that feed among the lilies," though perhaps if you find the right girl . . .

Either there is something addled about this troubadour, or he is not speaking of a woman. If he intends a city, namely Jerusalem, everything falls into place. To recognize this is not to deflect from other ways of reading the *Song of Songs*. It truly is a mystical love poem, the most radiant and daring, almost a scandal to find it venerated and preserved in the Jewish holy books. Bulgakov considered it "permeated by such a trepidation of love" that its eschatological yearning constituted a "verbal miracle."

Yet those who wish to reduce the poem to a dialogue of carnal desires certainly miss the point, and doubly so, for the meaning of fleshly embrace, both its humor and ardor, and the ultimacy it aims to consummate surely cannot be comprehended by so narrow a scope.

Sealed scroll

Right there, in the quiet, seeking without knowing, a kind of hidden knowing, it's in the green shoot yearning for rain, and the young kid goat and the foal, the lamb and the elephant calf, the gawking nestlings, too, with their wide little maws and their huge eyes and the wee pelt of feathers, but particularly the mammalian beasts where affection and singular demand unite, almost frightful need searching out the maternal teat.

Yet beyond mute, instinctive desire, beyond the immediate, innate determination to exist, to perdure, there is the cherubic child, the fatness of well-being. What that state of affairs is, I need hardly tell you, though you've barely experienced it except as a sort of prophecy that wakens in your birthing. You still feel the trail of it in the first breath of the journey that is goodness despite sometimes frail, sickly, wobbled legs, four or two, flying, swimming, slithering, rooted to the earth, secreted, encrusted, building the city in infinitesimal accretions, the reef descrying the sun in aqueous abyssal realms, generations of silent, yet insistent labor, this action that is quest, not quite lucid knowing, though imbued, enriched, carrying a message.

You feel the weight of it, you shake it and peer at the wrapping, or like a herald with a sealed scroll, your heart's desire written on the inside, so coming to some rational awareness, some speech, but even this language is both real and opaque, touching upon the underside of the tapestry. Following the music, charting an elusive surplus that often appears as nothing, as pregnant, unspoken hope towards the act in the acting of creation, it is the sign of eschatological flourishing.

This poverty of receptivity is the wealth of infinite gifts, and the metaphysical basis of the symbol. Before all else, that gift of attentive emptiness must be for other gifts to be received, so the gift that is suffered, that suffering so awful, hardly anyone will look for it and fewer still live in it, the depths.

Economics

There's nothing surprising in a dead thing. The sick, one may say, are somewhat less predictable, though one can readily admit that they are mostly to be found within the great arc of a probability curve. The entire logic of the modern world, the modern system, is founded on the sick and the dead. The closer to dead you become, the more stable. Absolute death is both the most predictable and the most bankable. You get a good rate of interest provided you are solidly dead.

Risk averse

What was this demand for a miracle, but the request that the risk be taken away? To discover a path mediated through signs is to accept the need to trust the one who has sent the message.

"Prove that you are good, and then we will follow you," said the Pharisee, unaware and heedless of whence the Good — that mystery of the Unknown Father that announces itself by hiding in plain sight.

And what of the sign of Jonas? Some think it is the entry into the abyss, the great whale as a tomb, and forget the anger of the prophet that the God should show mercy to Nineveh.

Kingdom of beauty

The way the vates work resists the experimental method, though experiment is involved. The Arthur material from the Continent and the prior Welsh deposit undergoes trial. Forms are tried out, some bear fruit, while others are discarded as spurious or malformed. And while the judgment of a particular generation may be lacking, over time, the vates discover by their own process of memory and work what is valuable and what is merely fashionable.

The failure of Camelot is the bane of historical man. It is the failure of time to attain the splendor of the mysterious Good. Perhaps failure is itself security against presumption, carrying a hidden relation to victory unapproachable by the powers of nature alone. There might be ersatz forms, idols of success that ossify the heart. Glittering applause, as Plato asserted, may condemn the wicked man to an approval that imprisons.

Mordred can be read in differing ways. Here is one: whatever his bitterness, animosity, and impudent rebellion signifies, it is certainly a refusal of what Arthur had come to represent. Arthur, who began in the desperate warfare of preservation and resistance to barbarians and who was later translated into chivalric romance, crystallized as the headship of a Court dedicated to a particular quest. The vates probed and felt their way into this discovery, that the kingdom could not be realized apart from the Grail. Arthurian man is called to be more-than-man as the seeker after an eternal realm. Precisely this haunting beauty of promised completion is what Mordred rejects in the name of rational politics, and the economy of struggle to survive.

There are other names to bind: a particular notion of freedom where choice is unconstrained, the indifferent plain of endless choosing taken as pure self-creation, which at the last might turn out to be the bitter pleasure of decreation.

The myth of the canny peasant

Those who say he was shrewd often think of Jesus as a canny peasant. They might honor him as a creative teacher, maybe even a genius, taking the views of his time as a basis for innovation. And then it is a matter of conjecture, just how different he really was.

And of course, if he was a man, born into a culture bearing the momentum of the sweep of ongoing history, he must have learned a language and engaged the thinking of his people. All that is commonplace. Yet few grapple with the mystery of the God-Man, some because they don't believe. They take it for a chimera like the centaur, a pseudo-concept where the signifier for the absolute alludes to incoherent perfection, a conceptual plenitude both empty and abstract.

Others, out of pious regard for a set of scriptures or tradition, out of humble awareness of the gulf between poles separated by infinite leaps, stick to the well-worn paths, heedless that in doing so they might risk a more subtle impiety. One could court dullness when confronted with the unique, forgetting the unending fecundity of revelation.

The wondrously capacious, dynamic flourishing that gifts joyous surprise is better encountered flying the wings of imagination, no matter how inevitable defeat. Grace kisses the bold. And there, too, he might have been bold himself. The Christ was hated for it. And if he is shrewd, it is possibly of a different ilk than the usual sort, the kind tamed by prior examples.

If Jesus is a tactician, the strategy must be measured to the attempted action of which we know the barest palimpsest of love's incomparable design. And here, so often, scholars are apt to project themselves or to subvert pious certitudes with the flash of fashion — it's pleasant to be congratulated by one's peers and to insult the sensibilities of the *hoi polloi* with a single toss of the dice!

The fierce Virgin

The Infinite was not a thought you could start from. How was it possible to think it, to even imagine it? Yet when Anselm made that little remark in his *Proslogion*, that small empty space, a nothing, the logicians all shook their heads and began to pick it apart — that "*nihil quo majus cogitari nequeat.*" They thought that St. Anselm was proposing a conceptual proof, a chain of rational links that was both definition and logical certitude, that the idea of God "*aliquid quo nihil majus cogitari potest,*" a being such that I can conceive of nothing greater, was a demonstration brought before the tribunal of academic acumen and scholarly debate.

And it might seem like that. It was wrapped in a dry enough treatise, this proposal to dispute and discuss. Though that is not at all what Anselm meant. He was not sifting concepts or suggesting a ladder of ascending thought to end in the inevitable conclusion that logic could not but agree that there is a God. He had caught on to something entirely different, so different that for centuries his critics tilted at an argument chimerical and utterly confused.

The idea of the infinite is not a concept. It is not a mental puppet of the mind to be commanded, to dance at the bequest of the little gray cells. No, it was impossible to command. One couldn't even think it. And yet, strangely, men and women have a sense of it. They could feel the immensity of it, tremble at their smallness, their fragile vulnerability, or triumph in the very approach to such a lofty idea. Either way, it was odd, that you could think limit. The beasts did not quail or marvel before the Infinite. The yearning for the eternal was a mute secret in their blood, but none pondered it.

It was the maiden who understood, the fierce Virgin. She'd been thinking about it her whole life. She did not call it thinking. She called it prayer. But at the highest level, they are identical. And this, just this, is what the scholars would never understand.

All her life, from when she was a little girl, the smile of the Infinite called to her. That is how she imagined it, felt it, and perhaps thought of it. She could not really imagine the face of the

Infinite, but it smiled at her just the same. If it was thought, it was not commanded. You did not rule it. You might start out that way. You might believe you were considering, judging, determining, and weighing the concept as one did with other ideas. Yet the very thought, the feeling for the infinite, what a strange thing, that men should ever think of it, that they should feel a secret whispering, a yearning, this gravity, this desire that could nowhere be discovered in the world.

That was what Anselm was saying. You are not thinking this thought; this thought is thinking you.

From her childhood, she'd been listening. There was music to the Infinite. It was not in the ocean or the stars, though they could suggest. It was often in the silence. And then one day, the herald of the Infinite came to her. So long she had communed in silent wonder, and yet it was still a shock, this announcement, the Infinite.

"Hail, favored one, the Lord is with you."

Lovingkindness

And let us not forget that charming story of St. Seraphim of Sarov. Motovilov has drawn a sketch of the saint's cell in which there were seven candlesticks lit before the icon called *Umilenie*, that is, Lovingkindness. Florensky comments that the icon is remarkable since it depicts the Mother of God without the infant and even before His conception. One catches the maiden at the moment the angel is announcing the triumph of her ardent soul, the great burden of her joy.

All this was drawn from the memory of Motovilov who remembered a feeling of astonishment before the flames. As a little boy, he began to dance and frolic about the cell. His mother was embarrassed and remonstrated with him, but the saint intervened, saying, "The Angel of God is playing with the little boy! How can one stop a boy in his carefree games? Play, play, little child! Christ be with you!"

Whispering in code

So, we walked the plain, the long plain. You might call it time. For some, you think it's short, very short. Men cry about it. Even the God cried about it, Lazarus, and that was a strange case. And then again, even for the long, it's short. Compare your mechanism to the tall reds, the giant sequoia. But that is all wrong. You're looking from the outside, and thinking about the way the lever works or the way the wind pushes the dead leaves on the pond. Artifice or nature, that's the efficient cause that doesn't touch the intimate, where truth discloses the hidden life.

Switch to introspection. It's different, but most likely you're still off, because now you are thinking of consciousness and maybe how you can choose what to attend to, perhaps not how. You might lack the range, though some have more to work with. Still, the object is measured by the powers of the knower. You might not have the powers to attend well. But all that's beside the point.

You're not yet close to that no place a mystic like Eckhart discerns where there are no images and the sequence isn't linear.

The heart rushes past the mind, it doesn't care about limits. Rushing ahead like a hound of love, it runs without thinking, with graceful abandon, because it desires and in desire, it refuses to be satisfied by a mere idea. Knowledge short of cardiognosis is not enough. More than knowledge, it wants the beloved. The call of the real, which eludes nature enchanted as much as the denuded object of rationalist intentions, can only whisper in code.

It's there, nowhere, without images, the plenitude in silence where the small isn't small, though everything is small.

From agony to agony

Affections dissipate, betray, even the best, end in death. This is the true sign of Cain. Folks read that as a legend, and the pious imagine the mark as an individual judgment after the fact of fratricide. (*Nota bene*: Cain became a founder of cities, so there is the ancient link between that sacrifice of innocence and civilization born of brotherly strife.)

Yet the sign merely manifests the nature of the origin. Cain, the first child born of the desire of man and woman for one another, the knit body, forming in the womb, tracing an embryonic path that comprehends in image the various beasts, what was happening?

What was brought, this curse, how masked, impure, bloody, life in time . . . Messy, painful birth, crying out, the tears, delight, the bearing of gifts, of siblings, the generation of family, then the attempted offering, the daily bread. Cain tried, but got it wrong. What came of it was the blood of Abel calling out from the ground, the land itself crying out. How to make it right? What was the point of it all if it were to go from agony to agony?

People never think, well, they just assume, because that's how it's always been, for everyone. How could death be all wrong? It isn't rational, to imagine the universe mistaken on something so fundamental.

Expiation

Sure, I could say what's what if you like. It doesn't make sense, though. Maybe, I dunno, maybe to a barbarian, if you're that sort. They go in for ritual killing. Incense, altars, lots of smoke and buckets of blood thrown on walls and stones with everyone chanting or singing. It makes for a kind of transaction. Kill this bull or this lamb that never done anything to anyone except trust, and in return for that innocent suffering, that death, you get points. A bad bit of math for the poor creature put to the knife.

The better the victim, the higher the points, that's why certain tribes thought, Why not? Slaves, women, children, and soldiers who lost in battle — most of them were probably drugged. Maybe they played music, made it special, better than most. I mean, we're all going to die somewhere, at some time, but you first.

Seems to me, everyone, well, not everyone, but lots of folks got used to it. Religion. Oh, I'm sure there are clever ones, the kinds that write books, think deep thoughts, they dress it up with fancy words that hardly anyone understands, and shake their heads all knowing like. You can fool yourself if you want it badly enough.

But for regular people, it's not something they think about. If they think at all, it isn't much. Just enough to get that glow feeling, all satisfied that it makes sense when in reality it's just what they believe because of where they were born or what their parents told them when they were too small to question it.

Let's put it like this. You can't so much as take the pain of my toothache, can you? It's my toothache, not yours, and even if you were crazy enough to want to, you just couldn't because my body is mine, not yours. You can say you're sorry about it; we all do that; it doesn't cost much — but the actual pain, that's a different story.

Blood and torture, and not just anywhere, but at the center, this Cross! So, your fella had a way. Clearly, he had a way. Women liked him; that shows you something. He wasn't a brute. All the same, what's his pain got to do with ours? How are horrible things happening to him supposed to fix all the other horrible things?

I know the word they use, those clever ones. They've got lots of theories, because that's their jam, they go in for that. It pays them off, if you like. Expiation, they call it, especially when they can get all the sad, scared, lonely folks to make a contribution.

The high priest

Gaston Bachelard says, "The blue of the sky is aerial when it is dreamed as a color that pales a bit, like a pallor that seeks finesse, a finesse that we imagine as yielding beneath our fingers like a delicate fabric as we caress, in Paul Valery's words 'the mysterious texture of the utmost height.'" And surely, there is something right about this dreaming aspiration, which seeks to join the eros of flight to the tenderness of touch.

Yet there is still the danger of the heights, which is not a measure of literal miles as a Russian cosmonaut might imagine, but a metaphysical distance beyond the reach of rockets. This sacred fear may be penultimate, but it cannot be conquered by mere audacity. It is not a question of will alone. Ignorance of limit is exposed by the waxen wings of Icarus.

But still, that doomed youth is poignant, because his desire for the infinite was not only a crime against a certain Greek moderation, but prayer disguised as titanism. According to Josephus, the bells on the high priest's robe were reminders of thunder. The robe itself was a picture of the sky. Bachelard's dream is too ethereal, melting to a vanishing point. The priest is an aerial being who pleads for the earth.

Chosen beloved

All names are actions, you understand? Job was a noble friend from outside the People. The story is perhaps told to Israel in order to meditate upon the condition of exile. Moses saw the splendor indirectly, in a euphemism for the impossible, he was allowed to perceive "God's back," though even Moses did not see what Abraham and Isaac were granted. Notice it is the father and miraculous son together that prepare vision . . . Compare Daedalus and Icarus with this journey that encompasses three days.

The God who answers Job impresses with overwhelming majesty, with the distance between a creature's ignorance and divine knowledge, though all that is beside the point. That God comes to Job at all, well, he names him friend. Yet, the father of the people of hope was gifted a greater intimacy.

Look, Isaac was the apple of his eye, the child of Sarah's laughter, God's generous joke. Many rabbis have pondered this request for sacrifice. Some, for instance, have taken a popular stance. They supposed some moral necessity. Abraham was required to offer the promised son because of some unspecified sin. It is for this reason that a ram was substituted for Isaac, since redress was still needed after Abraham's hand was stayed.

This is not true. There is no indication that the God ever requested the *Akedah* on account of unrighteousness. Further, it is a mistake to see the whole affair as a pseudo-sacrifice. Isaac was indeed given by Abraham, and the precious son willingly offered himself to the knife. The ram, well, the ram is a sacrament of that offering, a participation of the whole creation in the personal obedience of the father of nations.

And the place where Isaac became the twice-given, the miraculous birth and the return from death was named by Abraham *"Jehovah Jireh."* Some have translated this as the place where the Unnameable sees, but that is incorrect. It means, the Lord is seen.

Of course, the theophanic glory of the cosmos that humbled Job and was praised by St. Paul is not to be dismissed. Nonetheless, it is not lightning, floods, earthquakes or constellations that intimately mirror the face of the God. Abraham did not look out upon a spectacle of overwhelming power. All *that* the pagans would have understood with their cosmic gods who battle chaos.

Remember that the land of Moriah is the destined place of Jerusalem. The high altar of the mountain is where the Temple abides. That this insignificant mountain should suddenly be revealed as a site of utmost importance is one of those lessons we are always forgetting. The God chooses with perfect artistry, claiming from obscurity love's fascinating discovery of the unique.

How then was the God made visible, you ask? In the performance of unbounded devotion by the patriarch, in the radical trust of the son, God showed himself. This is the heart of liturgy. Romance begins where the irreplaceable boy of wonder is offered as self-sacrificing gift. It is in the reciprocity of gift, return, and gift again that the mystery of life begins to be told. Sacrifice is more than remediation for wrongs. It is ascent, translation, revelation of the endless play of divine bliss.

Odd kind of wisdom

"I am like that," He said. "Giving everything all at once, holding nothing back."

If it was prudence, it was an odd kind of wisdom, keeping nothing in reserve to see how things go. He wasn't that sort, the God.

The Binding

The least of sinners, the least of sins, wounds Jesus eternally. There you have Christianity. And I, history, can do nothing which does not interest Jesus, God, naturally and as though physically. I cannot commit anything temporally which is not inserted, physically, as it were, into the body of God himself. There, my child, is Christianity for you. Real . . . It is the binding, the eternal, temporal binding, the link, the inlay of the one in the other, the incrucification as it were, which makes Christianity. The rest is good material for schoolmasters. Otherwise, it would not have been worthwhile, taking so much trouble.

— Charles Péguy, *Temporal and Eternal*

What cannot be fully expressed

And how did the *Shekinah* manifest itself? Rabbi Naftali said to Sky: "It is written that 'a fire went forth from before the Unnameable and consumed the elevation offering and the fats upon the

Altar; the people saw and sang glad song and fell upon their faces.'
Now, my dear, listen, this is the reverent response, the falling upon
the face, it is the sign of the appearance of his glory. This is why the
elders asked Moses to cover his shining visage.

But here, it is not fear, but joy that dominates, because the
creation had drawn close to joyful mysteries. The teachers say that
this fire descended upon the altar. It was added to the ordinary fire
of the sacrifice. *Rashbam* suggests the fire emanated from the Holy
of Holies, but Solomon indicates it came directly from heaven.

On the eighth day, the fire descended. According to the Talmud,
the fire from heaven carried five miracles. First, it seemed to crouch
over the Altar in the form of a majestic lion. Second, it dazzled
with the brightness of the sun, so that direct vision threatened
blindness. What is counted third through fifth is related; the fire
was not mere appearance, but consumed all variety of objects, both
the wet and the dry, so that all of creation is intended, and finally, it
burned without smoke. *Maharsha* observes that it had the nature
of elemental fire.

Whether this is so or not, the miraculous fire no longer appeared
in the Second Temple. It is my opinion that something more is
intended. Smoke is death and judgment. The fire without smoke is
translation. The created is lifted into heavenly realms. The essential
teaching is this was no ordinary fire, the Uncreated light, for the
essence of sacrifice is not at all destruction."

Alien fire

The approach to the Unnameable, to that Unspeakable frontier, how to do it? You could make a dull hash of it, thinking the effort could be turned into morality without passion, apart from heartbreaking beauty, separate from the danger of adventure. All false and bad liturgies do this. The whole world might try to forget, manage the pain, and live in distraction. Football and news and the movies, maybe even crime. You could run away and hide, but there is still death and the frontier. At best, worlding it is a delay tactic.

Things repeat, with a difference. It's non-identical. The first pair, the Adam, the Man-Woman, fractured, despairing, told of death, a doom, maybe a mercy. It happened again, in history. It happened to Noah with the ambiguous vine, and then there was the Temple. The Torah knows — if you can read with discretion — that the entire creation was still not yet, that is key. You think it is finished? It might be finished, but not from where you're standing. The Jews, they thought it wasn't finished. Even the six days, they waited. And the garden was the seventh, and the Temple was the eighth. On the eighth day, it should be finished.

The Temple, golden and silver and bronze, woven in threads of azure, crimson, and purple, could be understood as participation in celestial forms. At the same time, it might be speculated as an aspirational essay upon meaning that is synonymous with philosophical wonder. The High Priest, too, dressed in his vast robe, the breastplate of rainbow gems, the sash, the headband, he wore the cosmos. To glimpse him who entered the silence, the penumbra of glory, folks caught their breath. He was the Temple's secret incarnate. Miss that, and you miss all, trap yourself in ink dribble.

The Fall *is* time, the dark mystery before and outside history, yet begetting history, so that the golden age is a dream, halcyon days, the trace of forgotten innocence — and this, too, the priest must approach, and it's risky. The pattern was set with the Tabernacle. It was confirmed, at last, with the descent of Shekinah. The Mystery of intimacy came near, but unlike the delayed judgment upon the primal pair, unlike the first advent of Shekinah in the desert, it went wrong immediately.

The sons of Aaron sought alien fire. Some scholars say this was a rite taken from the surrounding peoples, and that Abihu and Nadab tried to contain the Immensity. No one really knows. The priesthood of Ultimacy failed, and this time the death was prompt.

Something of a hoarder

That the water bearer is time is hardly remarked. In his house are many furnishings randomly strewn about; he is profligate and something of a hoarder. One might see a brass *sanggori*, an ornament of simple curved lines shaped like a serpent, or perhaps the exquisite dance of calligraphic art on a Chinese silk; immense silence transfixes one in the umber brooding of an Ivory Coast mask.

There's a fine supply of Chimu fabric, the wool of llama or alpaca in the natural colors of ivory, pearl gray, and glossy black augmented with dyed indigo, carmine red, or the yellow of false pepper depicting humans, gods, dragons or coastal seabirds. He's got whole rooms stacked from top to bottom and overflowing with pendants, sharpening stones, spoons, and all manner of implements made from bronze or jade, gold or ivory. They often assume winking identities, half-metamorphosed into beast or fowl.

And then there are the necklaces of mother-of-pearl, the ceramic bowls of delicate, iridescent flowers, and in a far corner the haunting stucco and wood sarcophagus mask of a plaintive female, her large dark eyes and silent mouth plead for the kindness of an answering gaze.

Cenacle of signs

On Thursday, they gathered in the cenacle, the appointed keepers of the stars. The room itself was prepared beforehand. The sign had been given, to enter into the house of the water bearer. No one had a premonition of disaster. Obscurity was in his words. The lamps were filled, they were congenial together. And what was he doing that evening, directing them, foretelling, initiating, he was taking upon himself the whole vast effort; nowise did they understand the extent of the room prepared.

The reason they went to battle

Those highlanders from the north were always singing. Repairing their nets, boasting of interminable genealogies, and telling fabulous lies about the prowess and antiquity of their various clans, they couldn't do any of it without breaking into song. Half the reason they went into battle was so they could sing about it afterwards.

Music of the inexpressible

On Yom Kippur, the holiest day of the year, the high priest enters the Holy of Holies in order to enact the rites of atonement. Initially, there was the unexpected disaster of the sons of Aaron. Nearness to the divine was known to be dangerous, yet Moses had made something of a habit of it. At its best, there was that singular event on Sinai when they came together; the elders, the priests, and the people of God entered into the celestial tabernacle, stood upon a foundation of heavenly sapphire.

Afterwards, the rabbis debated precisely what had happened. It was said they feasted, ate and drank in the presence of the Unnameable. Whatever that remarkable and unprecedented communion entailed, they could not sustain it. Things went awry; the gloom of death returned. And so there was the annual effort to return again to that mysterious festivity.

What was intended by that sacrifice may be inferred by the particular rituals surrounding a Jewish wedding. At the conclusion of the week of celebration, the bridegroom himself wore a crown, king for a day, while his robe emulated the brilliance of high priestly vestments. The friends of the bridegroom would also adorn themselves in splendor, usher him to the place of embrace, the hidden delight of joining. The People see them and rejoice.

"You must ask the Elder how well Naftali used to dance at them, my dear. We are hopeful wayfarers called to ecstasy. In the long season of waiting, we dance to the music of the inexpressible. Yet entry into the bridal suite, that was the almost embarrassingly frank aspiration of the People.

According to the Mishnah, the measurements of the bridechamber were intended to resemble the Tabernacle. The linens were dyed blue and purple and scarlet, the liturgical colors of festive joy. Did they know what they were asking? The bridal chamber where the nuptial union would be consummated held to the ratio of the Holy of Holies. Yes, well, think of the responsibility!"

Edith looks back

"You like that statue?" asked the Tribune. "There's a rather remarkable story told about it by Josephus, so far as I can determine, a generally reliable historian. Oh, I know that she reminds one of the Aphrodite of Knidos, but she's nothing of the sort, apparently. This lovely creature was taken as the spoils of war when Jerusalem was sacked. Naturally, one was surprised to find her hiding amongst the Jews.

Their religious teachers claim she is not, in fact, a work of human artistry at all, but the result of divine judgment. I had Crixus write it all down. It seems she was the wife of one of their patriarchs. As a young maiden, she was raised in Sodom and married off to the nephew of a tribal chieftain.

One day, their desert god was in a foul mood and determined to destroy the city of her birth. Edith, that was her name, I believe, had nearly escaped with her life, but could not refrain from looking back to see the ruin of her ancient home. Rather, poignant, that.

It's a shame about the arms. Protracted siege angers the men. Once the legions break through, everything ends in shambles."

Suspicion

Have you read the *Enuma Elish*? Those Babylonians were more honest, or at least guileless, or perhaps simply brutally masculine, arrogant and indifferent to other opinions. Marduk clearly wrestled with the waters. His order is a victory of battle over the forces of chaos. Any freshwomyn can see it — the tyrannical, overbearing male with his rigid laws who cannot abide flow, well, we know what that is.

The anxiety of dependence creates neurosis. There is no suppleness. But look, the Jews are shrewd. You have to admit, they're clever. The bankers are like that, careful with their pennies. But what can you expect from a people who celebrate Jacob the deceiver? And so they evade the truth by denial. Oppression nearly disappears. They create out of nothing — though the Spirit broods over the dark, maternal waters.

Every once in a while, in Isaiah or a Psalm or two, the evidence slips past attempted erasure, and it comes out that their supposedly unnameable Divinity has fought with the waters as well. Why, it's Marduk after all behind the curtain demanding the witches' broomstick.

I've never trusted Jesus. Yes, he liked the company of womyn, especially wealthy womyn — his toadies rarely tell you that. But all his talk of the Father was blatantly projection, some compensation, probably to get back at the whisperers who were always casting aspersions upon the ever sore subject of his legitimacy. One knows his kind, their rabboni: an adventurer, a dreaming boy, secretly beholden to womyn whilst chasing after his absent sky daddy.

Battleground

The burnt offerings of the Temple were a continuation of Abraham's breakthrough into the mode of eternal life. Where everyone saw propitiation of an angry god, the Jews lived out an entirely different liturgical existence.

The purification rites were dual, aiming at both culpable sins and the taint of a world diseased and mortally wounded. The everyday sins of the people might be blithely forgotten. Folks forgot. When time passed, the wrong seemed less. It might even fade into zero for ordinary conscience, yet a metaphysical wound remained. The latter quality of damage due to simply living within a social fabric that inevitably involved acceptance of global iniquities made one impure, but did not entail intrinsic moral failure.

The cleansing from both addressed wickedness and milder improprieties of circumstance, often unavoidable, served as remedy to make ready for an apocalyptic expectation — the actual center of Temple activity was strung to a vaster bow. The arrow of prayer and priestly service was joyous preparation for ecstatic approach to the divine. The fire offerings were acts of translation into angelic tongue.

The Jews understood the Temple to be the site of healing, because it was also the place where evil accrued. Blood as life was an antidote to contamination. What is perhaps harder to comprehend is the strange gravitational pull of the holy for the sins that persist as shadow monsters that manifest from man's perverse heart. Naturally, this will be taken as mythic imagination run amok, but nonetheless, this the priests observed.

Grant that within the religious narrative that propelled priestly action, the rite was logical. The sinful deed is not limited to a punctiliar temporal instant, but ghostly seed that seeks to spread flowers of evil that are paradoxically impersonal or perhaps better, depersonalizing, so that wickedness takes on the image of a life of its own. What could explain the attraction of the Temple for the demon hoards?

The answer may lie in the equivocal quality of existence. For a creature, existence may be taken for a bare assertion of a state of affairs, a shallow positivist register of verified fact. One could think of a time and place where the creature no longer exists or of a fiction that never achieves factual reality. Yet for the God, existence might be dynamic plenitude of Being, infinite joy, radically creative. No distinction occurs between Divine existence and essential being.

Juxtapose the two concepts as thin versus robust existence. Perchance, the monstrous simulates life, but desires a more perfect autonomy. What it wants is impassible integrity, freedom from a precarious dependence it simultaneously denies, but cannot escape. The God is both hated and envied.

It was thus that the Temple bore the people's sin and fought the onslaught of demons. Think now, how it was that the unclean spirits could hardly contain their shouts of recognition when the Nazarene came into their paths.

The guild of soldier artisans

Pax Romana is the triumph of Caesar, which is the Roman legions, and engineers of roads, of Seneca and Cicero, and laws. We are great ones for duty and for following the legal codes duly drawn up by an obedient Senate. And while perhaps the city of seven hills cannot boast of Homer or Aeschylus, one need not falter to mention Virgil, Horace, and Ovid. Catullus, too, has his admirers. Creativity is not lacking, even if the tendency is towards a certain bureaucratic correctness. Empire insists on the latter, as it is the rectitude of the civil servant that makes the whole thing hum.

But you can ask the Jews where the real creative impulse finds its way. Thousands of crucifixions have given wide scope for every conceivable talent. A man can be hung in any number of positions. A cross need not be set up in the traditional perpendicular. The aesthetics of pain, the lesson so crucial to the wellness of imperial polity is not lacking in novelty. The nuances of the human flesh are a special study of the guild of soldier artisans.

Recipe for despair

Pilate seems to have thought the whole thing one of their over-heated affairs, but you can't take it lightly in Palestine. Probably be like that for millennia. Endemic hatreds, religious mania, some desert insistence on taking things to maddening extremes mixed with fatalism and whatnot, it's a recipe for despair.

The fellow was a deluded dreamer, sad really. Not a zealot, but in spite of himself, he managed to stumble into the maelstrom. Certainly, there was nothing else for it. No one foresaw the extra-ordinary hysteria that followed.

Of course, there are all kinds of absurdities that human beings find convincing. Every day is plenished with stupidities. In that, at least, the well never appears to run dry. So, the Galilean was dealt with as these things must be.

Time's double action

George Steiner writes eloquently of Plato's supreme achievement. "Does a Hamlet, a Falstaff have greater 'real presence' than Plato's Socrates, is there a more various sum of humanity in Don Quixote?" Attend: It is in approaching the fictive that the historical is transformed.

The gadfly and the Nazarene, between them they bear the questions and the mysterious response that is also question. Of the former, Steiner asserts "the ripening complexity of his role across successive dialogues" as "proof of Plato's art," an art that enlists "the compositional and corrosive agencies of time as does Proust" in order to produce "a mosaic of snapshots."

There is greater power invoked in the writing of an icon, but a similar choosing of representative moments intends a living witness to a dynamic, integral presence beyond the limited aims of mimetic art. The double action of time is crucial: how the transformation of the literal into heightened truth requires the abrasive washing away of quotidian facts.

This is why the Gothic in Western art exemplifies an important distinction from the general oeuvre of the Renaissance, which moved in the direction of pure naturalism. This shift in attention ultimately degraded into the dullness of journalese that thinks being as a sort of "verified appearance." The irony is that appearance only has meaning as message bearing, and precisely this is denied.

The art of the icon requires an ascesis that sweeps away the heady gossip of the clique. Forgetfulness of surface chatter may allow for reception of reality, the eternal form that gifts vibrancy to temporal life. The Jews also understood this. If you like, the two goats of Yom Kippur enact complementary offices: the goat for Azazel bears corrosive time into oblivion; the goat for the Lord composes to the music of the eternal.

Eighth day

You understand what he was saying, the upstart from Nazareth? This outrageous boast that he would rebuild the Temple in three days — his followers made something of that, the will-to-believe cottons to every imaginative cloudland; and now the rumors persist for centuries, though the wild dogs probably made off with the carcass. Pious legends about secret believers begging the body are enough to satisfy the credulous.

Still, you have to hand it to him. He was a bold rascal. Not enough to aspire to overturn the Roman rule. If he was the Temple, he is saying his body is the glory of creation, the flourishing crown that all things seek. Not even the Caesars ask men to apply to them such a divinity.

Highlanders

"Little known fact; Andrew is a bit bow-legged. No, watch him when he walks."

"He won't like that, Peter. He's almost as sensitive as Iscariot when you bring up sea-sickness."

"Ach, fella turns green in becalmed waters."

"The master says we need 'em, so we need 'em."

"No one said different, Bartholomew. Bloke has his uses no doubt."

"He is a bit. Walks like a pigeon. Did you know a pigeon closes its eyes when it walks? Always takes a blind step, and then looks about to see where it is."

"This bit of useful information brought to you by Thomas."

"Some folks only know fish."

"What are you lot looking at?"

"Nothing, Andrew. Say, you don't happen to blink when you walk? The twin is pretty sure that you do. Now, how about a song, boys?"

Secrets of the Cherubim

Rabbi Naftali was reading a passage from the Babylonian Talmud when Sky entered his study. He was so intent that for a long minute he was unaware of the girl. Sky did not wish to interrupt him and besides, there was something charming about his face that she had not noticed before. Behind his grey beard, a childlike freshness suffused his features.

She saw that for the rabbi, to read the commentary on sacred scripture was a form of play in which he could barely conceal an innocent, nearly exuberant delight. When he finally looked up to discover her presence, he smiled as if he were seeing her across a distance far greater than the confines of the study.

"Ah, Miss Sky," he said. "A little bird informs me that you are curious about the Cherubim."

"And does that little bird wear a white beard?" she asked.

"We will not discuss the age of the bird," declared the rabbi. "The winged creatures are all related. The Cherubim are very fond of their venerable little brothers."

Sky felt warmth rising in her face. She worried that somehow she had insulted the rabbi with her joke about old men.

"It's only that the Elder was telling me about the Tabernacle in the desert. He said the golden mercy seat that covered the Ark was guarded by two Cherubim. I am particularly interested in them, you see. Then he explained that one was on the north side of the Holy of Holies, and the other on the south. It seemed the length of the wings were too long to allow for any kind of body to fit, if you see what I mean? The Elder was very happy about this. I think it's because he hates math. Well, really, it was because he said it meant the Cherubim did not occupy earthly space, so that is how they fit."

Rabbi Naftali began to make hot chocolate for both of them. Sky relaxed and justified the visit with a last bit of information. "When I asked him to explain more, he said to go ask you, which meant he wanted to take a nap."

Rabbi Naftali was very pleased with this story. "The Elder is correct," he said, "but he left out some of the best secrets. Did you know, for instance, that when Israel did God's will, the Cherubim would face one another, but when Israel strayed from the way of life, they were so upset they turned their faces away from each other?"

Someone else besides Sky might have objected that the Cherubim were metal artifacts and could not possibly act in such a manner, but as she was not a foolish girl, enchantment seemed normal to her. The rabbi placed some marshmallows in the hot chocolate and added by way of explanation, "Just as divine breath descended into the Adam, the golden likeness could be made living."

When he saw that Sky also shared his delight in the play of God, he was moved to tell her that one Cherubim is masculine and the other feminine. "There are those who think the angels lack these qualities, but this is not so. The principle of masculine and feminine patterns the whole of Creation. Moreover, the Talmud states that each face is a child's face full of purity and innocence."

"Oh, but I heard that they are fierce," said Sky.

Naftali's visage suddenly turned grave and solemn.

"Very fierce," he answered.

Timely decorum

What really wound them up, the professionals who knew about the God, was the manner in which the Nazarene spoke, as if the usual exigencies did not apply to him. Thus, "before Abraham was, I am."

And if that not so subtle allusion to God's speech to Moses were not enough, he acted out that parable about the bridegroom, casting his disciples as the friends of the bridal chamber. The refusal of divine prohibitions, the way careful men had construed them in order to preserve the clearly marked zone in which the sacred might be encountered, well, all that was tantamount to a claim.

Everyone knew that Israel was the bride. No man had ever thought to cast himself in the role of bridegroom. It wasn't just the arrogance, but the timing. Revelry was allowed by some at the end of time. To insist on festivity in the middle, well, that just wasn't done. There was a sequence, an expectation of proper decorum. You can see that, can't you?

Certitude

They thought the claim was outrageous, the Sanhedrin tearing at their robes and making as if to throw dust into their venerable beards — all because they considered the God, though incomprehensible, clearly unable to approach them with a human face. Of this, they were sure.

The face of eternity

He was himself, he was. It's what he does, the strange one. He is tender, harsh, too, because of the child in him. He never got used to our ways is what I think. His ways are different, the way he commands the wind, talks to nature like it could hear him and respond. And it does! There's no one like him, I tell you.

On this night, we came to the cenacle where he promised a new world, taking our feast, the Passover, and weaving in new words. All the time, he was filled with yearning and sorrow, it's an odd combination. He summoned us and spoke with candor that made you weep. I'd never known before. I tell you what it was like. It was like the face of eternity, like discovering you were loved and looked for, that before you were even born, he was practicing your name.

And then he clearly intended novelty, he was initiating us into a brotherhood, but murky, dark, I didn't understand it. And then always before, the Passover isn't complete without the *hallel*, the cup of praise. It's my favorite part, the singing and the sweetest wine. But this he held back. This he would not drink until he had come to his father's kingdom.

This abba he seeks, the invisible glory, I've asked Peter and the sons of Zebedee, but none of us really understand. It's like he journeys into a far country and when he returns to us we are greeted with his sad looks because we are never able to keep pace with his heart or comprehend his mind.

And now they have taken him. Iscariot fell in with the Jerusalem bigwigs. That's what I heard. Everyone is hiding, lest they come for us who know nothing.

Joy in living as a stranger

The Father of all things is a well-beloved kingdom.
Anyone who is in him,
Anyone who establishes his dwelling in him,
Finds his joy in living as a stranger
because he has for delicious food
the beauty of God's face.

— Evagrius of Pontus, Centuries, Suppl. 57

Spirit hides in strange places

For the cunning, low mind, spirit is a word for deception. It is a vague reference to emotion connected to an interpretation of events mistaken for revelation or worse, nothing more than a rhetorical tool to try and make one's advantage sacrosanct and beyond questioning. Of course, there are those kinds. They forget that Job in the dust and scraping his sores was commended by the God. Spirit hides in strange places.

The Proud Who Blink

Indeed, there was always some limit beyond which the shadow men were unprepared to follow. They are drawn to the fire because deep down they suspect that without the flame, there is no um-bratile mimicry, no secondary causality, and no pretense of creating themselves out of nothing. Yet to enter the Unfading Light is to truly enter into the Unknown, and this they refuse under pretext of principle or prudence, cloaking the nature they now inhabit in the language of self-respect, when it is frankly cowardice.

The same lack of trust is the immemorial sin passed on from the generations. Their weak eyes blink at the palest reflection of light so that light itself is readily diagnosed a malady of bigotry or deranged imagination. They pull back within the more comfortable imaginary of the possible. Within this immanent frame, they ponder the potentiality of a nature amenable to their reason.

They plot out the foreseeable, enticing the city with the prospect of wondrous achievement, forgetting that the world has depths it cannot presume to know.

If it is simply what you were expecting, it is not what you secretly hope for. If you think to arrive is to be done with the need for courage, you have not begun to see the radical beauty of love. The pious who try to remain open to the contraband faith, even they generally quake at the cost, for it is still true that no mortal can see God and live.

Secret garden

If the tabernacle is conceived by the Jews as not only representing creation, but much more radically, as contributing essentially to its completion, something quite startling about divine artistry is implied. First, the exile from Eden, the wandering, finds consolation. The tabernacle is a moving mountain, bringing the Akedah of Mount Moriah to the people.

Yet the ark was always more than the establishing of covenant. It was secret garden, a translated recapitulation of the peace of Eden. And so, perhaps more revealing, it meant that the work of the artisan was allowed to merit a role in the ultimate shaping of the festive bower. And likely, this is the gnostic meaning whereby Adam and Eve were intended to dress the garden which was potentially a centrifugal movement meant to embrace the entire created reality.

Despite or perhaps by way of the proscriptions against images, the artist was allowed to approach the unapproachable. The religious instinct to avoid all possible deformations, the horror of idols driving aniconic refusal, is not allowed to be the final wisdom. Like apophatic silence, plenitude requires the Word, must find at least an oblique image in order to make enigmatic contact known at all.

One might suppose, even, that the notion of the artisan may be extended to the simplest human soul whose actions are able to be included in the eternal design. And so the really confusing way the God has of acting, the manner in which he woos them, even when he threatens, because He bears the winsome hope, yes, this is the character of the God, he hopes for the beloved partner, the one who will spark in joy and answer creation with a new word.

Chapter Four

The Knowledge That is Not Power

So long as the present was supple, it was not monetary, compa-rable, sellable, venal. As soon as it was made rigid, as soon as it was fixed, it became all this. The property of a unit of measure-ment is to be fixed. So long as the present was present, one could not commercialize it, it was not negotiable. As soon as it was past, I mean as soon as it was made into a past, as soon as it was a result, it became negotiable, it could be commercialized . . . It is not some books of debauchery that are the antipode of the Gospels, the secret point diametrically opposed to the secret point of the Gospels: what the modern world's secret point of resistance is, what in the modern world is the antipode of the Gospels, the secret point diametrically opposed to the secret point of the Gospels in the Christian world, is not some books of debauchery (none would have the force), it is the bank account book. . . . They believed they were considering the event

*they were writing and they were considering another, an identical, a
falsely identical event, which they had written.*
— Charles Péguy, *Notes on Bergson and Descartes*

Mrs. Stupka and the old Guardian

Ginger, the cat, was old, thought the old woman. She is old like me,
only she does not know she is old. Still, she will enter a room and
look about and expect to be made a "to do" over. The old woman
looked over at Ginger all furry sprawled in the corner of the room,
the back of her round head turned to her, the ears twitching ever so
slightly to see if she was noted, admired, apt to be coddled. There
was something profoundly innocent in cat's agreeable witness to a
lifetime of being noticed, scratched, and petted, subject to childish
gurgling praises to feline existence.

I am still here, thought the old woman in a spasm of petulant
angst at the meanness of age. She looked at the mottled, spotty
patchwork skin hung haphazardly where her lithe, springtime self
used to sport in soft cotton dresses drawing bows, tipped hats and
admiring, hungry eyes. Oh, how she laughed and danced and held
a summer umbrella just so! And before that, before the eyes and
the promises and longing, longing, she was so young, with a muslin
pinafore and mother braiding her hair and she was there, too, and
she could hardly believe it was still the same girl in this harpy body,
all alone except for the cat.

"It might be better," she thought, "to be covered in fur, to hide
the sin of time."

How she laughed at age then, and said bravely it didn't matter and they mustn't admire her too ardently, because she wasn't she, you know. This body, those glistening, dark eyes, the whimsical mouth just short of new laughter, it wasn't she. So of course, neither would the crow's feet and the shrunken skeleton, bent back , and huffing old lady forgetting always her purse on the shop counter, scanning obituaries, though she knows no one, but at least, up to now, she has not yet read her name.

The hunger of their eyes had been quite alarming, never subtle and delicate. Ginger turned, blinked meaningfully, and thumped her tail. "Sweet kitty," said the old woman. "Poor Ginger, such a good girl!"

She looked out the window. She had forgotten to turn the blinds at night. You can see everything when it turns dark. But it was morning now. Mourning. That's all life had become. Someone, who was it? They had said it was blissful to mourn. What could that possibly mean?

She hadn't slept. Or she had nodded during the day, so she lay awake during the night. Tuesday followed Monday. Wednesday came next. And if Friday should resist the usual law and custom, would anyone faint? Would cosmic police come and arrest the day, archangels arriving with serpentine gold-ringed brushes to ornament the mourning doves, dressing them aqua, incarnadine, and golden-haloed with magic dust?

She allowed herself these few holidays of imagination free from dullness and the grudging need to eat. She kept looking out the window and forgetting that it was she and her eyes that did so. Nothing ever happened. Nothing had happened for a long time.

A dark shadow crossed the light. There was a hurried tapping at the door. Ginger, ears back, looked anxiously at the old woman. The old woman sat for a long time wondering if she heard rapping at the door, decided that she did, wondered if she need answer it. At length, Mrs. Bell called through the door.

"Mrs. Stupka, it's me, Mrs. Bell. Mrs. Stupka, have you heard?"

Slowly, the old woman dragged herself towards the door. "I'm Mrs. Stupka," she thought. Yes, I married that man. He was a tailor . . . or a watchmaker. Something. And mama said what a silly name and I laughed and said, "yes, but he likes opera." Mrs. Stupka answered the door, edging it a crack so that you could see her through a long perpendicular narrow from which waves of stale perfume exuded.

"Malchidion is dead!" announced Mrs. Bell. "The old guardian has passed on, Mrs. Stupka."

"Is he? Has he?" said the old woman. Her face broke out into a rubbery, embarrassed kind of smile. "Thought he already was. Nothing ever happens, Mrs. Bell."

In parenthesis

And at that time, there was consternation, for no one knew for certain who was lord of that realm. Some said that always it had been the lawyers and the clerks, that Malchidion was but a figurehead for an unending bureaucracy, and soon enough another would be delegated to hold titular power so that folk might have some name or other to supplicate, to curse, to grieve, to forget amidst endless cares. And others, mainly the old, who knew what the young did not believe, that the Guardian had long ruled when the aged were but babes in the crib, wondered that he should prove mortal after all.

These parties held various opinions about whether it should be welcomed or shunned. Then prophets came out from caves and taverns to announce the new age, which became a topic for the markets to proclaim and discuss. Yet never in all that tumult was there anything more than gossip and the pretense of knowledge.

In the darkening hour, when the tents were closed and the inventory taken from tables, the young went to their games, to their clandestine loves, and the toughs journeyed to the warehouses, where one bet on boxing matches. The Pilgrim Kheen wandered the narrow paths, peering anxiously, for the king of coins had departed. This hearkened the Great Change, something beyond the ken of blood.

Then there came the rumor of a rough man in the desert, a man who said hard things, especially about dancing girls. And some said they had seen this fella, and that he told them they had lost their heads a long time ago. The prophet would stop and laugh at this, a private joke no one understood. Then he said they could not tell the Good from the back side of an ass and made similar denunciations. Some folk liked that sort of thing and flocked to him, while others went to tattle to the priests because it made them

feel important to have news to report and besides, no one likes a sc
old.

A fever dream

The learned scholars, the lawyers, and the clerks, all went about
their business. It was as if nothing had changed, but very thinly beneath the customary actions was terror. A fever dream of madness
came upon them. It was at first a barely registered frisson. There
was no ostensible reason the machinery of exchange should not go
on. No reason the usual calculations regarding interest, scarcity,
demand and whatnot should not continue to provide the rule for
living.

Yet here and there, among a minor functionary in an obscure
province or a clerk in the City, hysteria began to manifest, a neurotic disease. One suddenly felt oneself to be playacting, and then
the entire schema started to unravel. Entire departments would
stumble about and look anxiously at managers who would query
supervisors who sought out department heads, who answered by
blinking or locking their doors. A fad of hanging oneself swept
over the clerks.

And then, it was never clear where the information originated,
it was decided that the malady was due to foreign influence. A
yarn about the return of a dead king was recalled and said to
circulate among dangerous, disreputable sorts. The functionaries
swung wildly and shifted from confusion and dismay to zealous

suspicion. Detectives, spies, and the network of agents who occupy the gray interstices sprung into action.

Strife whispered shrewd malice to the folk. It was found expedient to remember grudges, to note with careful neutrality the somewhat concerning behavior of a neighbor. It was enough to suggest in a tone of civic concern to bring the authorities to bear upon anyone you disliked.

Babylon

Yes, it was at this time that Benevolence began to crack down. It was like a great, wounded beast that senses some oncoming, decisive conflict. Blindly, but efficiently, it took precaution against the enemy it could not see, nor properly understand. Furious rage gave vent; violent partisan hatreds erupted in street riots, disjointed calls for freedom ludicrously linked to demands for more and more public control of realms traditionally private and personal.

The fourth estate reliably did their part. The rank and file of the journalist class quickly came to consensus, finding obvious culprits, the sources of danger. So, too, in the schools and theater, everyone denounced the easy target. For the barely literate, headlines gave the message, so one needn't trouble to read the article, and so few did. Why should they when everyone knew?

Few thought to point out that the drama was manufactured; folks were told beforehand what mattered, like gulls at a magician show, the eyes directed precisely where the trick was *not* taking place. Sky confessed to the Elder certain discoveries and suspicions that burdened her, and asked with increasing concern what was to be done. And the Elder said it must always be this way, for the adherents of closed economy hate to the death that which cannot be contained by the image of their appetites.

The festive table

The young men with their dark suits and long beards, the moist dark eyes that always seemed as if everything they pondered were made visible through a mirror of blazing fire, and the mirror was Torah, and all their conversation was a leap and a dance across time, one sage shouting the distance of centuries as one would speak to a comrade sitting at the other end of the raucous, joyous, festive table.

And there was Bene among them, telling some story; Sky could not hear what, but her face was kind, and it must have delighted Rabbi Naftali, because he clapped his hands and rose from his seat throwing his arms out as if he would draw the others into the blessing of her words. And there was the pale Ansharu, Ratcatcher, who said nothing, but smiled in a soft, wry way, as if soon he would be leaving on a long journey, as if all that they said in every language of the universe were stored in his satchel, and the priest Terence Bunn in his ivory alb was standing near the ancient, ramshackle throne dragged out from its place in the artists' studio, the Elder's staff in his hand and Sky thought any moment he is going to strike the ground and call everyone to attention, but he did not strike, only the Elder entered the room and with him silence.

"What is remarkable," said the Elder, "is that the vates and the sophist appear to the world to be the same. There is no difference. The words of the vates and the words of the sophist are taken as identical, the performance of the one equal to the act of the other. This is what the men of shadows believe, so much so that when Socrates, who never wrote a word, witnessed to his innocence, they could only scoff and summarily pass judgment. And the Son of Man, who wrote only in the dust, a trace, what words men can only guess, but I will tell you, it was his time that he was tracing, the time that men and women cannot capture, but that grows, like the mustard seed, until all emptiness and desolation is encompassed; it is the terrible exchange."

At these words, Sky was thrown back. It was not like remembering. She felt literally thrown into that moment in the hunt. The gentle eyes of the white hart offered no hint of timidity, yet so lovely, to be under her gaze, to be brought within an enchanted circle from which nothing ugly or cruel could be thought of or tolerated.

And Sky wanted to throw her arms about the hart, but felt herself unworthy, and so she simply stood and adored the demure creature, so impossibly pure and white like pearlescent lightning, and there was a gold collar wore by the white hart, and Sky discerned a writing on the collar, but no amount of scrutiny would allow her to make out the words, and then she thought, it must be in a language I cannot read. But none of that, she thought again, explains the hounds, and the cries, and the great fright.

Whisper

The arc of stellar light was crossed by a splash of purple that faded into magenta. In another corner, a nimbus of amber with deep veins of oxblood pierced the horizon where twin stars pulsated. As she walked along the plain, Sky felt as if she had encountered in a premonition just this impossibly exotic scene. In the distance, low, dark hills were lit by strange bursts of phosphorescence that briefly exposed a line of gnarled trees that stood like goblin sentinels watching her slow progress. In the midst of crossing a dry river bed, she suddenly stopped and stood vigilant. A whisper of memory, and then she gasped in recognition of the shuddering horizon, what had greeted her behind the mask of the Vendakar's face.

Secret prayer

Above her, the stellar expanse written in strange hieroglyphs, the images of history, innumerable tales, not scrambled, or merely bizarre, but made into a rhythmic pattern that suggested, but eluded, mystery pregnant with something, some vital thing, an intimate universal — or not. Perhaps it was all curses and putrefaction, nothing besides this appalling end. And the wind blew, whipping and stinging, and then soft as a gentle kiss on the forehead, and there were tender tears, and wailing, and slow, tremulous night songs, adagio, and sepia, waiting for the dawn.

She heard the tribes gathered, the kinship for all, fur, scale, and feather, the behemoths of unseen deeps, the poignant, gossamer life, the beetles, the wrens, fierce lion, and ram, and water buffalo, all were advancing, and men of craft, harpooners, fishermen, smithies of the forge, and those who dared to take from mother earth, the miners who crawled into telluric veins to bring forth the hidden.

Poets, and warriors, kings and merchants, slaves who knew their slavery, and those who did not, liars, thieves, saints, sages, torturers, idiots, craven, innocent, clerks, and lawyers, and nurses, professors, bankers, shamans, whores, tram drivers, teachers, gardeners, whimsical, sturdy, mad, weary, bitter, solemn, cruel, kind, whispering with lore, or utterly lost, drifting, herded, striding with purpose, they came, crying, crying with ardent voice, that someone, anyone might make sense of it, that book that was nature, that book that was history, that book beyond the cosmos, the song they y earned for, and knew not.

They were advancing and crying, helpless for justice, deranged, embittered, and covered in sores and flies, pathetic, but some noble, with a mantle of beauty like wings hovering above their tatters. Who will come? Who will answer for it? Who could unseal the scroll? And all their voices rose up like incense, the horror of the abyss deepened beyond thought, cacophony rendered into secret pr ayer.

Persephone

Sky felt beneath her the dry, flat earth, its skin baked and crackling into a dull mosaic that pictured only wasteland. The sky was heavy with storms, but the storm did not come. Nearly everywhere she looked, there was nothing but the endless plain. She recalled that her father once explained that the Inuit had several dozen words for snow. When one is surrounded by the stuff, careful attention to differences could play a crucial role in survival. Doubtless, there were also poets of the plain that would discern a word or two, if not an entire lyric, in what appeared to be pure monotony. Unable to be astonished by the inscape of the barrens, she plodded on.

Just at the edge of vision, she thought she saw something — a little blip of ground rising above the uniform dullness, though her sense of distance was distorted. It might be miles away. She might be seeing an insignificant mound. But it was something, so she pointed her way. As she grew closer, a grouping of monoliths rose up against the sheltering sky.

"Daughter," said a gentle, motherly voice, "it is well with thee. Be not afraid."

There was a scent of pomegranates, something softly incensed, a smoky citrus, and Sky leaned back into a warm, welcoming bosom. She felt tender arms reach round to hold her, and the woman began to sing a long, slow breath that felt like centuries in the making.

"Daughter, it was a good day," said the maternal voice, "and now it is night, and that is good, too. In the evening, we forget our cares, we let them go, do not hold on to those errant ones! Let them caper in the barrens, nothing will feed them. In the dark, we remember loves, we remember what is good, like that time your brother went fishing and the bear joined him. That creature was not sorry to visit the cold wet, the white silver babbling that brought her meals. She cried out her thanks, and brother was abashed by that. The bear was not offended by his sharing the gift ribbon, the presence of the boy, she tossed him a fish."

And though Sky did not have a brother, she was fond to hear it, and indeed something in her recalled the brother, and the story of the fish.

"And there was the time our uncle came, he had gone on a voyage and returned with many tales, and many rings, and that bauble, the one your sister stole while you slept. You saw her playing with it naively the next day. She loved it so innocently, and she forgot it was yours. Folks think everything is evil and dark in the heart, but it isn't so. You forgave her, were happy for her, and played with her and said nothing. When later she remembered, and came running to you, tears falling, and you offered the carving, it was a miniature hen that nested upon three wee eggs of lapus lazuli. She could not take it, but you put it under her pillow. We did not know the fever would come, that was our last winter with her, our dear."

"Or the day the Sage came down from the mountains and begged a meal. We all stared at him and were afraid to speak. That strange one, he walked as a man at that time, and we lit candles, and he prophesied. He said you would come back to us, and here you are."

In the morning, Sky saw where she had lain. It was remarkable that she had not recognized them in her twilight quandary. She'd reached them somehow in that vestibule of night. The quiet sun shone now upon a half circle of sentinels, standing stones that looked out upon the plain.

You are a duchess

Sky was still blinking into morning when the rider came upon her. He must have been following her trail. There wasn't any side path or obvious place from whence he could have come. The first thing she noticed was the armor he wore. It was old and creaky, and may have been an antique rusting in some barn. In any event, that was nothing on his horse. She'd never seen such a rickety nag before. It was nearly a mock horse, as if someone had found a skeleton in the desert and stretched a thin skin over it.

Then the knight raised his hand in greeting. He was sloppy in the saddle, unaccustomed to riding or half in his cups. So she was in a further state of astonishment, what with the Etheric geography and now this, when the fellow raised his visor and asked her if she might be a duchess. His face was haggard with a gray beard, though admittedly there was the ghost of nobility about the eyes.

"I am not," she said.

"Oh, but you must be a duchess," informed the rider. "You can't have adventures on behalf of a common girl. It's against the rules."

She might have laughed, if it weren't so absurd. "Whose rules are those?" she said with feeling, forgetting for the moment the nature of the road, and the puzzle of their meeting.

"What?" said the knight. "You're very impertinent for a duchess. The rules are immemorial. They have always been. Now, you cannot dispute that. Clearly, you need a guide."

"Clearly, you are mistaken," said Sky. "I am not a duchess."

"Most likely you just don't know," offered the knight with sympathetic courtesy.

"That's not the sort of thing one should forget," she said.

"People forget the most important things all the time," said the knight, still sliding about in his saddle.

"I really don't think you ought to be sitting that poor horse," she said with a sigh.

"Why not?" asked the knight, with just a hint of righteous anger. "This steed has the blood of valor. Besides, where else should I be? The inn was very fine, but the horse began to whinny. He knows when an adventure is up; and so we are here, and you are a duchess, whether you know it or not."

The idols

Sky looked sideways at the scraggly knight, and his narrow shadow of a mount. "Is that the best you could do?" she asked, half whimsy and brim-full with exasperation.

"Yes, it's the best. I only drew him this morning. Ever try to draw a horse, whilst keelhauled with a hangover?"

"Might as well ride a cock horse," she said.

"Indeed, that is how he appeared when first we met. I was well-nigh a toddler, though distinguish between modalities. Perception of form is fit to the capacity of the knower. In reality, he's sturdier than he seems."

They set off then along the plain, riding hard. To her surprise, the knight and his ersatz horse carried her along with ease, though she had a feeling that following this fella wasn't likely to get you anywhere. As they rode upon that stark and endless plain, a sense of her own nullity before unqualified vastness dragged Sky towards humiliated sadness. As she sank into grim silence, the knight spoke with sudden urgency. "Don't let them abash you," he warned. "You'll feel it now in your heart. They are a vain lot, the archons."

She raised her head to look around. The land was unbroken by any interval of mutability, the horizon low and hot with painful, smothering heat. Soon, however, images of lovely beaches, tranquil water, enchanting eyes and lips, and the suggestion of beautiful flesh under an artificial skyline of artfully chosen clouds, followed by a flurry of blossoming flowers, propelled themselves into Sky's mind. It was like finding oneself immersed in a commercial for a high-end fragrance.

"They like to forget belching and flatulence," said the knight. "And children. Nothing must interfere with pleasure devoid of honor. They are mostly all natural Docetists."

This snippet of theological opinion oddly vanquished the spectacle presented to her imagination. Next, Sky felt as if immense divinities invisibly presided from on high, gods of prescient and comprehensive ability, so overwhelming that it was folly to dispute their supernal judgment.

"Ah, and now they will be advising you of their beneficence and power, and of your good fortune to fall under their tutelage. You have to thrust them from your heart, dear one. Only then can you see them clearly."

The knight began to hum a childlike lullaby of surprising sweetness and gentility. As the notes unfurled, Sky recognized familiar rhythms. Someone, somewhere, had sung this melody to her before. Simultaneously, the inhabitants of the barrens were revealed to her in brute objectivity. Sky kept gasping in astonishment to see them — giant figures sculpted in soft stone and painted garish colors, or huge carnivalesque signs designed to attract roadside visitors.

She nudged the knight of fools and gestured towards the idols. Now that she stood outside them, they appeared as flat and second-rate as a painted scene for the stage. Yet the idols were not embarrassed. They kept on speaking as if their pronouncements were never more profound with misery or august disdain.

Certitude of Method remained convinced of its findings. Smugsloth rested its chin in folded hands, a wry expression of satisfied disenchantment marring the beauty of its features with sterile boredom. The Sadness of Sex brooded in faceless despair, while the pale and bloated ghost of the Outer Darkness gawked in blind imbecility.

She noticed the cadenced phrases of Certitude began to repeat. It was explaining the advantages of additional insurance for those who possessed out-of-warranty vehicles. Each idol was unaware of the others. Except for the unbroken muteness of the last, each followed a changeless script of endless repetition.

Hidden desire

"There is an odd thing about memory," said the knight. "It comes, and it goes, but always out of sequence, the way the past jumps out in front, as if it were just now coming into being, showing you what you could not discern when you were living it, because you were too busy, or likely recollecting some other moment.

We wander, always seeking after our own meaning, and it never seems to arrive, trapped behind the various props that linger like souvenirs of an inept, impossible enterprise. There are barrens enough where the pitiless moon groans from the cold, and the sun blanches beautiful bones."

"Is it all just this, then?" said Sky, indicating the preening fakes.

"No, my dear, our stretching out into the future is a form of prayer, or a desire to pray, often hidden from us. One must surrender to the imageless, the plenitude in the void. That is why the vates enter the desert. And the hermits of old, the holy seekers. The imagination that has not tasted death inevitably begets idols."

They should have gone with her

Having journeyed through that spiritual geography, Sky found herself back in the room surrounded by her friends. The Elder was sitting upon the throne of Prester John with a benevolent, softly ironic smile upon his face. Everyone was talking; there was vigorous debate, some laughing, a few shouts, the ordinary, lively human thing.

Sky edged closer to the Elder who was silent. He was remembering, catching hold of the non-sequential stream that speaks truth. Then he gestured towards Benedicta, spoke a judgment upon her companions of the earth.

"They should have gone with her, you see? The moment was ripe. The contemplation they lived out had roots. The act had begun years before they were born. If you really want to know, some of it began with John, that rough-hewn angel man who spoke out, telling everyone they had forgotten everything, when they became shrewd and cunning, calculating what was pleasurable, and what would benefit them.

And some of it was started after the Anointed had wrestled with the immense wildness, the multitude of shadows — he knew what we are afraid to remember, that the tongue of fire only comes to the one who has died.

Those who sensed this, you cannot reason to it through abstract logic, departed from the rabble of noise, lived in the solitude of the desert listening for the music of the Cross, because that is where we sing as one.

All that had built up a kind of momentum. It was the river in which their prayer flowed, so there was an opportunity for greatness. The first martyrs would have recognized it, and leapt at the chance — but they were afraid, like all of us, and though they wept, the veiled ones allowed her to be taken. They gave her up to the monster, she and her blood sister, Rosa.

If they had not abandoned her, of course, they would have died. Yet they died anyway, in little gasps, dispersed into anonymity, rather than together. The glory of that lost labor awaits us. We have to make good the lack, redeem the cowardice. That's how it works, Sparrow."

Antidote

Suspicion pervaded the City like a poisonous fog. Yet Sky seemed strangely immune to fears. While almost everyone became closed-lipped and cautious, she frequented all her favorite places with nearly frightening carelessness. The priest and the Ansharu re-monstrated with her. Benedicta was away. The Elder watched but did not intervene. He seemed almost to expect this of her.

And shortly after, the others found her. They met in the back room of a smoky pub, where the dark prince paced back and forth whilst making programmatic declarations. The problem had always been simple, he said. One was dealing with an arch-magi-cian, a power that did not quibble to stoop to deceive. A show of overwhelming beauty was cast before their eyes, and everyone bowed down.

It was like that, even for the hard men and women who ought to know better. It was that bluster of appearance that finally cowed the hero, Job. Job aspired for more. He aspired for freedom, but in the end he settled for restoration of his health, a bunch of heifers, and more children. "What is needed," said Mordred, "is proof against spectacle."

Mordred was bold. He believed himself a champion of humanity, though he might be a victim of the wasting disease that eats the world, and remains famished. He might be in that class of being the Buddhists name *preta*.

"The will must be strengthened to resist the smothering show."

Mordred produced from the folds of his cloak a thin chain with a tiny flask that served as a pendant. He said englobed within that droplet was inviolable freedom, and at least in that he was true. "It is our 'no,'" he proclaimed. "Not even the whirlwind can take that away."

The tincture of the ampule was a gray gruel, the color of dishwater.

"Oh, pretty!" said Wanda.

Denis said nothing. It was the color of his eyes.

"It isn't much," said Sky.

"A tear in the ocean," concurred Ned.

"It is enough," said Mordred.

Special delivery

Ned leaned back in his chair so that it creaked under his weight. He looked like he was ready for a nap, but he always looked that way.

"Say, Ned, do you think you could answer a few questions for a fella?" asked Sky.

Ned shrugged, which was as close to agreement as she was likely to get.

"I'm still wondering. Why is it you lot decided to bring me in? I'm not really your sort, don't you see?"

Ned gazed at her for a while, like Sky was speaking Portuguese, and Ned doesn't know Portuguese. Sky waved her hands in front of his face to make sure he hadn't gone to sleep after all. "Not my line," he said at last. "I don't pick'em. Wanda had a say. She said you bizzed her wrong. She didn't like your mug, maybe. I dunno. She's mean as a hornet some days, our Wanda."

"Well, maybe I don't like her mug, either," said Sky.

Ned grinned. "But that was just a starter," he said, getting a bit of momentum now that his mouth was moving. "The prince had a yen, so Wanda maybe just pointed you out. And then Denis; he's the delivery man. He brought you over."

"Brought me over?"

"Well, someone had to do it. Wanda could have. I wouldn't put it past her, but it was Denis that done it. I heard him chatting about 'where' and 'how'." Ned was blunt that way.

"Why didn't you stop him?" cried Sky. The incredulity and protest in her voice was unmistakable. Ned stared blankly back.

"Well, my dear, it didn't occur to me, is all. No, it just didn't."

A touching letter

Sky received a letter from Diana. It gave an amusing report of the countryside. They were all grown quite lazy with happiness at the removal of Aunt Elisabeth. Mama asked after "the nice girl." Rory had even come down from the attic to wonder about Sky.

That last evening before she left, they had all been quiet together. When Bunn and Ratcatcher had shown up to retrieve her, everyone suddenly felt that they were losing a sister. Narina had cried and told Sky that she must not by any means leave them. "And what about Herman; he's in love with you?" Herman was her rooster. Deco was back in the city. He wrote them of the unrest and how it was no longer safe. "It's certainly foolhardy to stay there now," wrote Diana plainly, with the added exhortation that Deco should accompany her as protection on the way back to the summer house. "You know that we all care for you."

Sky wrote back to thank her warmly, though not without the admonition that by no means should Deco come. "That day we played Characters, I can't explain. If we are to be ourselves, it is sometimes necessary to endure suffering if it should be required of us." Feeling that this was perhaps harsh as well as enigmatic, Sky tried to soften the blow. "And if we love one another, surely what is most precious is somehow preserved, come what may."

Musame takes flight

And then Benevolence upped the ante. Special agents of the Bureau of Information Retention were assigned to go from house to house and verify down to the last copper coin the income and identity of the occupants. This was an unprecedented level of intrusion justified by the heightened state of concern for general welfare, the peril to society indicated by dissidents, and the needs of Benevolence to continue the necessary work protecting those most germane to the continuation of Benevolence — the circularity of this last argument being somewhat obfuscated by induced terror and the graft of those always ready to take advantage of an opportunity.

Mrs. Takashima was in tears for Musame. Mr. Takashima was adamant that "daughter" should stay. He knew someone quite adept at forging necessary papers. Yet Sky could see it was no good. Midori could not contain her anxiety that Mr. T might end up in prison. Surely, they could secure some hiding place until the sweep of the Bureau investigators had finished. The Elder had many friends.

Mr. Takashima pointed out that the Bureau came unannounced and often returned now a second time to stymie efforts at evasion.

That evening, Sky took special care to observe proprieties, which was the way one showed intensity of feeling in that house. Towards morning, she slipped out. The note she left said they were not to worry. Benevolence was not so fine a net that she could not make herself small enough to escape.

The mackintosh factory

First, they said the factory processed sheets of dried dragon fruit brought by cargo ship and train from a distant island province, though Sky had yet to see workers laboring to unload, clean, or package dragon fruit. Then she was told the company was diversified, that, in fact, the branch she occupied had been repurposed to produce flax milk, prune juice, and avocados, though none of these items appeared to be available for inspection.

Her labor was in a warehouse barracks outside the city. It was one of the few places where they didn't seem worried about the recent ill-temper of Benevolence. What Sky did, surrounded by others draped in rubber coats — it wasn't clear why everyone had to wear a mackintosh — was sort pieces of paper that arrived in bins carried by conveyor belt. Each employee was responsible for a certain color.

For instance, there was a worker who sorted for shades of yellow, say, from lemon to chartreuse. Another employee would check for a different range of yellow. There was a German specialist who oversaw that group, the *gelb* leader. Sky was assigned the blues, indigo and cyan to cornflower, royal, and cerulean. Conversation was strictly prohibited, unless one was asking a supervisor for a second opinion on the shade of a particular scrap of paper.

It was only on the lunch hour when the laborer was permitted brief conviviality, but each table was presided over by a supervisor who made certain speculation as to what the job was about was never broached. An offense of that sort received a warning, a second of which was a warrant for immediate dismissal.

The point of it all

The factory grounds contained acreage dedicated to a series of additional barracks that served as dormitory space for the workers.

The barracks were segregated by gender, though there was a section building provided for those who claimed agnosticism or refusal of binary codes on that matter, as well as a separate collection of modular housing reserved for the small group of those with supervisory positions that appeared to merit allowance for family life.

The vast majority of laborers, however, were either single individuals or those who passed themselves off as such. Every morning, one would shower and perform organized calisthenics. Then there would be a team leader who provided an inspirational message speaking of the emotional benefits of colors or the tremendous service to the future accomplished by the labor of minions who had no idea of any concrete purpose at the end of their prescribed work.

A brief breakfast was followed by the claxon alarm that designated the work shifts. One day, Sky was sleepily between jumping jacks and the empty homily when she became aware of a solitary worker, apparently at pains to catch her attention. It was a spare fella with a slightly unkempt mug, reminiscent of Shaggy from Scooby-Doo.

He was first excited when he determined that Sky was approaching, then exaggeratedly careful to look about and make certain no supervisor was observing. When Sky was close enough, he whispered a single declamatory expression: "Puzzles," he said.

Unaccountable reality

Sky didn't stop to consider that flinging oneself desperately into a broom closet might appear rather worse than actually talking to the offending personage. Still, she did not want further revelations or attention from Shaggy, though he had made several hapless attempts to do so. Once her eyes could take in the chamber, which was lit by a pale light emanating from a small oil lamp, she stood for a long time in a stupor of incredulity. Then Sky glanced about and pinched herself to make certain she wasn't dreaming, though for all she knew, pinching oneself was as likely to occur in dreams as anywhere else.

It was a curious fact that the room that Sky had been shown by Lady Winterbourne as a hideaway for priests appeared to occupy a storage space in the factory. "But there are so many strange connections I know nothing about," said Sky, before stealthily retreating from the empty chamber.

The young man in the cupboard

The next day, Sky spent her allotted time for exercise and leisure retracing her steps in an effort to identify precisely where the impossible hidden room was possible. Of course, nondescript doors look alike, or they wouldn't be nondescript. *And if you are hiding a fugitive priest, naturally, one doesn't wish to advertise the fact.* And then, of course, it was not the sort of place where one could indulge curiosity without explanation.

There were a great many corridors and bays, stairways to the boiler room, and such. Sky only had a general notion of what part of the factory she had been in, and the clock of her time was waning. In desperation, Sky made a trial of her senses. Walking about in solitude, she pretended to hear steps to see if it would point out to memory which door was right. And then . . . Eureka, the room was right, but to her shock, it was occupied by a youth dressed in a plain tunic, though it was not the uniform of a factory w orker.

The young man was not at all surprised to see her. He turned to her an agreeable face, tolerant, very slightly bemused. And when he spoke to her, it was as if they were old friends who simply happened to meet one another by some happy coincidence in a secret room reserved for renegade priests.

"I am pleased," he said, the tone equally courtesy and natural warmth.

"I'm sorry. I didn't know anyone was here," she said.

"And why should I not be here?" he asked with an arch humor that escaped her.

Sky saw then that the whole room was both the same and different. It breathed with life, as if it knew nothing of neglect and abandonment. She daren't stay long. When she left, she suddenly realized it couldn't possibly be the same room. She had gotten flustered and gone in a completely wrong direction.

We give them twisted existence

Where Deco's aunt could see nothing but connivance and design, a refreshing indifference to how she appeared to his set made Sky all the more appealing to Deco. Her artless lack of vanity was the finishing touch in her devastating allure. Deco's sisters had refrained from speaking too much about the new girl, mainly because they sensed an unequal attachment. Otherwise, Narina would have quickly warmed to her; indeed, she had already done so in spite of an intention to remain aloof.

Diana was puzzled by Sky's avoidance of deeper friendship with her brother, but she could find no objection to her character. As for Aurora, she descended with ornery forbearance into any ordinary human interaction, though Rory, too, seemed to have made an exception of Sky, whose own eccentric solitude suggested spiritual kinship.

Deco had concluded that Sky was unavailable to anyone, though he rather hoped once she had worked through the dark clouds that had followed the trail of her sojourn to Elnaria that prospects might change. The alteration in the mood of the City, however, eroded what patience his youthful ardor was capable of sustaining. He was shocked to discover that Sky had fled the Takashimas and that neither the Elder nor any of her other friends were aware of her current residence. He suspected they weren't telling him everything they knew.

Deco, of course, was not the son of a merchant prince without having acquired useful contacts at various levels of Elnarian society. These he plied with skill and tenacity. Sky really shouldn't have been surprised when one day he showed up at the gates of the large, almost eerily vague collection of structures outside the city proper. Deco encouraged her to come away. Why should she endure her present existence as a worker in a dubious factory?

Sky was certainly impressed by the sober urgency of Deco. She had liked him from the first as an endearing, passionate soul, but now she balked, and Deco found there was nothing practically to be done if the storm should come upon her.

"But really, do I have enemies to care about so trivial a girl?" she asked with that frankness that only added to her beauty.

Deco tried to remonstrate with her. "Sky, there is nothing rational in this hate."

Vindictiveness towards those on the wrong side of Benevolence was bereft of pity, for Benevolence could only care for identities duly entered and rigidly accorded the respect of the system.

"We have given *them* a twisted existence," she lamented bitterly. The intensity of her expression surprised him. Sky was left to answer Deco's concern with natural gratitude for his offer, but she would not go with him.

Asylum

There was almost childish meanness in it. That evening, when Sky returned to the dormitory, she discovered a small bag containing a random collection of different colored bits of paper stashed beneath the pillow on her bed. With a panic, she saw the offending item and wondered who could have put it there. And then Sky considered if she should call for a supervisor or surreptitiously discard the item. It would be a low, craven thing to foist it stealthily upon another.

In the end, she pretended to have a need to check her locker, where the mackintosh was stored. On the way, she thrust the bag, which she had hidden under her shirt, into one of the burn bins located in various places to discard materials requiring combustible elimination.

Sky began to wonder if anyone in her memory had actually quit the factory or been fired and seen alive and well away from the institution. The runners on the street had all talked of the place as an asylum from the scourge of Benevolence.

The Horai

Sky was less astonished, yet not quite not surprised, the second time she met him. She had decided it might not matter which random utility room she chose, and it didn't. The youth was no longer sitting in a simple wooden chair, but instead he was seated with dignified grace on a throne painted in black lacquer and adorned with eight-petalled flowers, the bird that rises from flames, a strange creature she did not recognize, and lovely clouds of five colors.

He bestowed upon her a gaze that made her feel she had stepped into a solemn ceremony. Sky noticed now Asiatic features somehow missed before.

"I never know when to expect you," she said.

"Perhaps I am always here, and it is you who arrive unannounced," he said with the hint of a whimsical smile.

"Have you been waiting for me, then?"

Instead of answering, the young man walked over to a shroud of dark silk. He pulled this covering down to reveal a tall mirror shining so brilliantly that Sky could not even see herself. In the reflected light, the royal youth showed her a sacred sword and sparkling jewels that were spread out against the dark floor like stars winking in the firmament. She was silent and pleased and wondering all at once.

"Now we must go," he said.

Sky still did not ask his name. She could not bring herself to press him, or perhaps something in the youth forbade this. He had put on a long, cascading garment of raw silk that reminded her of a priest's alb. Her breath caught at the chill and the darkness. The time must be different here, she thought, for it had not been night when she discovered him.

He walked with a steady, brisk pace and did not look back until they came to the small, nearly hidden gate that gave entrance to a sacred grove. She heard the gentle whisper of a meandering stream beneath an arched wooden bridge that led to a meadow. Like a crown upon an ascending hill, the ivory dome of a pavilion gleamed in moonlight.

Inside the pavilion, the young man performed various rites that culminated in the rubbing of sticks of *hinoki* wood from the imperial forest until a flame sparked into life. With the new fire, he cooked rice grown and cultivated according to strict rules and reserved for this meal, cloaked under sable skies. Then he spoke to her words with meaning only half remembered once away from his presence.

There was ardor, urgency, and childlike, festive joy in his voice. He was telling her, it was all so compact, but not vague or mashed together, of the *Horai,* which was both the blessed land, and also the folk. She understood that the rice they ate was a sacred meal, shared, somehow a kingdom of souls. The Pleroma was nothing ethereal, radically real.

Azure was the color of the *Horai.* As he spoke, he laughed, and she saw the disk of the new sun rising and the youth was now dressed in the dawn-colored garment known as the *akebono.* The light of *Horai,* he told her, was unimaginably pure, brilliant white, and yet, milky, soft, caressing, speaking the truth with utmost clarity without burning or harm.

Then she was asking a most important question; only she found herself again in the hidden chamber, and seemingly alone, and she wondered had she ever really left it? The question echoed in some deep place she could not fathom, and there was the empty washbasin and the ancient dust.

The cure for evil

Peridin's house was built around an open patio. A fountain marked the center of the atrium, where he often went to reflect and have a bit of quiet. The bubbling noise of the waters would counteract the intrusions of the City, and he could almost forget he was a man at all.

It was twilight, and he was bemused by the silky movements of a tiny lizard no bigger than his thumb set upon the wall of the fountain, when a man's voice, low but spiced with a hint of thunder, startled his peace.

"Tell me, apothecary, what is indicated by pleurisy, gripe, an itching nose, and a feeling of smoke in the chest?"

"An imbalance of yellow bile," answered Peridin as calmly as he could. He reached for a cigarette and lit it. He was having trouble seeing his questioner. He could not imagine how his house had been so successfully breached. Strangely, however, after the initial shock, he found that he was only moderately alarmed.

"And what does one do for sore joints?"

Peridin felt himself back in school. The voice was definitely one used to authority and to posing questions. "One grinds sandalwood, clay, and red clover blossoms with a little camphor; add a touch of rose water and vinegar. The balm is then rubbed vigorously onto the joints," he answered.

"Very good," said the voice in the night. "And tell me, apothecary, what is the cure for the evil in men's hearts?"

The man stood before him then, a silver beard and piercing eyes most distinct in the gloaming. Peridin paused before answering. "I fear there is nothing in my house that can answer to that ill," he said at last.

"And yet perhaps some object has come your way that even now makes you seek solace from its power."

The apothecary gulped. Then he blinked and stared back at the intruder as blandly as he could.

"I know," said the Elder. "Your silent words reveal the secret so judiciously kept, Peridin. Think ye that narrow vessel large enough for the task? The Grail is no such thing, and even the truth of it is but a thimble for the infinite."

And then the vates began to laugh, until he roared so heartily that Peridin crept back within to muse upon his treasure. He found to his displeasure the residue of doubt.

Mute not mute

Sky saw him once more in that place. He no longer appeared like an emperor of the Rising Sun, though he might still be the Sun King. They were in the rooms of the *Grand Appartement* in the palace of Versailles. The sovereign entertained her with a display of its virtues. The Grand Canal ran through the park like a river out of Eden. The chariot of Apollo emerged placidly from the waters of night as it looked towards the East, the ashes of Phaethon but a memory. On the northern side, monsters arose from abyssal midnight, though the youth barely noticed them.

"It is from elsewhere that the ancient foe strikes," he said in passing.

On the West, alongside the gardens, the center was celebrated by statues representing the four great rivers of France, as if the original peace had found restoration beyond exile. "But you see, all this is rather like the summer house," he said with casual dismissal. And then they were back in the hidden room, and the king was a child holding before her a luminous flower of prayer.

"You wanted to ask me something?" he said gently.

"It's very important," she said, "but somehow I just can't find the words."

"It's alright," he said. "Spirit cries out for you. Abba knows what is in your heart."

The seventh chamber

Deco had told Benedicta and the Elder where Sky was. He hoped they could convince her to see reason. An enigmatic smile flashed in Benedicta's face. It was more like meeting someone across the fence of a labor camp. She whispered something Sky could not hear. When Sky breathlessly told of her mysterious encounters, Bene simply said, *"The seventh chamber"* in a wondrous tone of voice.

Then, louder, with quiet mirth, she said, "That room you came upon is not in the house you visited, nor is it in the factory. More like to say the house is within that room. It is within you, my dear."

One can pray anywhere

A young Jew stood very still next to us. His jacket was much too loose, but a grin broke through his stubbly black beard when he said, 'They tried to smash the wall of the prison with my head, but my head was harder than the wall!'

Among all the shaved heads, it was strange to see the white-turbaned women who had just been treated in the delousing barracks, and who went about now looking distressed and humiliated.

Children dozed off on the dusty plank floor; others played tag among the adults. Two little ones floundered helplessly around the heavy body of a woman lying unconscious in a corner. They didn't understand why their mother just lay there without answering them. A gray-haired old gentleman, straight as an arrow and with a clear-cut, aristocratic profile, stared at the whole infernal canvas and repeated over and over to himself: 'A terrible day! A terrible day!'

And among all this, the unremitting clatter of a battery of typewriters: the machine-gun fire of bureaucracy.

Through the many little windowpanes one can see other wooden barracks, barbed wire, and a blasted heath.

I looked at the priest who was now back in the world again. 'And what do you think of the world now?' I asked. But his gaze remained unwavering and friendly above the brown habit, as if everything he saw was known, familiar from long ago. That same evening, a man later told me, he saw some priests walking one behind the other in the dusk between two dark barracks. They were saying their rosaries as imperturbably as if they had just finished vespers at the monastery. And isn't it true that one can pray anywhere, in a wooden barracks just as well as in a stone monastery, or indeed, anywhere on this earth where God, in these troubled times, feels like casting his likeness?

— Etty Hillesum, *Letters from Westerbork*

Arrest

Sky loved the woods. She cherished them as a retreat from the folly of mankind. So it was disappointing that the net of evil should extend so far. The workers were allowed an hour a day to wander about in the bit of forest enclosed like a park in the factory grounds. Hardly had she set foot upon the secret path she liked to follow when a supervisor appeared with a group of agents from the Bureau of Information Retention to block her way.

Sky recognized immediately that look of legalized malice distorting their features. Every visage turned to her was wrought in cold, official iron. *You are shunned;* this was the message of their flesh. *You are not recognized,* said the blank eyes. *You shall die the death*, said the dull, workmanlike tone of their voices.

They formed a little band as they marched her towards a police wagon filled with others who no longer existed. Her thoughts, universally grim, *I shall disappear; no one shall ever hear from me again*, were interrupted by a line of bystanders that included Shaggy. Was he some sort of inside snitch? She'd never even said a word to the fella.

A bit of paranoid madness ended the episode. As she was pushed into the prison van, she glimpsed a tittering pair in the crowd of onlookers, who looked very much like Wanda and Phylida Angstrom.

What I cannot tell you Sparrow

What I cannot tell you Sparrow, because it cannot be told yet, though I have been telling you all along. Better to say nothing; if you could but hear the silence.

The mothers and the papas have yearned for everything, and so foolishly hoped, because they know the secret. Péguy called it the secret of forty, what a man knows when he begins to suspect his strengths and to recognize himself, when he knows what youth can never fathom, that one must commit to a path, and the choices shape you so that one discovers what has been invented, the secret of forty, the great secret everyone knows but never tells, so that the folks of forty look with compassion, and a bit of dark humor, at callow youth, triumphant youth, in its brave, proud ignorance, that secret, that no one ever in the history of the world has been h appy.

They know this, and yet for each, the child, the beloved, they hope, in spite of themselves, and in spite of the secret, they hope, and even believe, it won't even be hard, they believe it with the charm of spring, with the charm of the first buds of spring, that despite no one ever, not one, their child will be happy.

Because they are not bad people, they are not so hard as to celebrate their child knowing that it will all end badly, in dust and unhappiness, it is very natural, it will be easy, though no one ever has been happy, not truly, fully, without taint of sorrow, without that dark residue at the end of the feast, it dries in the bottom of the cup, that remainder death.

With serene confidence they hope, for this birth, there is joy, because this child is born to be happy.

I will tell you, though this will mean nothing to you. Bulgakov knew that Man is an uncreated divine spirit that becomes person through the acts of a created soul and body. Humanity contains within cosmic being the image of Wisdom made for creation. All our stories hearken to the lost homeland. When we fail, the stories recollect the child of promise. When the name is lost, it is preserved in the stories.

The stories are ontological; until we live them out, we are the shadows. And yet, even so, few truly desire everything, though no one knows what that means, not even those who know the secret of forty! For desire is the secret of the saint, but also, I tell you, it is what the minerals know, and the flowering plants, and the sweet little birds that come to the branches in winter and hop about robustly like a fellow shaking off the snow from his coat — and that is why they come here.

These are the words of the vates. "Thérèse looks at me and says, Only when you can't see him do you know you're there. She says, Can you see me not seeing you? That's when you see me." You don't know what that means, but you will.

He felt lost, your friend, but is not. You will find him. Already we are together. The ones who know where they are sleep the death.

Holding cell

The holding facility where they kept the prisoners awaiting trial was remarkably like one of the smaller barracks at the factory. The very same beds with a similar regiment, a factotum of the warden, at least, a functionary distinct from the guards, would come and give an exhortatory message before breakfast proclaiming the therapeutic benefits of subjecting oneself to the arrangements and dictates of Benevolence and calisthenics.

That dark prince, Mordred, perhaps he was of the vampiric kind. He had a way of gliding, of entering; he was in the room before you knew it. Sky was looking out a tiny window. She was lucky, many cells didn't have one. She was holding with her eyes the lone tree in an exercise square reserved for the prisoners when Mordred appeared. He was never much for introductions. He just began talking.

"It was the horses, I suppose. We riders know one another. And your contempt for their grubby, dim ways. My kind of girl. And so I thought you might join the party. I understand it might seem like an imposition."

So, this was an explanation, if not an apology. And the longer he talked in his serenely wicked, charmingly bitter manner, other images came. *Yes, I have known him before,* thought Sky. *He is an old man. He is a dusty gown. He is a large crow.*

The secret of cast shadows

Something else, Sparrow, I have wanted to tell you. Light is plenitude. All the colors musically arrive and differentiate from the comprehensive brightness. It is within this invisible arrival that everything announces itself. And light is darkness, too, by order of magnitude, by the nature of its gift. Its speech surpasses every expectation.

An early master of the Renaissance, I am thinking especially of Taddeo; Taddeo is set apart in two ways. First, he does not operate under constant light from above, which lends serenity to the scenes of an artist like Giotto. His light is interior, a lamp or candle, an artisan's artificial sun, or perhaps directed solar entering from a window. From this closed source, light approaches at sharp angles and pitches; objects within this falling light are more narrowly defined, subject to local constraints.

Yet there is a second element to Taddeo's work. He is keen to portray the attached shadow, the darkness connected to an object that reveals relief, but he is not interested in cast shadow. The latter renders an object's unique position within a poetics of space. Here is what is important. The cast shadow, my dear, is the signature of a distinct orientation in time and space. It is also a dynamic moment, nothing that can be captured as isolate, as separate from motion and the complex interrelations of the whole. No finite artist can control it.

The discernment of that moment is love. Only love reads the eternal in the flash of the evanescent. You see why it is hard to tell?

The girl in the cupboard

Sky was sure no one knew of her imprisonment, so she was surprised to be told she had a visitor. Someone with extraordinary powers would be needed to make it happen. The young woman wore a white peasant's blouse beneath a faded pair of denim overalls with a crimson sash. She smiled, and Sky recognized the lost girl — that aspect of her elemental friend, the one that told her of the Elder's early days in the City.

"You're coming along fine," said Rachel Moon. "Just fine. My man's real proud of you, even if he won't say."

In spite of the circumstances, Sky felt a momentary flush of simple pleasure, though soon panic returned. "I don't know what to say," said Sky in a plaintive voice.

Rachel spoke with quiet firmness. "There's only the one thing ever. But don't you worry. Shaa, the father of all is exceedingly hard to find, even harder to tell; trust anyway."

Rebellion

The bland man sitting behind the table could barely suppress a yawn. He kept glancing at his wrist as if he wanted to look at his nonexistent watch. A spasm of irritation flitted across his bored face. Then he folded his hands and began to speak to her as if she were a tedious imbecile who had to have everything explained to her and then was sure to get it wrong in any event.

"I don't think you quite understand your position, young woman. Right now, you are a cipher. Do you know what that means? It means we can code you any number of ways." The fellow sighed and fumbled about in his pockets. Strictly speaking, it was against the rules, but he felt unaccountably reckless. He pulled out a polished lighter and fired the end of a cheroot.

"Some of them are quite pleasant, have a bit of power, even. Others —." He paused to follow the path of smoke with squinting eyes as it danced murkily above him. "Let's just say you can disappear. We can erase you so that everyone will look right through you. Or perhaps they will hold their noses and run. We can write you up as a repulsive, foul smelling bit of carrion or a wheedling sponger, vulnerable, undignified, mocked, humiliated, sometimes pitied, but never loved. People say it is vain to want to be admired. Let them subsist as what is never wanted, to have no beauty whatsoever, to never be invited into people's joy. Yes, you will then beg to be forgotten."

The bland man paused. He was rather satisfied with that speech. He leaned back in his chair and smiled the beneficent, untroubled smile of a man who has conquered himself and done his duty. "Better by far to take the safe path. And that is what we offer you, a safe, secure, reliable way."

Sky stared back for thirty seconds. The silence was long. At first, she wanted to be sure there was no more coming. Then she scrutinized his shiny, pink skin and the vacant, sleepy eyes. Misgiving and slowly dawning confusion and dismay registered in the dull face of the official. She thought about telling him to "go pound sand" or "suck eggs" or any number of crude expressions of dismissal.

But then she suddenly remembered the words of Brother Timothy; it was odd that she did not remember them aright until later, what he said. He'd pulled back his hood, and she was surprised by the blue serenity of his eyes. Then his flesh began to inflame; it was like spontaneous combustion, but he did not burn, he glowed. It was really quite astonishing. Then he said to her, "We do not manage to die. It is done for us. We do not surrender ourselves, we are taken."

These were strange words, but she understood that even death was not quite what one thought, if one could really think it at all. This kind of death was not available; it was not the kind of possibility that always appeared at hand, as if suicide could finally achieve this death. All this raced through her mind in a quantum of insight, and then she hit upon what she really felt at the moment.

"I'm so sorry," she said. "It must be awful, to never find it possible to die for love."

The shiny pink skin blanched. It was quite wrong of her to act that way. He was still thinking about it, when he realized she'd been removed from the room.

Accountant's nightmare

Exasperation had begun to tilt into dullness. When two people of different temperaments, backgrounds, and interests are accidentally thrust together, there is the potential for a momentary connection, some spark might even ignite, but inevitably the distance reasserts itself. Courtship was partly designed to be a process of protracted delay because, first, it is in slowness that superficial masks and mistaken judgments drop away, revealing the more essential person; and second, it militated against entering into a bond of honor on the basis of an ephemeral passion.

The preternaturally tall figure with drooped shoulders, of course, had none of these thoughts for the simple reason that his heart was capable of exactitude, of cunning, of careful calculation, but had not even a squib of propensity for romance. Kandran Valmack pondered the gulf that had gradually widened and widened, so that the Man was increasingly an enigma, so different as to no longer invite the potential for solving. Hence, initial intrigue and excitement was waning into cold, reptilian dormancy.

With the resolve of duty, let no one claim shirking, the scholar Mage reexamined his accounting sums. Let us grant the sincerity of the project and the foresight of . . . And here, again, he grappled for words. In the end, Valmack settled with punctilious nicety upon the abstract, "Let us grant foresight."

Kandran Valmack tried to put the best case forward. He did a cost-benefit analysis, reasoned that one might run nearly infinite theoretical scenarios to arrive at the absolute optimal outcome. Given the freedom of the backwards and vicious bipeds, even with the best will in the world, there were bound to be some bad pots in the lot. The prophets of the God seemed to like that metaphor.

And here, the sage could not but concur that "justice must agree with foresight." The syllogism appeared airtight. Liberty required choice to be genuine. It was hardly likely that everyone, or even most, would choose well. The best of all the possible worlds must still accept some inevitable, or at least likely, loss. No, there was nothing wrong with it!

Kandran Valmack paused at the brief interpolation of indignation. He did not like to see the serenity of logic impugned, after all. Once the principle was admitted, it was evident that a perfect balance sheet required proper redress. The, ah, foresight, or at least its obstinate ape favorites, were often zealous for victory in battle.

Why, even they could understand that victory meant the subjugation of the enemy. When the blood of one's foe mixed in the dust, the champion rejoiced. But the Man did not rejoice. He stubbornly refused the obvious.

What they call honest

We did not understand; those of us who are the children of time. He was prophet, king, brother, and friend. And what does it mean to be bridegroom? It cannot be cottoned apart from the implied bride. What does it mean to be joined to the God?

The men and women who come at the dregs end of a cycle — the cunning, the insensitive blind, those who blink, and pretend there is no such thing — they are the ones who shudder at the thought. They do not want the cosmos, the world enchanted, the yearned for loveliness where the God is, where the cosmos is creation and not accident.

The very thought offends them. Better freedom apprised in the void, and death than the unctuous song of the pious, a grotesque, confining triumph of the dim. They prefer the honesty of surd existence without cause or hope of everlasting life. Well, what they call honest.

Don't you think we all should know?

As trials go, it was efficient and quick. Sky was brought into a room with minimal pomp. It was clear the juridical procedure was *pro forma*. So far as the state was concerned, Sky Odyssey was just another Offworlder requiring correct bureaucratic processing. The large docket made for haste. The presiding judge, weary and overworked, appeared so rigid that Sky first mistook him for a puppet effigy. Whenever he began to nod off, a clerk would come by on the pretense of bringing some necessary documents in order to reestablish a semblance of consciousness.

The official charge was failure to declare identity, as well as residing under false pretenses, and thirdly, sedition. The last was the most serious, though it amounted to a reiteration of the previous, for the crime trebled remained existence outside the boundaries prescribed for lawful citizens.

When asked if she had any defense, Sky tried to tell them that they were hardly real, but that love was coming for them anyway. Some words she had gathered from her friends sprung rather eloquently from her lips. Whether because of her words or her beauty, the young prosecutor attended carefully, but did not deign to answer. The verdict had already been stamped on the paperwork.

Afterwards, Sky was taken into yet another room to await the next phase of her criminal history. She was surprised when the nearly boyish prosecutor entered her cell. Some quibble of conscience, perhaps, was to blame. Something about the prisoner unsettled him. He smiled ruefully and remained quiet. He had no wish to bring her pain.

"There's something you're not telling me," she said at last.

"We don't know everything," he responded almost in a gasp. "And the archives are filled with forgotten knowledge. So, all our pronouncements are provisional, you understand?"

"Yes, of course," she said, feeling her mouth go dry.

"It is only that, for something like you speak about, well, there are myths, the kind of tales wrapped in ritual that are very primitive. I have no doubt they express something vital."

"Yes, of course," she repeated mechanically, almost against her will. Sky felt a surge of emotion welling up, and was embarrassed by the way he tried to talk as if he were conversing with a twin, someone next to her, just like her, but not on the precipice of tears.

"It's just that something as momentous — the claim overwhelms, you know, that a kind of ultimate change has taken place — and yet, nothing has changed, has it? Something dusty in the archives, maybe, but that sort of thing, don't you think we all should know?"

When he had left her cell, she felt the hot tears falling down her face. "You should know," she said in a hard voice, almost cruel. "You should, but you don't. Everything is the same. And everything is different."

We are not like the Greeks

Normally, they are not yet finished when the body has done with breath, is nothing but a carcass. Normally, the flesh is left to the wild dogs and for the carrion birds. Joseph of Arimathea knew someone. Nicodemus, too. Those good men sent word to Pilate, that Roman, dutiful in his cold way, resents us, resents being here, we are quarrelsome — and the heat.

We are not like the Greeks, accommodating, cultured. And so, they begged for his body, the body of my beloved. And that is why now we are bathing the poor flesh, we women, the ones who did not run.

His mother is here. Silent. All that weeping along the way and beneath the cross; now she is quiet. Doesn't say a word. I wonder if she is thinking anything like — she loved him, too, after all, and I am absurdly jealous. That she held him in her womb, suckled him, and told him her stories — how she was taken as a child and dedicated to divine service so that she might learn the ways of the Temple.

We have the spices, the useless balm. When he cried out, at the end, I can't stop hearing it. It was not like the common criminals, the one on the right and the other on his left, grim counselors to that sorrowful throne. They groaned and cursed and asked for pity. It was something you might expect. Not with him. Until then, I yet felt the power of his love. I was confident; strange madness. But that cry was something else.

We women are always at the portal of the secret we do not know. Birth and death. She says nothing, and I can still smell the nard, the ointment of our love. He is mute, too, though his body speaks. I want to dress the wounds, but cannot. I want to follow him into the dark lands, to merge time into his stillness. I am crying for both o f us.

The grammar of love

Words are clumsy. The intimacy of flesh speaks in silence and touch; in smiles, and playful laughs, and shattering moans. The mutual tenderness and care and fierce protectiveness for the honor of the other; loyalty and the daring lengths to which love might go to en-joy the other — this was a grammar utterly beyond Kandran Valmack.

So he knew nothing, yet even he began to sense the audacity of the Man, the sheer, stubborn refusal that *anything* intended by the Father should come to shipwreck. No one and no thing should be lost. It was . . . intemperate. Why, even the scribes could see it, couldn't they? Where was the justice in it?

Yet the Man did not consent to their wisdom. Mercy was not an abrogation of justice; it was justice. It must be the new maths.

There was something awful in it, and before he knew it, the devil was trembling and fled from him.

Lost sheep

Pennyfeather was prepared for stealth. He expected to need it. Yet now that he had discovered the primary chamber of the late Guardian, he was surprised to find it almost casually disregarded. He entered the room and swung his lantern about, wondering whether the living book had been returned to its occult hiding place or was part of Malchidion's private treasure.

The clerk had a shrewd nose. *If it is here, I will find it*, he said, and he did. Probably no one knew its worth. Trembling, he held the book. Ever since the Guardian had first made it known to him, a thought had come. He'd done his best to forget it. He did not want that thought, but no matter how far he ran, its whisper crept into the farthest reaches of his fleeing. Trembling, he opened the book, and thought the thought. Come at last, always circling, approaching, then putting it off, he'd forgotten how he was tired of it, tired of the fear.

And there he was, in the middle of the Night Garden called nowhere.

"All right," said Pennyfeather. "What is it you want to tell me?"

And the Man turned to his brother, that exasperating, foolish brother, the dragon in the garden, and he said, in a bold, laughing voice, it was like they had met in the pub and were sharing a private joke, he said, "You really are a most clever wooly-headed, citified, stubborn, scapegrace of a sheep."

And the rest, no man knows.

> *Strayed from among the nine and ninety Aurignacian beati*
> *that he has numbered at his secret shearing*
> *as things made over*
> *by his Proserpine*
> *to himself.*

— David Jones, *The Grail Mass*

Registry of names

A convicted prisoner by the old law was permitted the witness of friends to the installation of sentencing. In the current climate, Benevolence was of two minds. In the first instance, it was conducive to useful terror to take away any semblance of consolation. In the second, the revelation of friends eased the burden of contact tracing of contagion. In Sky's instance, friends were permitted.

And so it was that Father Bunn and Ratcatcher walked with her. The Registry was a kind of architectural joke set against the edge of an ancient forest. They had been walking a path that led away from the large, imperial edifices, the blocks of arcades, and impressive municipal structures meant to exude power. Away from the theatre of authority, they followed the well-preserved remains of what evidently had once been a main throughway.

Now, it traced a journey past rusted-out warehouses, vagabond shacks, pasture land, and a decrepit aqueduct fallen into disrepair and half defeated by vegetation. Further on, a spur became a walkway that appeared to studiously complete an itinerary into wilderness. The guards were bored. To them, it was a familiar route, and familiarity dulls the senses to lingering mystery. Sky puzzled aloud at the purpose of placing an important office of the City in so eccentric a backwater. The answer was an unsatisfactory "it has always been there."

A high wall of marble the color of black earth, dark mulch, and coffee grounds stood opposite a wall decorated in saffron and mild, noon day dreams. Between them, the walkway became a series of steps and extended terraces, the end of which concluded in a tall, relatively narrow building covered in a facade made from some viridian stone.

The Registry was located in the old Exchequer. The nearer they came to the building, the more they encountered sporadic congregations of the citizenry. Rustic folk mixed with townsmen, and everywhere, soldiers. Some stopped to stare at them as they passed. Sky guessed, for there were no others to be seen, that Anshari were rare in these precincts, but it was really the priest that interested t hem.

When they were close enough to see into the windows of the edifice, Sky noticed the heads of clerks facing outwards like the shadows of malevolent owls. The great bronze doors that barred the entrance opened with august slowness, and a golden-robed official departed. At the top of the steps, they discovered Sergeant Folkes. The retired soldier had fallen on hard times, dressed in rags, cried out piteously. When the official ignored him, the old warrior tried to follow, his ancient limbs flimsy as he limped forward with the help of a rough-hewn staff. His debilitation was too much to keep pace, the exarch deaf to both pleas and imprecation.

"My son, my son. You took him. Where is my son?" lamented the unremarked suppliant.

They tried to go to him, to speak words of consolation, what words? But the guards intervened. The papa tumbled into a pool of dust. He rifled his hands through his sparse gray hairs, lamentation rising from his frail chest.

A gust of cold air suddenly kicked up, badgering the soft veils that curtained the windows of the clerks. A coven of papers floated down from the windows in a billowing dance. Was it Sky's imagination? They seemed to sprout into fledgling wings, and scatter into the wind.

Copper is restless

The Chancellor of Names peered closely at the prisoner cards taken from the file. Then he chewed on the end of his pen and moved ponderously about, shuffling a collection of yellowed papers. The clerks scribbled industriously at their desks or moved with studied finesse through the carefully balanced stacks of files that rose like stalagmites from the depths of the archives. After an interminable period of deep concentration, the Chancellor looked up with an impossible combination of weary surprise.

"Ah, Flipthrop will see to you," he sighed with a modest shake of his head.

Flipthrop was a junior clerk with ginger hair and a thin Van Dyke. He smirked at them with professional malice. The Chancellor admonished them with sad resignation.

"I'm afraid the young lady should have been stamped when she came in. She'll have to start on the irregular list. That's the way of it."

Flipthrop led them through a maze of texts and whirling scribes, a murky odor of ink and dust perfuming the turgid air with an incense of bureaucratic decay. They descended a level and found themselves before a tiny desk. The monitor sitting behind it had the same sallow, triangular head as the Chancellor. Indeed, he could have been his twin. Flipthrop steadied his gaze upon Sky before declaring,

"Off-worlder. Female, apparently."

Sky gaped back, offended and astonished. What does one say to "apparently?" She and her party were made to sign a log, and then they were escorted to an anteroom that let onto a long metallic corridor, which ended abruptly with a wall entirely made of mirroring material. It subtly bent the light, and distorted images so that one had the impression everything would come crashing into the center of the glass.

A sensation of frigid cold abruptly swept through the hallway. The center of the glass became darker than night, and then they were walking again along the corridor, the mirror now located behind them. This disconcerting process was repeated several times as Flipthrop led the way. Father Bunn had initially attempted a polite banter, but the clerk remained silent with bored and malignant insolence. When Sky glanced over at Ratcatcher, his visage barely concealed fury that was instantly suppressed by her regard.

A new monitor appeared before the ingress of yet another corridor. Sky noted that the twins were triplets, and wondered if there might be an entire race of innumerable replicated clones. This time, however, they were not required to sign for their admittance. A hushed conversation between the clerk and the monitor was interrupted by the exasperated declaration by Sky that she was most definitely a girl.

This was likely not the subject of interrogation. The monitor's brow furrowed at the possibility of an addled client. This, unfortunately, sparked a spasm of giggles that did nothing to deflect his concern. Then the Ansharu stepped forward. Sky could not rightly tell from behind, but some message was concisely conveyed.

Next, they entered a lift. The clerk darted furtive glances at Ratcatcher. Sky had little time to gloat in triumph. When the doors of the lift parted, they found themselves surrounded by tall columns and vertical cupolas attached to the exterior of a building the size of a small city. The architecture was largely made up of rounded arches, some of which were wide enough for two elephants, and others were so narrow as to hardly constitute an arrow slot.

The building material was a kind of warm, pearlescent marble. An open portico looked out upon the dark obsidian sea of space.

Far below them, like a gem in a setting of velvet, was the aquamarine glow of Elnaria.

"But, how?" gasped Sky.

The beauty of it, and the pristine brightness of the stars took her breath away. The vision remained with her as she was ushered past a forest of pillars. Flipthrop was saying something about the Library, but her mind was elsewhere. She was thinking about Elnaria, and how when she stood upon it, its spaces surrounded her like a cloak, giving shape to her imagination. To be in a place was to be part of it, the borderland between body and world more permeable and hard to pin down than one was wont to recognize.

And yet, when she gazed down upon the planet like a child spying a delectable agate, it was circumscribed by vast, empty space, something small she might put in her pocket, too tiny for her soul. The paradoxes of perspective were still distracting her when she discovered she was being asked to go on alone. The clerk had recovered himself sufficiently to stare at her with surly contempt for having clearly ignored the counsel and admonitions he had been freely offering her.

Father Bunn looked upon her with an expression of anxious and hopeless care.

"Aes she seeks aurum cor schnell," said Ratcatcher.

"Copper is restless to become gold," said the priest.

The Library

And then she no longer saw or heard them. For a brief moment, she glimpsed a tall, distinguished-looking man in a brown tweed jacket. He was standing before a map set upon an easel with a mad, determined gleam in his eye. She could not see the map, which purported to show an impossible entity in the Amazonian basin of Peru, but she felt unaccountable warmth towards him, and equally held certain knowledge that he was ridiculed and doomed to frustration.

And then she was standing before a wall of books that reached several feet above her head. Adjacent to this wall was a similar wealth of texts. Turning around, she noted that she was in a hexagonal room shaped like a cell in a beehive, four sides of which were devoted to housing books. Five bookshelves per wall, the spines of each volume were inscribed in manifold languages.

Each paired wall was separated by an open space. One of them led out into a vestibule with a mirror and two rooms on opposite sides, one for sleeping and another for bodily necessities. The other open side of the cell was traversed by an iron railing about waist high. A staircase provided access to further levels of the honeycomb.

A great echoing height and depth was palpably present even if one did not peer over the railing. When Sky investigated, she had to fight back a swell of vertigo, and an irrational fear that she might climb over and jump. Either direction she looked, there was the prospect of an endless display of cells, so that one could imagine a jumper from centuries ago might decay into bones that were still falling.

Sky called out for some time to no response. The cell was covered in dust. No one had perused these shelves, perhaps, for many years. She pulled a book off a shelf at random and discovered a script she could not read. Another contained the Latin alphabet, but was scrambled into a meaningless sequence of unpronounceable verbiage. If it was a cipher, she lacked the code.

She wandered across the vestibule to another cell, equally abandoned. Seeing it, the silence became forlorn and vaguely threatening. She cried aloud then for Father Bunn and the Ansharu, and even for the disagreeable clerk, but no one came. At length, with nothing left to do, she tentatively climbed the staircase that led onto a new level, and entered a new vestibule that appeared exactly like the one she had left. Again, she investigated the walls of books and searched for signs of habitation, recent or otherwise. No one had left a notebook or scrawl of a diary. Everything was suffused with a sense of the abandoned.

She climbed upwards for a long time, and then reversed her course. It was impossible to tell the place from which she started from anywhere else. She began to think she had been relegated to a perverse kind of prison, a solitary confinement of exquisite eccentricity. A familiar horror and despair gripped her, which she recognized for the wandering she had first experienced when she walked upon Elnaria without a name.

This time, no spectral hero appeared to save her. Nothing did. Nothing ever would. Even the books were closed to her, so that she wondered if she was literate. *I just don't know how to read. I thought I did, but I don't.*

It was shortly after this sad thought that she entered another vestibule that led to another identical cell, only this one was where she discovered the librarian.

The Librarian

Afterwards, she could not tell exactly what he looked like. She had a clear memory of his hands and his height. She was sure of his eyes and the timber of his voice, but when she tried to unify the fragments into a coherent image, the accidents escaped the substance, leaving behind a peculiar sense of disembodied qualities.

They had walked, and the librarian had gestured towards the books. There was a dispute, he said, among the scholars whether the library was coextensive with the universe and also whether reality was a function of language or if language was itself a gift or a disease, and if a gift what had happened so that it so often was used for lies and to take advantage?

"Are there very many librarians?"

"There are many vates (this was not probably the same thing, but that is what he answered), but the library is so large that one may wander for many years before finding one. It used to be different."

He had become silent then, and she could not tell if it was embarrassment or tact. When next he spoke, the librarian was discussing the problems of translation. He said that the perfect work of translation would attain identity between the original text and the translation, but that such was an ideal fraught with dangers, for languages grew from the soil and the blood, had histories not abstract. Words and actions grew together, the very possibility of action was a feat of imagination, and so it was rank foolishness to claim, as some did, that words were empty signifiers pure, and separate from the actions of unique men and women.

Language carried the trace of memory and lived on even when the flesh had rotted into bones and forgetfulness. The translator must empathize, live within many worlds, and so natives of any specific tongue were apt to distrust him, fault his efforts and suspect him of treason. This was, of course, quite a lot for Sky to take in, and she did not really understand him. Still, what he spoke remained with her, even as his bodily presence eluded capture.

"I had no idea it was so dangerous, but I seem to recall a friend saying it is very low paid and hardly anyone respects you."

At this, the librarian merely smiled. He said that one fellow believed that the differences in language derived from the secretive nature of the tribe. To know a word was both to live out the life of one's people, and also to defend against the hostile aggressions of others. To share a word was thus a sign of great hospitality or treachery, depending on the circumstance.

The librarian added that conversation was indeed full of verbal jousts and wonder and endearing commitments and betrayals, and so much went on that all of us miss and perhaps must miss much of it because the weight of significance would render everyone mute with trepidation were they to see as the angels see.

Thereupon, Sky properly and frankly asked about angels and the tongues of angels, to which the librarian spoke in a manner her memory could not fully preserve. He mentioned the Sha-rule, for instance, and he said that all the human arts were lit with the fire of the Seraphim.

Then she recalled her own dilemma and mentioned the clerks. The librarian paused to look down into the dizzying pit, whose prospect was held in fragile abeyance in each cell by the fig leaf of the balustrade with its low iron fence.

"They have tried to make everything straight and flat and safe; that is what they call reason, though it is only so much whistling past the graveyard."

Then he broached the topic of the secret of naming, and her heart beat just a bit faster, but all he said was, "The reason they ask is they are hoping you will tell them."

From within, she could not determine if it were her own thought or something he said, came the certitude, "This is a bad infinite."

Then, with a kind of mirthful panache, "Do you know what I'm doing now?" It was evidently a rhetorical question, for the answer immediately followed: "Picking the lock, Sparrow." And then, quickly and without warning, he tossed her over the railing.

Chapter Five

Garden of the Infinite

*P*eople, human persons, you are not hopeless, you are not really *the nothing things that you have appeared to each other this long time. Here are your depths revealed in their true aspects, which can only seem allegory to your uninstructed visions.*

— R.A. Lafferty, *Arrive at Easterwine*

Puddle splashers

Every man and woman I pass on the street feels trapped by the boundaries of their skin, but, in fact, they are delicate receiving instruments whose spirituality and corporeality vibrate in one specific manner because they have been set at one specific pitch. Each of them bears within himself a multitude of souls and, I maintain, of bodies as well but only one soul and body are at their disposal, the others remaining unliberated. By changing civilizations, time continually liberates new souls and bodies in man, and thus time is not a serpent devouring its own tail, though ordinary men and women do not know this. Once, a very long time ago, walking down the street in a Polish village, I grew thoughtful at the sight of ducks splashing about in a miserable puddle. I was struck because nearby there was a lovely stream flowing through an alder wood. 'Why don't they go over to the stream?' I asked an old peasant sitting on a bench in front of his hut. He answered: 'Bah, if only they knew!'"

— Czeslaw Milosz, *Essay in Which the Author Confesses . . .*

This Message only for You

It is a long time since I have been here.

And yet, I am always here. There is a paradox in time. That is how the man called The Elder put it to me. When did we meet? Have we met? Perhaps I am meeting you even now, at the bridge, wondering if I am seeing a ghost.

How shall I begin? What I have to tell you, this message, only for you.

I used to think you were too large, too abstract, impossible to know, and thus, impossible to love.

People talked about loving you, but what did it really mean?

A lachrymose gushing, some weird projection from the subconscious,

Something, that was nothing,

a fairy tale for children.

And there was something else. How shall I put this?

Not everyone, no. Not everyone.

The truth is I do not like many people. Or, it is strange,

I like them well enough, but in the aggregate, not so much.

And most of those who claim to speak for you, not at all.

And so I used to think,

If those are the sorts of people that He likes,

If that is the kind He wants,

He does not want me.

For I could never be like that; I do not want to be like that.

That would be betrayal.

"And what do you think a lie is?" he asked me in that tone of his, you know the one.

So of course, I naively answered. How anyone would. "A lie is telling an untruth."

It seemed simple enough.

"But that assumes," he said, a glint in his eye like a hawk bemused by the mouse, "that you know what truth is."

Falling

The shock of the fall came first. Her mind reeled, panic racing through her body. There is a poem by Szymborska about 9/11 and the people who leapt from the towers. They were pushed out to the ledge, to the high windows, by the choking smoke and the fire. When they leapt, it was desperate, resigned, and made hopeless by gravity.

Sky once saw an acrobat, dressed in a costume of radiant blue fabric with a face painted silver and cat-like, leaping from a hidden trampoline into the air, accompanied by the sound of a haunting, undulating cry. The acrobat seemed to leap into an abyss, graceful, flying without destination, serene. But the leapers from the tower were closed off from the ambiguity of a nebulous dark. Body of flame, burning flesh, terrestrial meteor, photojournalists snapped the flux of time; uncrying lens captured the despair of the jump. Limbs flail or rest in a semblance of free abandon.

There is yet time for a thought, a memory; the particular face is composed, infinitely apart from smash and blood. And so the poet shared the small mercy within her power. She refused to add a last line. Frozen in their leap, they lived.

Presentiment of sound

"Tier her," said a voice.

Sky felt herself slowly being cut away like a tree whose bark is split, an outer ring peeled back, each concentric layer removed as a series of visible veils until the very last blush was taken from her, and she was nothing at all. So that is how she knew she was in the abyss.

She discovered that the sense of down becomes problematic without a finite limit, without the sharp edge of earth. The longer she fell, the more she wondered if she were not in fact flying, though this quickly gave way to vertigo. Her sense of self had been so much constituted by specific, concrete relations to persons and things within the vista of time. Here, she drifted endlessly, and she began to envy the leap with a definitive end. But not too much.

Then she was very angry with the librarian. She was composing for her own satisfaction just how she would express her complaint, though obviously someone who would throw a nice young woman who was very politely listening to every word one said over a rail into infinite descent was hardly likely to be impressed with rhetoric. She was in the middle of contemplating this sad probability when not so much sound, it was a perfectly ghastly and sterile muteness that surrounded her, as the presentiment of sound came to her.

There was the ghost of a second where she thought she saw a tiny speck of something far, far below her, and then she was looking as a child watching a magic lantern show at the image of the upward flight of an impossible creature. For a long moment, she was staring into the determined, yet peaceful face of a Shiriloth named Rut. Then she was lying upon the warm, palpable flesh of her godson with the mug of a Sphinx (but not a Sphinx)!

The Shiriloth's back was so vast a field that it allowed for a dozen or more riders that anchored themselves to the creature through a system of saddle and tackle as strange as such a horse. The riders were feminine, though their faces were uniformly hidden behind a metallic mesh that resembled the front of a sabre fencing mask. One of these riders made her way over to Sky, and managed to lead her to a seat secured to Rut.

Soon after, there was a lurch, and then a tantivy of ferocious joy. Sky looked down and back at the shimmering marble spires, the corridors and arches from which she had contemplated the solitary beauty of Elnaria. They were gliding through the icy dark, racing past astral belts and galaxies, moving so swiftly that distance became almost an odd fancy.

And then there was a sensation of drifting with the plangent insistence of an aerial lullaby. The dark rider who grasped her pointed a lithe arm in the direction of a small copper planet with verdigris seas and ice-capped mountains steep and sharp as needles. They had come to the abode of the Sha-rule.

Empress of the Sha-Rule

Tall among the Pleonax, spires sharp-toothed against the milky sky, the Sha-rule dwelt, familiar with the eagle's cry. The servants of those dark ones caused fright in the people. The alabaster columns were softened in the golden sun, and the arabesque patterns of ocher and magenta, cyan, and umber, blood rust, and viridian adorned the mosaic work of floor and parapet. The Empress of the Sha-rule thought of all those tasked to her care.

"They forget," she said. "They do not know that they are children."

Mother Anagianna Miska Veronica of the Loving Face sighed. She allowed her mind to float upon the surface of the mirror. It was glistening, iridescent, with a darkening gray depth, like a dolphin's back. And why did the Unnameable proceed in this fashion? The Sha-rule did not know. The irony was that the secret was somehow kept in the flesh. Perhaps the flesh did not know.

Such living were hardly living, yet the Unnameable had tasked the Sha-rule. She could not help but feel that they did know something, even if they did not know what they knew.

Threshing towers

The narrow edifices rose to vertiginous heights like giant's fingers, some with triangular caps and others with gabled roofs. Many towers seemed to be spun, as if they were made from the thick golden web of some incredible insect. Others glowed with red warmth, like a lit jack-o-lantern with tall open windows from which the Sha-rule and their helper Anshari could be seen carefully unpacking a kind of cocoon made of silvers, blues, and greens.

This oblong shroud opened into a rounded hammock. The Anshari tilted this one way, then the next, rocking it like a cradle. The air swirled, thick with echoes. Soon, the end of the strange object began to shoot forth a thin net of fabric, which lifted above them, and coalesced into a herd of gauzy clouds floating above the towers. The gleaning of life, the threshing of time — this was.

"Listen, listen," said the Anshari.

"Be silent, the Word is in the silence," answered the Sha-rule.

The crossing

The moment crosses so fast, flowing, towards what? Emptiness? An ocean of infinity? It can't be captured, so elusive it's a wonder to try and think about it. Of course, events occur. Things happen.

Everyone believes that, yet the moment is already over when you think you are living it — a blink, unknowable in its present.

It is only afterwards, not in a space, though we tend to spatialize, to think of that first microsecond in which the moment has entered into that irretrievable alterity the past, the written, the unalterable, in that tiny, nearly imperceptible geography that subtle insight, or more often, dull, bored interpretation renders flux into form or at least into an episode within a vast story whose beginnings are wrapped in darkness.

Though not all agree upon the plot, many are indulgently ironic about the very idea of an author, even themselves. Who is to say? An inch, not a mile, though why not fathoms, galaxies? The inch is no less beyond recovery, innocent, vital life stolen forever, receding into immemorial loss? Perplexity will come. Bafflement.

Pull back, if you can.

And yet, in the first blush, in the first breath, in the cry of life, there is also ecstasy. There is the child's wonder, time not yet detached from the plenitude by forgetting, wonder before what? Never a static thing, only concepts lack drama because abstract, dead, untethered from the mystery, the reverent acceptance, ungrudging receptivity, trust.

Only here, the crossing.

All things lie concealed

The warrior of the Sha-rule, the maiden-creature, turned from Sky and removed the dark helmet of night. Even before the virginal face had turned towards her, Sky felt trepidation. And yet, it was nothing bold or terrible, though still a shock. Because she had listened to the people, Sky expected some monstrous visage. It was not. The warrior of the Sha-rule showed to her a face as mirror, Sky's own face, only unimaginably bright with a light that ought to have winced her eyes with pain, but did not. The Sha-rule smiled a kind, grave smile.

"We have known each other from the beginning," she said. "I am the keeper, the cup bearer. We laughed together as you were born, wet and bawling, from the womb of flesh."

Suddenly, it was as if they had entered within the pearl of Sky's orb ring. And Sky's angel took her hand and led Sky to the edge of the luminous globe.

"Human creature," she said. "Take a careful look at humankind! Each human being contains heaven and earth and all of creation and yet remains one whole figure, and within every human being all things lie concealed."

The bees of the invisible

It was the deepest night, black as thick velvet. Sky lay on the bank of a river that flowed like golden honey. Arboreal columns reached up even to the edge of the current. The earth itself, the water, and the trunks of the trees glowed with a warm light illuminated in autumnal hues aureate, fiery tangerine, and the soft browns of sparrow's wings. For a long time, Sky listened without realizing that what she heard was the most subtle musical caress. When she did attend to it, Sky was wrapped up in its soothing melody with such tact and graceful courtesy that the word "purity" echoed in her heart.

But this was not, as some might imagine, anything at all protected and insulated. This purity was cognizant of wounds and terror, of the exsanguinations that violently tear life away. It knew these things or intuited them, but pardoned us for them. The music was an innocent heart Sky felt beating next to her own.

As the music grew stronger, Sky sat up. A golden coracle was approaching from downstream. When it was quite close, Sky understood that the vessel was Benedicta. Her head and bosom formed the narrow prow of the craft. A tall man in a cape of burnished sun stood within, and pulled the crown of Benedicta's hair back with a comb to form a span of chords. With his other hand, he lightly bowed the music that had preceded them.

The vessel nestled in beside her, and Sky silently entered into the boat, noticing for the first time that the stern flared out into a fishtail that provided the propulsive force.

This body

This body is not like any other.

Of course, mother. He is beloved, unique, irreplaceable.

All that you say is true, but that is not what I mean. If his flesh was no different, just the same as everyone else, he wouldn't have been able to offer it as the antidote, the cure for what we call life. It wouldn't have been able, this body, it wouldn't have been capable, you see, to become all things. The connections would have been too slight, the kinds of relations we all abide.

This is difficult, poor woman. She must have suffered a lot. And there were the whispers, you still hear them. Who knows what happened all those years ago? He was born in Bethlehem, they say, not at home in Nazareth. Something was amiss, though the census, of course . . . And then they say he was abroad, came back as a toddler from Egypt. People should let it go, especially now. A mother has a right to think well of her son.

If it were not for this body, there would be no spring, the ice wouldn't thaw. It is because of this body that the industrious beaver builds the dam and clever ants construct entire subterranean kingdoms. Because of this body, the gentle manatee raises its head to the sun, and wise men remark the belt of Orion.

Grief speaks in hyperbole. She forgets herself, so deep is the wound. All these things precede the birth of her lost joy.

This body, this flesh, he brought the hope of the world, to make all things new. He came to bring them what was promised. He brought in his broken flesh the ways of love. This body is like no other.

Well, let us leave her then to weep if she will. It's a sad end for a mother to see.

This body, my son, my son!

Cryptic admonishment

And the Benedicta-craft navigated the slow, sinewy waters that worked their way deliberately past the night forest illumined by the river itself. The waters were mostly of soft golden amber, that in larger spaces splashed emerald or even amethyst. The trees sunk down into the soft, receptive glove of earth, held fast in the moistness. The mangrove was floriated with fragrant, orange-petalled flowers and downy orchids that flashed memories of brothers and sisters that bloomed in Brussels and Tokyo at the same synchronized hour.

When they had reached an opening onto a larger pool, Benedicta advised Sky to look upwards. The horizon was veiled as if by a scarf of Impressionist incandescence, painted in swirls of azure and silver against a midnight ground. A virgin star, brightest of all, pointed north.

"Remember," said Benedicta, "that the first love is like Juliet and Romeo. It is wrong to think them foolish and young. The ardor of love is always for greatness. If you are unwilling to die for love, you cannot love, and this is why the 144,000 cannot tolerate the lukewarm."

Sky pondered this cryptic admonishment from her friend. Then the placid lake gave forth to a branch of the river that gradually grew stronger. At first, the momentum of the current was invigorating. They passed obscure fishing villages and rustic cabins. Small lanterns lighted the buildings with homely warmth, and Sky imagined the inhabitants at their hearths or snugly wrapped in toasty bedclothes. But then the pace of the river sped faster and faster so that one could no longer attend to the passing scenes on either side.

Sky closed her eyes, and grasped hard onto the sides of the boat. And then, suddenly, the vessel calmed. The music softly played, but never yet did the caped figure speak. And Benedicta's voice rose into an aria. She sang that all true names were divine. And by this, Sky understood that everyone was called by such a name. And then Benedicta sang out, "Fearfully, we listen to the tale and wonder. Shall they obey their highest calling? If the tale ends in woe, it is not yet finished. It follows us into our dreams."

Sky opened her eyes and looked about. They had come to a dock that jutted out into a placid bay, at the end of which the Elder sat whilst humming a tune once sung by Otis Redding.

"The story remains, a haunting," spoke the Elder.

"And we shall have to do something about it," said the Benedicta-craft.

Golgotha

Sky hunched over and squeezed herself through a narrow, dimly lit passage. She was following the Elder, who explained as they made the uncomfortable journey about the many forgotten paths that following twists of perverse willing come up against dead ends.

"These are our bad stories, but we insist on them. It's what we mistake for freedom."

There was one singular route stretched out beyond the bounds of the outer limit — the limit of what he did not say — that alone leads to life and freedom.

"Where are we going?" asked Sky.

"To see Benedicta's chickens," said the Elder.

He did not tell her that the place was called Golgotha.

A mystery to be endured

The fact that individuals are frequently vile, cruel, and stubbornly vicious is a recurrent testimony of history. Anyone can know this, though lots of folks blink. They shudder before the horror of it. It's a kind of survival mechanism, that blinking. Maybe Nietzsche thought he saw this timid dullness in his Last Men. Still, whether he was ultimately a swaggering, pretentious would-be hero or not, Nietzsche is at least earnest in his attempt to say "Yes" to a cosmos beset with corruption, weakness, and an inability to face reality.

There's another side. Evil is not a problem to be solved, but a mystery to be endured. Some folks are incensed by the injustice of the world. They are permanently angry, furious at the cancer of evil. There's dust in everything. Each time disease is fought back, a criminal kept from felonious intent, every triumph in battle is but a happy delay for every mouthful of life, no matter how sweet, is awash in mortality.

All our loves end in death. All our essays at love, our desire to love and be loved, to experience the real as an ever-deepening novelty of discovery that is full with the plenitude of delight, yet open to fresh innocence, to frontiers that ever expand into infinity — that is what the dynamism of heart and mind require — all that seems to lose out. We grow old and stale, stupidly repetitive. We tire, are humiliated, and betrayed by our own failures and compromises. Cowardice accompanies the loss of powers, of beauty, the accumulation of sorrows, errors, and our own secret and explicit complicities with evil.

Canker within is met by cosmic despair without, by inveterate, tenacious refusal of eternal life, whose generous gift comes wrapped in dust. The folk tremble before this terrifying disappointment that seeks to destroy in advance our hopes. The death, bitter waters — Who grows beyond jejune childhood without acquaintance of it?

The House in the Forest

They walked a long while, long enough for the Elder to tell several stories, the point of which remained obscure to her. He spoke, for instance, of the fire birds that live in chimneys and appear to mortals synonymous with the flames, about Rodin's charming book on cathedrals in France, and how one should never play cards with St. Jerome, because he cheats and blames his bad eyesight.

They came upon a sharp, downward gradient and then a rise in the floor. The Elder's lantern cast an eye upon quartz rock and tree roots that reached down like veins into the walls of the passage. "Take care," he said. "This is from the earthquake when the Lord cried out."

Then there was a refreshing bite of cooler air, and they emerged onto a forest trail. "This is nice," said Sky, though if she had known about Golgotha, she might have expected desolation and unending fires. The brisk air stirred in her a desire she could not at first place. Later, when the Elder was trying to explain the need for such a journey, conveying to her some idea that human experience was unstable and often prey to untrustworthy alliances, she suddenly exclaimed, "I want a pony." She meant, of course, a horse.

At this, the Elder laughed. "You were born wanting a pony, Sparrow," he said.

Before them a new vista appeared, a lush green meadow and willows and birches and a stream not too shallow, nor too wild, and further on, the House in the Forest.

"Oh," said Sky.

The House stood welcoming, its tall towers embroidered with living gingerbread, rustic kin to the trees, yet stately and far-seeing. As they approached, a young deer drinking at the sweet water of a brook looked up with curiosity. A shock of crimson briefly blazed within the Elder's lantern, and then hovered in the air above them, a billowing smoke with the face of an old man.

"It is Petrus, the watchman," said the Elder. "He guards the House."

Sky was astonished. The House was too large to have a veranda, yet the portico had the simplicity and warmth of one. There were no liveried servants, though everywhere men and women, human and Anshari, moved about with lively purpose attendant upon some office in a spirit both playful and intent. Among them, she caught a glimpse of the dwarf who had warned her about Mordred and his folk. As he passed by, Elmerlin waved.

The door to that House is the mystery of Love. The entryway led into an atrium that promised to open onto a nearly endless supply of wings, towers, staircases, and chambers. Now Sky truly marveled.

"I mean, really," she said.

The Elder seemed suddenly younger, his voice both tender and strong.

"To know love," he said, "is to know that which is always greater, beyond the compass of our affections."

To Help Bring Things to Life

The Elder made a gesture down one of the branches of the House. "If you follow that long enough, you come to the ideal pub," he said with the bittersweet satisfaction of a man who must now take a different route. Further in, past a marble staircase and an oratory wafting thick incense, a smaller wooden staircase in the Victorian style was tucked away in a discrete corner. The Elder took Sky's hand, surprising her with an unusual intimacy, and bound up three flights with even more astonishing vigor. A large, rounded orb window was embedded in the slanted roof. "We saw that first," he said without explanation.

Then he whirled her through a hall filled with Anshari nurses and many, many Nocturnes. As they walked by them, the Elder seemed by turns stern and filled with pity. An unpleasant murmur punctuated by occasional, shrill cries echoed across the entire space. "The heart becomes trapped by its own desires. The pure fire of the quest is lost and wanders in fear and sorrow. The urge to protect oneself, to avoid censure wars with a thirst for glory, and to push oneself forward, neither of which is love. A narrow, ungenerous soul clogs with nether dust, winds a tangled labyrinth."

Before the Elder's words had ended, they reached a chamber devoted to bathing. A Nocturne covered in sores was undergoing an immersion at Benedicta's command. The disgruntled child in the iron tub was sopping in suds. It opened its mouth and bawled vociferously, perhaps broadcasting uncouth curses in an unknown tongue. In doing so, it displayed a set of jagged teeth that would have done a piranha proud.

None of this affected the serenity of Benedicta. She calmly directed the young terror to close its yap and proceeded to scrub and rinse with firm efficiency. The Nocturne, sensing inevitability, settled into a quiet frown and resigned itself to unwonted ablutions. How tenderly Benedicta dried its scabrous body. Quickly, it slunk away from her without a touch of gratitude. Yet Sky felt that only now did she see Benedicta, her warmth and strength, the courage of her kindness.

Caught up in admiration, Sky did not notice that the Nocturne had approached. It peered with half-frightened curiosity at the orb ring on Sky's finger. When Sky raised her hand that it might inspect the ring more easily, the orb began to glow, and a rush of warmth came out through her hand. The skin of the child was instantly cleansed and flush with health.

Sky and the child stared back at one another in equal astonishment. Seemingly only Benedicta was not surprised. "We are the ones who cross the Hallow Ways to help live, to help bring things to life," she said.

Hospitality

Then Sky was whisked off to other rooms devoted to various purposes. She was shown places where the solemnities of stone were honored in the sculptor's art, though unlike any she had ever known. One sang to the minerals, and soon they began to shape themselves, revealing the story hidden within. There were wild, magical gardens where Sky discovered that a governess was not intended for unruly children but as a guide to adventure into hidden realms. The Elder, indeed, wanted to show her the place where the icon masters attend exclusively to the saint's ears, but as this was only reached by a long passage on the far side of the ideal pub, he practiced patience.

There were rooms in that House where one swam in oceans and listened to the chorus of whale song, and others where the stars were near as chandeliers in a ballroom. Of course, there were chambers that appeared rather normal in comparison. Sky was taken to a place of wooden floors and ballerina's slippers, where dancers leapt and twirled, came together and departed in tempo, grace, and mood evocative. The mistress of the dance looked out upon them with kind severity. One look at Sky told her there was no future swan of her realm.

Just next door was a different music. Épée and Sabre, the lightning slashes and thrust of the fencer's art. A thin, sprightly Frenchman who compensated with an enormous white mustache was shouting out instruction and encouragement. When he saw the Elder and Sky, he broke off his shouts, handing over the job to an assistant. The master swordsman moved with a dapper gait that was evidently always prepared to accommodate the need to erupt into a duel.

Up close, his merry eyes and droll manner belied a life devoted to martial interests. The Elder and he chatted amiably, and Sky delighted the fellow by expressing a preference for the sword over slippers.

Last, Sky was brought to a place of heat and smoke and hammer stroke. Men in leather aprons cast sparks from the grinding wheel, forged blades, and armor. One of their kinds silently eyed Sky and unrolled a tape measure, making a quick assessment. "He wants to be prepared," said the Elder, "In case you are drawn into the sacred fellowship."

Sky, however, was suddenly like a child kept up well past bedtime. She simply could no longer take in what was said to her. The Elder spoke soft words to an Anshara. By her amiable expression, Sky understood that she was to follow her. The Anshara kept shyly glancing at Sky's orb ring, all the while she led her to a sleeping chamber on the ground floor. They passed a dozen tapestries and interesting alcoves, descended bright stairways lit by singing flames, and ended in an arch and recessed doorway that opened into a room fit for a princess.

Her guide attempted to describe the riches of her new place but ended in a rush of giggles. Sky thanked her and offered to let the Anshara try the orb ring on, but this provoked terror as much as embarrassed desire. The young girl blushed and quickly took her leave. Once she was alone, Sky fell back into the sumptuous bedclothes and yawned.

Then she suddenly sat up, wakened by curiosity and freed from the anxiety of everything and everyone; that's how it is sometimes. Sky examined the exquisite little writing desk adorned with enamel-decorated shelves, lovely paper, and an ink pot filled with lilac ink. The charming ceramic wash basin decorated with the likeness of woodland creatures, the lacquered screen covered in birds of paradise that set the boudoir off from the sleeping quarters — it was so perfect she began to feel hungry and wondered how one went about finding the kitchen.

Just then, a line of ivy began to visibly grow along the baseboard. As Sky watched in amazement, the ivy grew vertically before her and took on more girth and heft until it presented a small table. Then a miniature silver tea service and a plate of biscuits were placed by invisible hands upon the newly sprung table.

"Thank you very much," said Sky, and she felt as if the very room shook with pleasure in her joy.

Nomad

Sky woke to the first kiss of sunlight filtered through the shimmering draperies that veiled wide bedroom windows. She rose softly, nearly forgetful of where she was. The savor of life impressed with fresh innocence, free of cares and reserve. Peeking out onto the meadow, Sky cried out in delight. There upon the green, like a dream, stood a dappled Arabian stallion, its silver coat stately and regal. Quickly, she went to the wardrobe, where dress fit for riding awaited her. "I wonder whose card I have drawn now?" she asked. Of course, it was her very own.

Stepping out from the window onto the green, she walked in the quiet of the morning towards the Arabian. The horse stomped and rose on its haunches when Sky was at a distance, but the closer she drew towards him, the more he settled, his ears pricking at the advance of her footfall. Then the stallion lowered his head so she could embrace his neck. It was as if they had always known one another.

Without a moment's hesitation, Sky leapt. She wasn't worried about bareback. The stallion cantered brightly, and then his rider urged him into a gallop in the cool of the morning. It was a glorious run that ended in easeful pasture. Sky slipped down from her mount and walked slowly towards a field covered in bluebells. The gift of that morning spoke to her of knowledge held by feeling. Her sense was that unity was this strange combination of discovery and recognition, all at once. You are a surprise, but I know you. The beloved was always a presence whose arrival was somehow outside of time, borne upon a logic that could not be anticipated, so that familiarity was also ecstatic.

Returning in the afternoon, Sky wanted to stable the Arabian, but she was told he belonged to no one. "That is a wild horse," they said. "He comes from the desert."

"He is not wild. He is noble," protested Sky.

"We will find a place for him if he wishes," said the stable master. "What is his name?"

Sky put her cheek against the stallion and closed her eyes. After a long pause, she answered. "He says he will stay so long as it suits him. You can call him Nomad."

Necessity of Journey

The Elder sent for her in the early evening. The Anshara that brought her to him was older than the young girl from the day before, her manner reserved, polite, all business. Sky discovered him in a private study filled with books, maps, a cello, and numerous cats lounging at their ease. Again, he seemed somehow younger, more rested, and happier.

"The House welcomes each according to their loves. I am told you have already made friends with a Bedouin horse," he said.

"He's perfect," said Sky.

"Nothing less is allowed. The Father is easy to please, but hard to satisfy. I thought, perhaps, you might have some questions."

Sky had lots of questions. She'd thought up enough to fill days while she was riding, but confronted with an opportunity to ask them, she suddenly felt dizzy and could hardly think of one. In the end, she blurted, which was the usual way for her.

"I did wonder how long one could stay, and also, why we didn't simply come here in the first place?"

The Elder did his best to respond to perplexity, though metaphysics was not, perhaps, Sky's favorite subject.

"Yes. What you are actually asking, Sparrow, is why one can't begin at the end. Part of what it means for us to be, what it means to be a creature, is the necessity of journey. We come from nothing; it is inevitable that finite beginnings are ignorant of plenitude. The briefest answer I can give you is that everyone is brought into the House of Joy as soon as they are able, but while the story is always love, the path of that love is unique for all. In one sense, you have always been here, and so, of course, one is meant to abide forever. What is not evident to most of us is how joy is threaded into trial, sorrow, and time's wandering. And that is God's secret, perhaps, though we come to understand it as we learn love's ways."

Procession

The procession was decidedly ceremonial. Sky saw tears in the eyes of some as they waited. There were creatures, sentient, but strange to her; evidently they had crossed from other worlds. The robes of some of the monks were saffron and red. They told her what was meant by the nothing equated to the silence of plenitude. Nonetheless, they were surprised. Anticipation made them fidget like schoolboys, reining in the great desire to frolic. At the far head of the line, Sky had to jump to see, there was a shimmering she recollected, a Vendakar was there. And all about, ordinary men and women, many at their beads, others rapt in some interior prayer, perhaps.

"Where are you going?" she asked.

"To the chapel," answered a sturdy matron who nonetheless could not resist adding a sparkling ribbon to her dress.

"Is it anything special?"

This must have been the wrong thing; the matron frowned.

"Why, the Holy Bread," she said. "What could be more special than that?"

When Sky's place in the procession finally reached the portal to the Silver Chapel of the Birds of Desire, she found many folk kneeling, some with closed eyes, some weeping, others silently astonished before a monstrance that held like a jewel a pure white wafer shaped like the sun. Sky knelt like the others, though she felt confusion where everyone else was clearly in a state of reverent adoration. Of all the things she had seen so far, none seemed quite so baffling as this universal bowing before a piece of bread.

The Bread of the Face

Rabbi Naftali could have instructed Sky on the lore regarding the Bread of the Face. The Tabernacle in the Wilderness was designed to house three sacred objects. The Ark of the Covenant is well known. The golden Lampstand, or Menorah, is also recollected. The third object, however, is apt to be forgotten, a table of acacia wood overlay in pure gold. There were also plates and dishes for incense, flagons and bowls for libations, also of pure gold. Upon this golden table, Israel was instructed to set "the bread of continual offering." A sacrifice of bread that hearkens back to Melchizedek, who some say was Shem, the son of Noe.

According to the Mishnah, this Bread of the Presence was loaves with small pieces of dough rounded upwards at the corners like horns to emulate the bronze altar of sacrifice. The Hebrew word, *panim,* rendered "presence," is more literally "face." Ibn Ezra and Ramban asserted the bread came from the Divine countenance. Sacramental Bread carried the creature into the Uncreated Light. During the feasts of Passover, Pentecost, and Tabernacles, the Bread reserved for the sacred space unseen by the people was taken out and shown to the folk who had gathered to worship. The priests would display the bread, proclaiming, "Behold, God's love for you."

While the secret may be discerned in that mysterious priest who enacted a liturgy of bread and wine before Abraham, it also looks forward to that rite initiated by the Christ on Holy Thursday. Already, from immemorial times, men had carried a dark knowledge, that they were wayfarers on the earth, and some were thought to have the blood of gods. Yet always they stumbled upon Fate's cruel unmaking. Whatever human effort had thrown against the enemy of love, making could not resist an ultimate desolation. Thus, even a cosmic god like Zeus has to keep his distance lest the undertow of oblivion drown carefully preserved order.

The Anointed was different, yearned for the unmaking. Where humanity hopelessly waited to learn eternity, a wisdom incommensurate with finite capacities, beyond what could even be imagined, Christ, who came from the UnCreated, took to his bosom all that men had wrought. Time was to be made new, the made things reborn. Human love became bold, discovered within itself the fierceness of the God.

And what was this Bread offered by the Anointed, the Face of God? Ordinary eating devours dead flesh; the savages who cannibalize their defeated foes hope to absorb the power of the eaten into their own prowess. The Bread of the Presence was not that sort. It was predicated on a different, Resurrected flesh that no mere creature could fathom.

What the body knows

They laugh when the faithful kneel down instead of "considering the matter." I could tell a rare story of conversion, in which the superiority of a great thinker collapsed in front of the dumb knees of an even dumber spirit, not as something demonstrative or sentimental, no, only because the buried sources of his own soul ventured to flow there for the first time and threw him also on his knees, transforming him bodily.

— Eugen Rosenstock-Huessy, *The Fruit of Lips*

Waking dream

The longer Sky stayed in the House of Joy, the more vibrant she felt. Instead of sleep, she found herself often drawn into contemplation. The smallest creature, a sprig of ivy, or the way light transfigured the alb of a young priest as he swung a censer of fragrant smoke — nearly anything seemed to lead her into a state of serene waking dream. There were whispers from Anshari and some of the other folk who observed her.

"She is a sensitive. I have long known," said Benedicta. "Do not rush the gift. You know that it is dangerous. Besides, there are less glamorous acts of love that are ordained for those who would progress farther into the Mystery."

All bowed to this wisdom, of course, it was true. Then they hurried off to tell their friends about the new girl.

Riding the wave

Above the lintel of the obscure side chapel was a carving of a great sow on her side suckling a row of happy porcine children. Sky was disappointed when she entered the Chapel of the Suckling Pigs, though one could hardly blame piglets. She had expected, though instantly she recognized it was an unfounded assumption, that she should be alone with the Bread of Presence. A young woman in the garb of a novitiate had preceded her and was evidently deeply moved in her devotions. Sky felt she was intruding and made a perfunctory curtsy, it seemed a thing to do, before rising to leave. As she did so, however, the girl reached out to stay her.

"Wait a bit," she said in the twang of an Australian accent.

Sky knelt and tried to focus on prayer, but all the time, she kept glancing at the religious to see what she would do. After a while, the young woman rose and gestured for Sky to follow. She led the way down a side corridor to a window seat, which looked down on a view of a square filled with the white and pink blossoms of cherry trees.

"I was in the Hallow Ways," said Adelaide. "Not very far, mind you. I mostly follow the same path and step back before anything too crazy."

"Benedicta spoke of these Hallow Ways," said Sky. "Could you show me?"

The novice flushed. "Oh, but there's very little I could show you. Besides, it's dangerous. If you don't know what you're doing, it can get away from you very quickly."

"But what is it, exactly?"

"Oh, sorry. It's a convergence, that's what the older sisters call it. Not everyone can do it, I guess, but if you can, there's a way of tapping in, a sort of sharing of consciousness, so that you become another. That's what it feels like. At the root, we're joined, so the great saints say."

"And this happens how?"

"I don't know really, but it begins in prayer. It's a form of prayer, actually, but strange. Do you know the way of dancing, the little floor that floats along the great waves?"

"Do you mean surfing?"

Adelaide smiled wide. "Aye, it's something like directed surfing. You follow the waves, they show you something connected to your heart, then, it's hard to explain, the moment is never isolated, it's part of, well, the Event, the Love — and you ride the wave, it takes you to the next connection; if you're doing it right."

"And what happens if you don't do it right?"

"That's not so good. You wipe out, and that can be very bad indeed. That's why you should never attempt the Hallow Ways alone."

"Didn't you just say?"

Adelaide shrugged her shoulders, a puckish grin on her face, and pointed at the Monstrance displaying the sacred Bread.

"Technically, *he* is always there."

Surfing lesson

They arranged to meet at a time likely to be propitious, open to mystery and silence, in other words, unwatched by their elders. At the appointed hour, Sky and Adelaide sat in the very square filled with cherry blossoms that they had peered down upon on first acquaintance. Adelaide tried to explain some basic truths, though she had not yet experienced them herself, sufficient to speak with authority. She said, for instance, that aridity was frequently encountered in prayer, especially by those who advanced beyond the initial steps, which were often quite pleasant and sugared with enticing delights.

There were also those who were plunged into anguished perplexity that seemed unendurable, a dark night of the Cross given as a special favor to the saints deemed worthy of it. This, of course, did not sound at all pleasant, and it was not, yet it grew out of intimacy with the divine humanity, and only thus could one truly begin to know beauties that rescue and beauties that sustain the eternal rapture of lovers.

Afterwards, they entered a side chapel to pray. At first, Sky was too self-conscious for anything to happen, but then she forgot about Adelaide and began to simply contemplate the Bread of the Face. And then she felt a soft touch, and she knew that Adelaide was with her. Soon they were together in a sensation of floating in the air. They flew beyond the confines of the chapel and entered into aerial heights.

A creature, aqueous in the ether, sapphire, silver, and white — it was like a starfish of that celestial sea — greeted them in wordless amity. Then they were brought gently to the rocks of Alverno. A solitary man in a wretched tunic was communing with a circle of little birds. He seemed not at all surprised to see them, addressed the girls as if they, too, were charming avian friends. St. Francis is like that.

Afterwards, Adelaide pulled Sky back to the chapel. She dared no more. They were both smiling after the visit with Assisi. "Isn't he sweet? Yes, he knows everyone," said Adelaide.

Vanaya

Sky slipped into one of the many chapels, looking for the Bread of the Face. She wanted to be alone with the Presence. The chapel she came to just before dawn was called Patience, perhaps because of the carved donkey that stood just within. It had a straw hat so cunningly devised one was tempted to lift it from the humble ass only to discover how firmly it was attached to the head with long ears. It was still dark, and the hushed quiet of the world seemed as if all this time it had been waiting for her to enter.

Sky had been praying for weeks of small forays into the Hallow Ways. In spite of Adelaide's warnings, she'd struck out on her own. Sky wasn't always certain where she was sent, but so far all her journeys had been gentle. Once, she watched the tide come in on the Iberian coast with a monk scholar who told her that all things pray in their own way, that the plants and the beasts yearn after the Good as deeply as those classified rational beings.

On another occasion, Sky found herself chatting with a crowd of Indian women gathered around a mandala drawn in chalk upon the ground. She could not quite follow the gist of the conversation, but everyone laughed when the eldest told a risqué joke at the expense of men. Sky was amused by these encounters; however, she had brought a particular care. The idea had come to her, and she'd put it away. But soon it would be back, and she couldn't see why not, so she prayed fervently and hoped.

At first nothing happened, which also was the frequent result of her praying, at least from her side. She'd been told that some of the most adept saints spent years in that kind of prayer, which made her nearly cry at the thought of it. But then she remembered her friend, Vanaya, who was still falling.

What happened next, perhaps the Sha-rule know. She found her, that's the short version. Afterwards, when they laughed and hugged, Vanaya told a funny story. She said her falling had been broken when a Shiriloth approached her. She'd never seen such a strange creature, but it won her trust by peering out upon her with the likeness of Sky's face.

A fierce and holy blaze

Sky saw many strange and wonderful things, some of which are chronicled in the Light Book that is kept in the Enchanted Chapel of the Convent of the Virgin's Smile. There is a word of prayer that opens its pages. Here is one of them:

On one of the last days that she stayed in that enchanted peace, Sky rode upon the strong back of the noble horse, Nomad, and she gave him free rein. She expected Nomad to gallop hard, but the horse sensed they would part for some time (the beasts naturally commune with the Wise, especially in the House of Joy), and so they traveled softly, crossing fields and meadows in quiet sympathy until they had gone a long way, and come near to the sea where gulls swept the gray horizon. There, Sky saw another rider in the distance.

"Let us go and offer greeting," she said.

The occasion lifted her rhetoric, some grace ennobled her cadence. Then Nomad indeed began to gallop, so swift as to rival Pegasus, nearly a flying horse. A maiden awaited them. She watched their progress with admiration. A young woman near Sky's age wore armor as white as snow and carried a blue shield upon which was blazoned a white dove that declared the bearer "commanded by Heaven's king," and they were glad to see one another.

"I am Jeanne," said the young woman who sat a spirited, good horse.

"I have come from the House in the Forest," said Sky.

The two riders followed a path towards the shore where children were playing, and all the while, Sky was glancing shyly at her companion as if she wanted to ask her a question. Jeanne smiled, for she knew the girl was wondering about her, to see a maiden dressed as a knight. Then, when one could hear the sharp cries of the gulls and the bright laughter, she answered.

"And they asked, the venal sort, do you know the Morweni? They asked, 'Why join up? Why enter the service of the king's beauty?' Well, they didn't put it like that, though that is what they meant. They said something like, 'If all are saved, why bother? Why bother to suffer the Cross?' Everyone, however, suffers. 'Why be good?' As if anyone is good; they are that sort, the Morweni. They have, I hate to tell you, such a stale odor, like the dead air of a crypt doused in terribly sweet perfume. That's what they imagine the sacred smells like, it's how the dead imagine the divine."

Sky said that it wasn't likely the dead would have a very sound notion of the Living God. Jeanne certainly agreed. "And what they intended, at bottom, is that there must be so much suffering that is lost, good for nothing. That is what they insist upon. That is what they call justice."

Sky thought of Narina then, and the conversations they had about the beasts, who frequently did not come into the ambit of Morweni concerns. Then one of her voices echoed in Sky's memory. *The entire cosmos stinks with murder. The animals are wounded. The spirit cries. A trusting beast looks to man and hopes for love and healing. It's nearly unbearable anguish when you can't help them.*

"And the Morweni, they have long lists," said Jeanne. "They have entire lists of sainted names. And they have the scriptures, by which they mean the letter strictly observed when it serves. And they have God, by the same rule, but never, I believe, can they quite suborn the one who consented."

The children were playing, their limbs caked with sand and the cold froth of the sea. Jeanne looked down at them with a pure, merciful assurance, as if to say, "See what I mean?" And Sky did see, she saw a little, how it was kind and gentle, that it should be like that, if only it could.

"They say the past is unshakeable, that it can't be changed, you can't fix it," stated the Maid of Orleans.

Then Sky saw her, a tall, stubborn farm girl, dressed drably, they'd taken away her bright, shiny armor, looking a bit grimy from the prison. And the folk about her, the magistrates and the soldiers, but the people too, the people who should have loved her, the betrayers, they tied her hands behind her, then tethered her to the stake. The dry hay quickened at the first touch of the tiny flame, it smoldered and smoked, and the girl began in prayer and then was screaming, crying out, and calling, it was strangely erotic like the throes of a lover, an agonizing moan.

Stamp me in your heart,
Upon your limbs,

Sear my emblem deep
Into your skin.
For love is strong as death,
Harsh as the grave.
Its tongues are flames, a fierce
And holy blaze.
—Song of Songs 8: 6-7

"But they're wrong," said Jeanne with a merry laugh, because she knew Sky had been with her at the Passion. "They didn't count on him. They didn't know how he hoped, the future that is God."

The Mothering Tree

Jeanne rode then with Sky. She wanted to show her an aspect of her youth, the faerie tree. In the distance, a solitary tree stood in the center of the plain. Sky scanned the waves of heather dotted with dabs of dark crows, like in a painting by Van Gogh. Nomad hastened his pace. The closer they came to the tree, the more the little jabbering shadows became apparent. When they were quite near, however, the chattering stopped. All the faces of the Nocturnes turned to the newcomers.

Sky did not know if these were residents of the House in the Forest or refugees from the abyss that had congregated about the great tree. Now that she was near it, Sky felt regarded and sheltered. For a brief moment, she fancied the tree had a face, and that maternal eyes rested upon her with the tender strength of enduring kindness and patience. Sky even fancied that the roots of this tree reached all the way to the House, and that the magical tea that had been served in her room was but a single work of the Mothering Tree. Whether it was the same or no, let another tell.

Seeking

The happiness of finding Vanaya emboldened Sky. Everything suddenly seemed possible. The very edges of her lost memories called to her with tantalizing immediacy. Sky came questioning, searching in the Bread of the Face for the hidden depths. The Hallow Ways were not silent.

And so, her prayerful longing brought forth the image of a young man not yet twenty. Henry Ellwood stood upon a heath in the glooming light, a collie dog at his side. The tweed cap and walking stick served as romantic insignia, symbols of aspiration more than anything practical. His heart was open to her; she read it as her own. She felt how the land spoke to him as history, as thick with story. He nursed a youthful ambition to join his voice to the earth, to sing in its chorus some great tale to move the spirit, to adventure the unknown, yet also to cherish the homely and honored dead.

I know him, she thought. *I know him! But he is young, this is his before, so new and shiny...* What she saw next caught her breath. The man was older, with a thin, dark beard and a merry expression that nonetheless she felt but a brief holiday from watchful, pensive meditations. On his lap sat a fat dumpling of an infant, whilst a toddler poked at his pockets. He rewarded the auburn-haired nuisance with a miniature brass top, he had a knack for acquiring such curios and the little girl was fond of them. How precious that time, how sad that it cannot endure. This thought, she knew, was not hers. It was his melancholy, the bass that reverberated beneath the melody of his life.

Another leap, she could not account for it. Neither the man nor the children were in sight. Sky had forgotten that the connections did not follow sequence, stick to an isolated subject, or regard the narrow confines of time as we know it. It is likely that Sky had not yet fully believed that the Hallow Ways could bring peril. Everything that had happened to her there was pleasant, or at least not in any way brutal or disturbing.

And nothing yet was to make her feel as if she could be harmed at the very core, but now began a quick passage of searing cold. The ice of frostbite was mild in comparison. First, she was amidst a tribal people in small craft that dared to adventure in frigid seas. They were marked by bonds of honor after their own fashion, but given to sudden outbursts and brutal humor that could quickly escalate into violence. What they made of Sky is hard to say, though one who saw her evidently accepted the girl as a customary presence, a demigod, an ice maiden, someone venerated as coming from a kingdom mysterious to the realm of ordinary practical cruelty.

In that moment she knew that it was so, and then she jumped; she knew not where, only there was darkness and mist, and something that seemed slimy and cold, a sea creature powerful with an ancient knowledge, though simultaneously, a woman, the black sorceress, Arthur's enemy. She did not look at Sky, but smiled, aware, telling the girl she might yet come in useful, be swallowed whole.

The Hallow Ways offered yet another opening for Sky. She followed a narrow path, walking the steps of the goose girl, though she had little time to inhabit her thoughts. There was a high-pitched scream of intense urgency coming from a nearby field. The goose girl ran to investigate. The cry of anguish belonged to a mother goat in distress. Something had gone wrong, and a newborn was blocked in the birthing. Already, tears were falling as the girl reached into the warmth of the mother goat and pulled, maneuvering to release the kid. Terrible fear and concern made her bold. The girl acted quickly, did what needed to be done, so that the kid emerged, wobbly, but alive. The mother goat began to lick her young. The girl turned away, relieved, and was going to seek help. And then, a second kid smoothly entered the world. Capricorn and Gemini cryptically announced a year of marvels.

Then Sky found herself in a cramped apartment. A different panic, visceral, despairing raced through the thin poet, a Jew. He was rifling his books where he had hidden rubles, the wealth of a lifetime set aside for the time when the nets of suspicion closed in. His wife watched with cow eyes, warm and deep, sympathetic fright already sensing the butcher. Later, when the man was long dead, she would pen a memoir, *Hope Against Hope*.

The next jump returned Sky to the man who had pleased her, the one with a dark beard and pockets with surprises. Only now he was alone and wrestling with himself. Brooding anger had erupted in his soul. Nothing seemed worth the horror of living in a world of death and injustice. The trivial nagging of his wife continually renewed itself, never flagging like relentless water torture, pre-occupied with petty appetites and the silly opinions of fools. In desperation, he planned another journey, some quest, some new residence where the cards would be reshuffled.

Sky began to feel dizzy, nausea tipped her into a vertigo that ended in a damp hut. A slow, constant drizzle found a path through a roof of reeds. An old man was telling her to tend to the fire, which was already filling the hut with smoke that hurt one's eyes. Before she could respond to his command, she was pulled into the whirl, the stops brief and merging into an ever-increasing acceleration. In quick succession, she ran with a Greek hoplite dodging Persian spears, sat in a cold library with a Lithuanian graduate student who pondered the enigmas of non-Euclidean geometry, was crammed into a truck with bodies packed tight, breath a luxury; collectively, they hoped, though some of them were dying, all this to cross a border that might allow one to get a job washing dishes.

The whirl showed no sign of slowing, though intermittently, she sensed the siren of dark waters, the unkind sorceress, and then there was a slow chaos, the churning of an Amazonian river, and the man again, older, a bit haggard, but brilliant in his courage. Everyone else was falling apart, and just this called him to his best self. *I've got to get to him*, she thought, her heart swelling, but already she was swept away, thrust into the foul-tempered tirade of a merchant in the Roman slave market. She wanted to get off this ride.

Desperately, Sky sought the Presence, but the Face showed to her only the withering night, the silent absence. *He has walled me in; I cannot escape; he has made my chains heavy; and when I call and shout, he shuts out my prayer. He has blocked my ways with cut stones, he has obstructed my paths.* She was tangled with her brother and sister porpoises, they were drowning in the sea, where they had often played and called to the stargazers on their silent ships, the ocean had caught them with plastic tentacles.

She was an old woman who sat in the same chair on the same lonely porch, too poor to die. Everyone she had loved and known had left long ago for the shadows. Her body kept breathing, and so she sat there and waited, though she couldn't even remember her name. An opera singer lived in an attic apartment; his broken voice sang arias to the crows, who at least appreciated Puccini. A young boy slid on the toboggan, picking up speed, how quickly life can end.

A mangy feral cat, old by the standards of his ilk, had discovered late in life a fella who showed him kindness. The cat stayed in the shadow of his benefactor's roof, was fed, and even offered a soft word. So grateful for this unexpected consolation, the cat tried to rub against the fella's legs, but the man pulled back from the wrecked body, the gray leonine ruff and mournful eyes. And then one day, the benefactor moved.

Who would grieve for a nameless cat?

A soldier dressed in a ceremonial outfit spied a timid woman, her hair covered in a babushka in the old style. She walked slowly with an elderly man, perhaps he was her grandfather. They must have come from the country, the way they stared wide-eyed and uncertain, afraid to speak to strangers. They had come to the place where the faceless country folk petitioned distant powers. He turned a stern face upon them. Any sign of pity only gave false hope.

Wipeout

They weren't sure what happened to her, but Benedicta more or less guessed. Adelaide found her, Sky's body fading in and out, stretched thin. She was returning to a Nocturne state, the flesh dispersed into that night known only to eternity. There was no salve for her condition. She'd have to find her way, or rather, Providence would discover what became of her, whether it could be brought back together, that was the work of Spirit. And then she disappeared, leaving a blank space where she'd fallen prostrate on the floor of the chapel. Many were long-faced and weeping, a young girl in the background broke out into shuddering lamentation, Vanaya.

Benedicta turned to them, emotion shaking her body. She spoke with fierceness: "Do you not know that this is the way of the Cross? You expect the Savior to taste the terrible despair, but would refuse the Cup yourselves! Or do you think the truth is sweet and known beforehand? The Life that is Love cannot be possessed apart from risk. If you do not want the Unknown, go back, make peace with the dead, who will console you with their lies!"

The king's beauty

When the hero Rāma, who is destined to defeat the demon Rā-vana, appeared upon the earth, the salutary advent of the incarnation of Vishnu was readily apparent. "He always smiles and his face is radiant and pleasing to look upon. His skin is tinted blue like that of Lord Nārāyana, and his strength, dignity, and radiance are unsurpassed." And while Rāma can admirably embrace the asceticism of the forest after the betrayal of Kaikeyī, he is consoled by nearly universal weeping because of his suffering.

Everyone feels his absence as an obvious loss to their own well-being. "When they reached Ayodhyā, their wives, whose love for Rāma was like a mother for a son, chastised their husbands. 'What use was it returning without him?'" The response of the city is swift. "The loss was so great that the whole city of Ayodhyā plunged into mourning. No women cooked food, no men decorated their shops; all were overcome with memories of the happiness they had once enjoyed and thought of future glories blighted."

Hildegard of Bingen also discerned her Lord bathed in celestial azure, but his appearance was less pleasing to the people of Jerusalem. "Living with Him, one could fail to notice Him; looking at Him, one could fail to see Him. He did not compel people to see Him with signs or with lightning bolts from the sky," says Bulgakov. It was worse than that. "Everybody was against him. Everybody wanted him to die," writes Péguy. "It is curious. People who were not usually together. The government and the people.

So that the government bore him a grudge as did the rudest of carters. As much as the rudest of carters. And the rudest of carters like the government. As much as the government. That was awful luck."

There is, indeed, something very strange about his beauty. It is the beauty of his strange kingdom, the kingdom of the God. It is the beauty that calls to the deepest yearning in human hearts — and also the beauty that men fear and run from, as from the wave of the tsunami or the leper's kiss.

Lord of Hosts

Inescapable, remarkable how exacting, giving no smidgen to messy tolerance, what cannot be said except in words that fail: the doom, the doom, the doom. It was quiet, like the hush beneath the ninth wave, the silence of the little town astonished on the shore, rapt in wonder before the inevitable tipping of towering waters towards calamitous descent.

And it was in the silence when the doctor paused before his charts, mortal sentence pronounced in his tired face. And it was the silence of the tiny, besieged outpost, as overwhelming numbers of the savage foe, pitiless, revealed themselves as surrounding the hopeless. It was vertigo, despair, the infinitesimal blush of denial that knows futility is already there, covert in the shock that is slowly warming into sorrow.

Relentless, implacable, beyond any bargaining, any shrewd gambit — but it wasn't death. Death was the winding down of breath, the shadow closing eyes, departure into oblivion. No, this shattering is different, from inside, the walls of Jericho coming down, the idols of protection, every casual, sad little lie, every moment of every wearisome day, and the false victories, the shady deals, the times you tricked your neighbor and defeated yourself, all that, collectively, and alone, unique.

Light that sees, that cuts, that sears the comfortable places, overthrows every refuge of forgetfulness, of self-pity, every figure and pose that was imperfect, unjust, unjust to others and unjust to oneself, to what one should have been. Tender this holiness, deft, knowing with precision, but not harsh, though feeling so, this holy, this beauty, the holy is beauty, burning light, monstrously tender, refusing to allow the lack that is evil, and the surplus of mindless cruelty, that shabby plea that one was only human after all, when the human was intended for so much more, a quite different destiny.

This refusal, this cowardice, this dull, culpable, unimaginative practicality, this mediocre, tepid rebellion of stubborn complacency, especially not that — evil, this is what was bound, shackled from within, privation, awful, this nothing, this canker, this shameful nothing, unable to escape because you can't run away from yourself. And so we waited, and it came, quietly, softly, without weapons, needing none.

It came, this fierceness, a demanding clemency, a mercy that demands, fierceness that wants, it can desire only perfection. It came, they call it grace, and there was no escape, no fleeing from this justice, so that everyone felt their joints become bone broth, terror rising in the bowels, the heart breaking. It was unspeakably sad, because it could have been so lovely, enchanting, nothing like time, the time we knew, the abyssal time, the clock time of our death.

He is nothing simple that might have been anticipated. Those religious hymns the folk sing often miss it. He is not an escape from the anguish of our finitude, or an ideal projection of our perceived best qualities. Neither fable nor fact, he explodes the ordinary categories. Our mind reels before the advent of a kingly strength so unsparing, this delicate, kind terror, not of this world, this child, the Lord of Hosts.

The hidden alchemy

The gnosis of hermeticism is not for vulgar eyes. Yet, like all wisdom, it is protected not only by arcana and rhetoric that must be assimilated through a slow process of preparation that includes a difficult ascesis and years of contemplative patience, but also by the burning sword of the cherubim, which is the purity of innocence.

Yet innocence and purity are more wondrous, more mysterious than those with stone hearts imagine. Angelic fire is not a form of exclusion, as moralists think. The moralist lives in the land of a famished reason and incomplete justice, and therefore in the realm of calculation. Rather, it is the radiant ecstasy of creation that is wrought in love and can only be understood by love, which does not count the cost. The holy throws itself into the darkness that is brighter than light.

Still, there is at least the structure of words, a dull surface of teaching that must be burnished by the Spirit. So, the metaphysical axiom upon which the alchemist proceeds is that everything below is a mirror of that which is above. This simple Platonism is not even the truth of Plato. Yet there is a more hidden thaumaturgy known only to the saints. Such alchemy does not yield serene equations. It is a science of the night, with all the ambiguities and confusions of night.

Translations from the celestial realm to earth are torn apart. Beneath the silent heavens, no parables are of any use. And this was the risk the Man was preparing himself to make, which no one, least of all the Tempter, had the merest idea. Thus, no one but the Man himself was aware of the supreme irony in the parables he used to convey to his friends the nature of his battle.

Oblivion

You can't say what happens there. It isn't in the past, so it can't be read off as something finished. It isn't in the imageless future. It's happening now, though that now is everywhere, every time. For us, the moment, excised from the full stretch, the tether before and aft, becomes unthinkable. Lacking future, its justification fails, an event without consequence. Apart from language and memory, the thinking of thought wanes into mute perception, and it's not even that, because unintelligible.

It gets worse. As you go along, they tell you about the birth you can't remember, though some have magic, they believe they can help you with that. Still, whether you recollect that beginning or not, you hold onto this and that, some things stick out, and after a while, there's a yarn you're spinning, and that yarn is you. But here's the unsaying, it can't be helped. There's a kind of oblivion, but not the nothing some predict. You think maybe you're going to bring your story with you. There will be a great tribunal, the gods will review the spiel and let you know, but it's not like that at all.

You think maybe you're carrying a bowl, yes, a bowl of water, and you're careful not to spill a drop, because that water is the sum of you, the life you have to offer. And some might want to dash it all into the ground before it comes to that. Either way, it's a hash. When you look into the bowl, something else is reflected back. This isn't you. It's someone else. And someone else has your bit, and then the tangle is out of sorts. The Egyptians are building their pyramids to the trumpet of Louis Armstrong. A peddler in Bangladesh offers a copy of Joyce's *Ulysses* to Sir Isaac Newton. The martyred Romanovs are hailed as the rightful rulers of the Hittites. Shakespeare jots down notes from the internet to figure out the ending of Macbeth.

Then maybe you come to a doorstep in front of one of those old brownstones. There's a fella there, an old man who looks a picture, like a king from a storybook down on his luck. You've seen him on the rooftop playing his cello to the setting sun.

"Justice begins when you become unfamiliar with yourself," he says.

Chapter Six

Taliessin's Song

H e bowed down the heavens and descended
with darkness under His feet.
He rode upon the cherubs and flew,
flew on the flying wind,
and made Himself a hiding place in darkness . . .
He reached down from the far heights and took me,
and pulled me out of the waterfloods.
— Psalm 17: 10 - 12, 17

If you are in search of That

O traveler, if you are in search of That don't look outside, look inside yourself and seek That. I am blasphemy and religion, pure and impure; old, young, and a small child. If I die, don't say that he died. Say he was dead, became alive, and was taken by the Beloved.

— Rumi, Thief of Sleep

The barns of idolatrous eternity

"Access to the unforgettable," wrote Jean-Louis Chrétien, "far from being retention and conservation of indestructible memories, passes through loss and through forgetting." This is an essential step, though it is important not to mistake it for resignation to oblivion. The river Lethe is necessary, but there is a paradox. Chrétien cites Kierkegaard: "When a person links himself to an eternal power for an eternity, where he accepts himself as the one whose remembrance time will never erase, it is as if you lost yourself, as if you cease to exist."

A coincidence of life and death emerges. The ambitions of the individual are, indeed, bereft of promise if grasped tightly as a mode of self-assertion. Then the person is diminished in what Eric Voegelin termed "egophanic revolt." The new life, eternal, can only be received, not constructed as a project of radical autonomy, so that "every promise has someone to whom it is destined, and none is destined for itself."

The other's reception of the gift is precisely the creative instant of eternity where the person discovers what is unforgettable in themselves. The man who would collect everything and store it in his capacious barn is the fool who would resist this passage into the other. "We begin, and truly begin, only in promising, but we never begin already at the promise. If there is a parousia, I am not it and I cannot be its place. Its place is exodus."

The writing of the icon

The gold of the icon is more than a solar designation. That it points to eternity is well known, whatever that term might intend. Pseudo-Dionysius asks, "Why is it that theologians sometimes refer to God as Yearning and Love and sometimes as the yearned-for and the Beloved?" To which he replies, "He causes, produces, and generates what is being referred to." Language of that sort is comfortable enough, instantiating a causal metaphysics that many folks, albeit in a vague manner, implicitly accept. But then he says that "He is the thing itself. He is stirred by it and he stirs it. He is moved to it and he moves it."

This is a way of saying that God is beyond Cause. The incisive movement of Dionysian inspiration is towards a dynamic plenitude that finite minds cannot help but betray, for we inevitably spatialize fore and aft. Even as time is ungraspable, the present a strange remembering of the untouchable past and prophesying of the as yet unrealized future, it is imagined as something reified, the preceding memorialized as a stable mechanical succession that must result in a particular trajectory. All of modern science is convinced by this method.

The confidence often spuriously placed in statistics nods to the uncontainable multitude of variables, but presumes a speculatory expertise able to fathom necessary results, sometimes given the cover of "perhaps." And yet all of that is presumptive, a forgetting of freedom and the drama of the unknown.

The writing of the icon is the transcription in time of the hidden eternity, which is both judgment and promise of liberation. Its silence is not static, but an irruption of luminous freedom into the space of contemplation. The story can only be approached within the joyous dark of divine ecstasy, demanding of those who would dance with love intrepid trust in realities that far outstrip the narrow confines of any conceptual apparatus, or of any imagined array of choices.

The wreckage grasped from a certain point of view

The very nature of the gift refuses possession. Belonging is not possession. The jealousy of the God is not the despotic vanity of a petty deity, nor a refusal of generous, even lavishly overwhelming endearment. The God, after all, wishes to bestow divinity upon the strange being called forth from nothing.

So, bad readers tell bad stories. And yet, the cruelty of time remains several-fold. Within the deathbound tale, the blow seems irrecoverable. Though Arthur may retreat to Avalon, his grave mysteriously lacking, and the folk may hope in that amidst the sorrows of history, what boots the amity of mutual kindness when the lost appears to have vanished from sweet embrace?

And yet, beyond irrecoverable absence, where love proves unequal to the heart's cry for eternity, there is another darkness. For while fury in mind, heart, or body fades, as all things do, that is the nature of appearance, an aspect that could perdure only in memory, there might be a sense in which every creaturely moment persists in irretrievable stasis separated from cohesion, from unity, from any abiding name.

The deviously monumental quality of time emerges even as it mocks the person, its vanishing elusive nature somehow carrying sickness of guilt, a tomb, the momentum of our evils, entropic resistance, the weakness of the flesh, the weariness burdened with so much failure, fatigue, malicious, lazy, brutishness hidden in a thousand nasty duels of competitive recrimination.

Sin is that weight, the timely ghost, the forgotten that persists, the bloody thread frayed into a bad infinity of endless dull repetition. There is an old word for this metaphysical horror, much maligned. Be certain, there is a hell. It is related to a particular malady. The sickness called leprosy in the Bible is not Hansen's disease. The corpse-like condition of the flesh manifested from invisible, spiritual misery, the ironic contagion of souls isolated and cut off, we no longer recognize it, the living death.

This was, indeed, the sacrifice to idols. Today, what the ancient world still recognized as terrifying fate manifests as ephemeral celebrity and very dubious success. Just as the liturgy of the House of Joy is a living sacrifice of endless gift and novel receptivity in the dance of creative delight, there is a counterfeit that does not sing, but shrieks in agony, grimaces in stony silence, a metaphysical latrine where one drops forever, gagging, into noxious, leprous ordure.

Apocalypse noir

It is said that when the City fell, there was lamentation. It is said there were great fires, and that men and women became crazed, ran about screaming, fighting, and killing one another, even that the survivors envied the dead. At the last, what was left of them sought the Outlands, crying to the pitiless gods, and calling upon the earth and the seas to cover them so that they might escape the orb, the glowing monstrosity that followed them everywhere.

Some blinded themselves, only to curse and rage that they had not escaped. The running game was ever a fool's errand. If you waited, the urgency of violence abated. The voices thinned. The dark prince kept walking, not running. There wasn't any point in running when there isn't anywhere. Walking was an exaggeration, too, but he allowed that indulgence. It made you feel that you were getting somewhere. Memories came beckoning, looking for a mind to take them in. He told them to piss off.

He'd walked a long way, though of course, long meant nothing. Sometimes, the words came to him as if the ghostly cargo of great ocean liners or messages carried by transoceanic cables, invisibly under cloak of darkness far from the sun, the words of gossip, reportage, the usual conversations domestic, economic, the strangely ugly commerce of academics, everything, it was like an interminable hum of the long ago, the cadences of laughter, orders, commentary, all of it divorced from the urgent present, nakedly dim, no longer spoken or attached to a face, an impersonal noise unaware that listening had become obsolete.

When the voices had gone away, he was at first thankful, and then, utterly indifferent. Folks take the invisibility for non-existence. There's nothing there. Paranormal interventions, ghosts and the like were recreational tales. Death is the truth of life. Ask experts in neurophysiology; some of them will tell you there's nothing there now. The inescapable irony of the inquiry is that nothing is asking a deterministically derived illusion what means. You've got to laugh.

But let's just say, hypothetically, that the default atheist materialism of a certain world technological order is mistaken. Whatever a soul is or might be, cultures through the ages have thought it is a term worth preserving. It referred to something metaphysical. The Vedantic sages developed a highly sophisticated awareness, of which the West remains largely ignorant. There might be a peculiar, parochial bias, after all, in the science that captivates the globe.

He didn't care, really. He kept walking, regardless that the gesture towards motion in itself might be hypocrisy. Motion implied potency or appetite. It was difficult to speculate that the desire for oblivion was the deepest reach of freedom. Maybe freedom itself was the trap. Drop it then. Mind is a ridiculous burden.

The pretense of landscape had drifted into barren, dried-out plains, the earth hard, brittle, and veined with a network of crackled fissures too narrow to fall into, but measured by uncounted depth. Random geysers of scalding heat sent forth unnerving eruptions. Consciousness was just real enough to register the hellish drift of imaginary existence.

The final ghastly and provocative conclusion to the debacle was designed to humiliate. He was not surprised. The non-existent deity was relentlessly unwilling to allow the tortured facsimile of soul relief from unpleasantness. Kandran Valmack appeared with his ungainly stooping gate. Even with nothing but an empty sky above him, he dipped his head as if it were in danger of smacking against low ceilings.

The Sage informed him that the unfortunate circumstances were both due to the shallow intellect of his charge, and nonetheless an entirely discardable permutation of an endless supply of parallel universes. When asked rather indelicately why then he continued to haunt this particular wretched variation, the paragon of statistics saw fit to vanish into a nearby explosion of subterranean gases.

Next, the triumvirate of associates: Wanda complained bitterly that the whole universe was rigged against her. Denis pretended the entire nauseating doom was precisely the result he had expected and longed for. Ned shrugged and said nothing. He was already dead. Then came visitors from speculated realms: Mercutio, who went to his death punning, told an obscene joke, the Delphic Sybil gave him a glance of sardonic appraisal, whilst Holden Caulfield shook his head at yet another phony.

And then there was the girl. Sky was so vibrant, lovely, nothing one could properly imagine beforehand. He could not bring himself to call her illusion, though in a spasm of self-loathing and regret, he refused the gift. He grasped the sharp crystalline casket enchained about his neck, the gray amulet of his despondency, and closed his heart. Free, not free, what did it matter? It was just words. In the end, it was something at least to keep the spurious God from subverting everyone.

The Mobracht's taunt

And so the demon, which gorges on sorrows, ever keen to display the joints ready for the cut, laid out for the delectation of his old friend in bitterness the innumerable frayed ends, the endless fragmentation of the tale. *Just try to put that back together,* he said with a silent smirk. You could spend a bad infinity cataloging all that. "So, old man, time has ravaged you good and well." The Mobracht expected no answer. None was needed. What is time, but passion, this enduring of what comes? The body in its pain, its pitiful vulnerability, ripe with sorrows and that might have been the end, except for the silent acquiescence, putrefaction, rot, and the slow decay into mineral obsolescence.

This is what men thought when they could bring themselves to think of death; or jejune, gauche, they celebrated the macabre with adolescent glee. All our vital energies squandered in futility. As if he did not know that all his life was failure. Nothing remains. Nothing endures. Everything fails. He could not protect his child. This is the predictable tale, the consummation of caused causes, the sequential histories of our linear pride.

Only, it was not the vanquished body of the Elder that presented itself. Love alone mattered. Love alone was worthy of risk. A small boy brought with him the fragrance of the meadow, of a summer pond, his little hat askew. Henry Ellwood carried in his hands a porcelain basin filled with tiny life rescued from the waters. The trailing voice of his mama called after — "Do be careful, Henry. You know they'd be much happier where you found them." And the little boy stopped before the Mobracht, and displayed the treasure of the polliwogs.

"Look, look," he said in simple delight.

"Attend," said the vates, Taliessin.

The Mobracht drooped his head. There was a kind of vanishing light, something might be happening. It wasn't quite sure. And then . . . Then the man, Soren Blake, was standing before him, with that grim, ironic smile. Only now there was something gentle in it, a kind reserve for a dim pal who can't quite get the point.

"This isn't right," growled the Mobracht. "You're breaking the law."

"Alright," said Soren softly. "I make myself large."

The Green Man

So the folk know better, but they're not telling. They are silent, unlettered. They left no records. They are "the innumerable, the tacit, the vast ocean of the silent people." They know how to remain silent. Hence, the scholars think he's just a figure, a legend, a kind of symbol, though they don't know what that word means.

When they say the Green Man, they have in mind an image of nature, of natural vitality, of the humor of sap and resurgence; that's what they think, if they think of it at all. And perhaps he has been understood in that manner and made to glisten in springs and wells, to adorn the lintels of certain doors. So they imagine the Green Man as deathless in his way, and that is why Bercelak can be both reckless and courteous towards Gawain, because he does not feel the pain and risk of the unique, of the once and never more.

And no doubt, behind such a figure one touches upon those chthonic giants and dismembered gods that so often appear in ancient cosmogony. Cryptic and baffling, one discerns remnant knowledge in the Second Branch of the Mabinogi, in the magical properties of Bendigeidfran's head.

Yet time is not etched by the eternal in that way. A symbol is neither abstract nor reduced to an object of historicist interest. A scholar is apt to give priority to the first in a series of time, though that is not the best reckoning. Bercelak is not an image of that nature, and the Green Man is more than a legend. His courtesy is not frivolous or without pity.

Gawain's strike was true. It killed. That is what they do not treat soundly when they take it for mere fantastic tale, the logic of faerie. It is that as well, perhaps. And the Green Man laughed, because his flesh was no longer his own. It was beyond the cycles, and besides, his head had once already been severed by the sword.

Mercurial month

January has been a mercurial month, with heavy rains and swings of temperature presaged by strong winds. An old oak was uprooted and crashed into the abandoned cabin seventy-five yards from the farm house. Little field mice have invaded the house, practically all head and tail, like a tadpole. Henry sweeps them up into a coffee cup and deposits them outside lest they become playthings for the indoor cats.

There are folks who find this sentimental, and Henry soft. So be it. It is the world that is awry, lacking gentleness. As Henry grew old, he increasingly withdrew from writing speech. Words were unwieldy and, as Plato's *Seventh Letter* explained, too easily misunderstood or hostage to manipulation by malicious or ignorant souls.

And yet, there is the necessity of speech. He resolved to seek the prayer of silence so that words of healing might approach in a timely hour.

Vatic work of love

What if the markers of memory, so tenacious, and yet also fragile, are not utterly at the behest of our attempted retrieval? Certainly, one could misremember — an entrenched interpretation might distort objective reality. Equally, a partial perspective might yield to greater comprehension. Instead of individual possession, there is a frightening openness: what if each object of memory was also creatively porous to others, crossing boundaries that are the same as the discovery of new frontiers?

And then the story is revealed to be geometrically bountiful, bursting at putative seams. If the vital, living face peers out from each and every particular, the dramatic depths are suddenly renewed as both novel and inexhaustible. This begins to suggest an intimate relation between memory and imagination. Just here is the site of care. Memory may be either healing or pernicious, damning or kind — and this is the secret of fidelity, the vatic work of love that seeks the Origin from which all gifts flow.

Golgotha is not a new thing

The Virgin, betrothed to the infinite, was not gullible and was not made an offer trading on her ignorance. From the beginning, she was given an intimation of the inevitable. She saw before the darkness of the crèche in a Bethlehem stable the immense night of the Cross. Mary had those tidings in her heart from the start. It wasn't a shock, some bait-and-switch on the part of an inscrutable god.

For the God, while immeasurable and inexplicable to finite minds, is nothing other than unfathomable love. Golgotha is not a new thing for the God. Already and always, the God is sacrificial love, and there is no true joy apart from love. In the unspeakable depths, the Triune Bliss gives all without anguish or grasping or anxiety for justice.

The Book of Life

Rabbi Naftali says, "Consider, nu, that they never ponder what is meant by a book. They have forgotten their fellows, these bad and sullen readers, the false ones, cold and wrapped up in their narrowness, these feeble and tiny egos who are no longer a folk. Indeed, they have no gratitude; these clever dunces, their hearts shrunken, are the result of emaciated conscience.

They think like those who retreat into a private chamber. They presume their thoughts, or what they take for thoughts, and no longer speak out the words. Taking away the musical body of language, they render mute and solitary what is no longer a book; they mutilate, this mute. They forget their very speech is from the other, carried in the babble of their forgotten infancy, in the bathwater they blithely discard, the worry and soft care of their nurse, their oma, the chatter of their elders, they forget — and before all else, they alienate and mistreat their soul, pretending the vital gift in sinew and sap, in the kiss of breath is vapor, lost without delight.

Thus, they abide apart from the reverent awe, the holy waiting, the anticipation of revelation that makes possible hearing, apart from hands unrolling the scroll; from lips reading out the sacred memory, apart from the liturgy of ages — nay, this is what happens when they ignorantly despair, lacking understanding of what is entailed by the book.

And even yet, they presume to name the Unnameable, the mystery that is life!"

A knock at the door

Henry sat at the desk, staring at the ancient Remington bequeathed by his father, Lucien. Then he stretched and leaned back, listening for the sound of their voices, the many-colored, fantastical chorus. They always came this time of year, as they had for Dante centuries ago, if one goes by the standard, somewhat dim kind of clock. The Lenten hours were dwindling; the Triduum neared, which he knew was truly the beginning.

There was a knock at the door that led onto the porch of the old green farmhouse. Henry waited, for he did not receive visitors, expected none. But there it was again, a polite but persistent rapping on the door. With a sigh, and not without late grumbling, he moved, rumpled, tired, but yet with a dollop of hope to answer, to see what he would see. Two children, elven and mischievous, waited at the door. He knew them well.

"Ewa! Hal!" he shouted out in delight. It had been a long time, even if half of it is yourself.

"Hullo, Taliessin!" they cried.

The Weaving Cup

"Why can't the Elder see Lady Winterbourne?"

"That, my dears, has to do with the nature of the Weaving Cup, the way story works, the labor of the vates."

"I think they should get together," said Ewa.

"And who says they don't?" said Taliessin.

"How does it happen then?" said Ewa.

"All that is a very long story; it's still happening, truth be told, has to do with the four rivers, the ones that flow from their source in Eden," said the vates.

"What happened to Joss? You left him talking to Pennyfeather," complained Hal, who was apt to change the subject.

Taliessin removed the cat from his lap; she'd come begging for a treat. He stood and walked over towards the door of the side porch, staring out the window panes at a mated pair of cardinals supping at the birdfeeder. "Joss wasn't expecting Claire, you see. He didn't know about Sky. He only saw the girl with the red flower."

The girl with the flower

Joss saw her coming from afar, the girl with her brave little face, carrying the red flower, the long stem bouncing with her every step so that the crimson petals bobbed above her like a downy parasol.

"That must have been a whopper of a flower," said Hal.

"Yes," said Taliessin. "It was the umbrella she kept misplacing in its hidden aspect."

"Do stop interrupting, Hal," said Ewa.

Taliessin sought the thread of his words . . .

What did she mean, picking her way across the dark expanse, seeking a path with a look of determination, as if there were any point in arriving anywhere? And all the while he was watching her, just to pass the time, a tiny thought began to tremble and then to stand with spindly, shaky limbs like the first coltish tries of a newborn foal.

He did not give it notice. He did not think about it. He felt it; he knew it like one knows the flesh, alone in the wilderness. When there is a visceral, blind, yet seeing thrill, the flesh tells you — another has arrived. And so he suddenly knew, watching her, that she was coming for him.

Symbolon

When they stood before one another, there was a quiet joy that surged so strong within them that a soft glow radiated from each other's skin. Without embrace, they held one another. But still, Sky had to fight back the shadow of sorrow and did not want to lessen the gladdening heart with accusation. And then the girl took from her hand a signet ring that glowed like a living moonstone and placed it upon the finger of her friend.

"Now you must find for me a special kindling," she said. "It will be a long journey, a difficult burden, dear. But we all must bear one another; bring the gift of ashes."

These words furrowed his brow, yet Joss followed her gaze to where a dappled stallion was waiting. His saddle was studded with sapphires, rubies, and emeralds. The golden caparison about his spirited head was woven by Anshara skill. If you have to ask where he came from, you're one of the thick kind, I'm afraid. It's that kind of story, is all.

"Take my Nomad with you," said Sky. "He is a noble and free beast."

And then Joss was walking up to the steed without looking back. He was actually full of trepidation, but better to fumble about, make the best of it, rather than admit one had never ridden a horse before.

Metaphysics

Sky was so lovely his heart started to beat like bongo drums at a hippie jamboree, but Joss did not know her. This is partly, I'm afraid, because he simply didn't expect her. Joss wasn't prepared to find Claire, so he could not properly see her, yet it was something else as well. And here, dear ones, metaphysics!

Folks believe when they imagine things, especially say, when an artist imagines, that perhaps he begins with something or someone he knows and either tries to fix it in paint or stone or words as close to life as he can, and if it looks right, they say the artist is good — or it doesn't look all that close, and folks tell you it is interesting.

Though if it's a lively image, they allow it to be done well enough, only not real life, a mere fiction, supposing, right enough in its way, that what the artist did was to take a bit from here and a bit from there and pulled it together like Frankenstein's monster.

They don't know about Mumbo Junkies, or rather, they think all artists are confined to that, denying altogether the Wise.

But the Wise is different, and the knowing is different, because the vates listens to the silence. Sky came from the silence, and what Joss saw was right enough, a genuine aspect, but he wasn't prepared and didn't know she had that in her.

The images do not come from a pother of ideas in a fool head, but from the object so-called. And that is why when she came to him under the sign of the red flower, all he knew was the lovely maiden who proposed to send him on a quest. He should have told her, but then she was so beautiful, and Joss hated to admit that he was not, in fact, a knight.

"Where did Sky get the flower?"

"Yes, we're out of sequence, but you did want to know about Joss. Would you like to hear about the red flower?"

"Not now. Go on about the horse."

"You see, when Sky put him on that path, the searching, the bringing back, the return to the kingdom, it was really the long way to ask him to see her face. And then she knew better about Joss than he knew himself, always had."

The translated void

How did he find the thing in that trackless waste? It isn't possible. They say that you aren't even missed there, if you can call it a place. It's simply a missing, a negation, so thorough anonymity is too close to a name. Some might be inclined to invoke miracles. Maybe it was.

Joss considered the wisdom of the animals, how when men lived vulnerable in the time before sheltering cities, they learned to hunt and gather in the forests by following the trails made by their brothers and sisters, the beasts. So he gave free rein to Nomad, who did Sky proud. That was some horse; he didn't fall off once.

To say they covered seven leagues would imply that distance had meaning in the worldless dark. Yet the horse and his knight discovered that the void had been translated, somehow made navigable so that not so much light but the memory of light held them in motion. Joss leaned into the horse, the very act the body in prayer. It seemed as though the ground formed beneath them as they searched. Then there were the low, sleepy shrubs sheathed in the veiled touch of an unseen moon and pale forms that appeared like spectral driftwood or the collapse of an ancient hovel.

A kindling

It was a thing so slight, a shadow's shadow to the nth degree. Joss found it hiding in the raw, foul thatch, its glint of watchfulness equal parts abject fear, wretched despair, and a knot, tiny, bound, compact of unthinkable density, and this was a dark matter, the product of diabolic alembic, hatred so pure it was nearly selfless and no longer knew anything but distrust and revulsion towards anything other.

Indeed, so frail and empty was this odious wisp of resistance, Joss had to exercise extreme care and delicacy in order to grasp such nothingness, to nestle it within a cradle of swaddling cloth, a shroud of gossamer from the loom of the Anshari happily discovered in the saddlebag.

The body of the creature was tiny and feeble, with a heavy head like a coconut and a rough patch of ghostly hair rising above wizened, suspicious eyes. It was old, decrepit; bore ages of agonized brooding, unimaginably slight, fragile as an eggshell of dust. When Nomad moved with silky grace, the head bobbled against Joss with the sleepy consent of an ignorant baby. Around its neck was a little chain with a tiny pendant of gray fire.

"So this is the kindling," thought the knight, and he almost felt recrimination towards the lady who had set him such a quest.

Tethered and perplexed

The ethereal coconut cocooned upon his shoulder shifted, and Joss remembered its presence, for the monotony of their trek through the Expanse had caused his body to momentarily forget its burden, so feeble was its hold on being, so insubstantial was its shadowy casting forth. Undeniably, a change had occurred, though it might have defeated the measure of even the most discerning and sensitive scale.

When Joss looked back, a single lid half-raised to reveal a dark glistening eye like a sliver of raisin in the nodding head, and shortly afterwards, whilst he scanned the horizon which was now milky and pearlescent with a soft, slumbering maternal peace, he detected the quiet sigh of an instinctive, infantile yawn.

The infant creature born from that insubstantial kernel, something dead perhaps, yes, or as close to nihilation as possible; he'd grasped it with revulsion, and Joss sensed it would have gladly disappeared into the void, releasing itself from the risk of discovery, which is to say, existence. Yet it was sustained, tethered by an invisible care that nurtured this repugnant, wretched bit of vileness.

The question that began to trouble Joss: What does it mean to return? How does one return? Was it really as simple as reversing an itinerary? And how could it be, really, when you were changed by the wandering? You might find yourself in familiar territory, but you'd altered, inhabited an alien story, so when folks took you for restored, they embraced a changeling. The more he journeyed with the shadow child, the more he was convinced that he had no idea how to carry out the request of the beloved.

Betrayal

The betrayal of the shadow child was like this. Joss had grown accustomed to its presence. Already it had grown past the stage of a toddler, past perhaps the beginning of the questioning of why. The creature was now beginning to demonstrate signs of pack identification, where the friendship of peers is the nascent stretch of the soul towards social activities and bonding.

And since Joss was all there was of the tribe, he became the sole beneficiary of this emerging potency. Joss was lulled, so that he forgot — at least, it wasn't in the forefront of his thoughts, vigilance. Because the thing of dust was devious, looking always to claw and bite and scuttle away, since away, by its lights, was freedom.

So, while Joss was talking with the people from the first village they had come to in untold miles of emptiness, and the folk had gathered and were speaking in grunts and hand gestures, not because they were brutes, but because they did not speak English, leastwise, the tongue of Joss's time and place, it was then it saw its chance.

An old woman dressed in tatters entered into their midst, and the crowd parted. She was evidently a wise woman, for the elders and youth alike gave her the glance of respect, and the woman came up to him and whispered into his ear in perfectly modern parlance: "You are seeking the place of Weaving. Regrettably, it will take you longer now."

And when he looked back to trace the arrow of her vision, the burden child was releasing the stallion. Nomad followed his heart; his part in the adventure was done. Now Joss knelt, his spirit wobbly with dismay.

"Was this needed?" cried the knight. "Was it necessary?"

And the child beside him was momentarily abashed and shook its head, no. They walked in silence through the land, which quickly became barren, matching mood of soul, smoke rising from abyssal cracks in the gray and endless plain.

Misbegotten

There is a legend, said Taliessin. It is an old story, so old and feeble, but tenacious. It goes like this. Once there was a child, innocent and loved, so loved; our Abba loves all his children. Each of them is different, no matter how alike they appear. Into the womb of time, the seed is cast. And some fall onto a hard path and are trampled underfoot, whilst others are eaten by mice and the birds of the air. Yet other seed finds the sweet earth and blossoms in its day, though all grass dies. They call that nature.

Now, this child came into the naturing time amongst whispers. It was said the child was misbegotten, something shameful to be put away. Before the infant had taken the pap of milk, already his name was deemed poisonous. The nurse maid liked him not, bathing him with tepid hands and harsh words. And so the years progressed, and the child grew into a boy, a surly lad who pulled the wings off flies and trapped small creatures in order to torture them. Already, he would pay back the earth for bearing him such a fate.

From such deeds of beginning, the temper of his character was set. A prince he was, but armored in darkness. If he would not be loved, he'd cultivate flowers of hate and fear. In the chamber of his heart, this name he held his own, but I tell you it is an impostor, a false idol.

All true names are forms of love and lovely. They are prior to flesh of begetting. Nothing of violence, no birth taint touches this gift. Even now, Abba looks upon this child and knows him. Despite everything, he is cherished. When the idol dies the death, the truth shall live, and all will rejoice at the face of their brother.

Creative necessity

"You think that to forgive seven times seventy is a moral prescription? It is creative necessity!"

— Soren Blake, *Chronicles of the Forgotten Dreamworld*

There is something naively brash about the futurists and proponents of fascism in the early twentieth century. Like the bombastic cheerfulness of a brass band, there was a monstrous insensitivity in its celebration of heroic strength. The fascist aesthetic was incurably adolescent, a teen-aged boy incapable of discerning the nuanced enchantment of the passing, irrecoverable moment. Its predilection for the gigantic and the narcissistically monumental overcompensated for soul so tiny it was thinned to the vanishing point. The compelling beauty discernible in the weak and disfigured requires visionary capacities beyond its preference for the obvious, multiplied by the megalomania of the triumph of power.

Where Velázquez catches the surprising glory in the anguished countenance of a court dwarf condemned to jig and banter for a living, the poorly developed consciousness can only see titillation or revulsion in the face of the grotesque. The harvest of bad art proves the interior convertibility of the transcendentals, the way beauty and the good corrupt into kitsch and spoliation of the innocent. Victory for titanic will is precisely the suffering of the unique reduced to abstract numbers and dead bodies thrown into mass graves.

Though Nietzsche was correct that the judo of *ressentiment* perpetrated by the victim can equally distort, it can become an indulgence in vitriolic hatred for the oppressor that also forgets complexity, the profound integrity of art that insists on forgiveness as a prerequisite to accurate vision.

All our times are cherished

"Do you remember, brother, our chair?" said Ewa.

"Yes, Ewa. I remember," said Taliessin.

"Sometimes, that seems like a long time ago. But it's not like that. It's living, brother; all our times are cherished."

"We have to forget them in order to get them back," said Hal.

"And now, brother, tell us about Sky," said Ewa.

The song of the wise woman

When Sky awoke, she found herself inside a tidy, humble stone cottage. A kettle was heating above a small fire in the hearth. The woman hunched over the pot, singing so softly and beautifully that Sky closed her eyes and listened in motionless content. The woman's voice was gentle, with a little hint of husky smoke that Sky fancied in a singer.

There was a story and a teaching woven within the song. The story was all about loves that were pursued, lost, and found again, but differently, because love is the freshness of always beginning. There were quite a few characters, though every one of them searched for love. And the teaching was also about the heart, which is the spiritual place where your will resides.

The song said that spirit seemed a vague thing, easily disbelieved when folk grew hard and dim. And then they could no longer believe in the flesh, could no longer see with the eyes of love, and soon enough they refused to act as if they had a will at all. They did things without thinking or because everyone else said it was the thing to do. And yet, they could not help but desire. On the inside, the profundity of the gift; when you think you are alone, you are with the others. The harmony is from the Origin; the scattering was later.

There was more to the melodious lyric, but Sky began to smell pancakes, and her body stretched in spite of her. The woman turned, revealing a face furrowed with wrinkles like the rings of a tree, yet her limpid eyes were as young as the dawn. The last bit of the song, slipping already from Sky's memory, told her that the perfection of freedom is not endless choice but total bliss, where the others are found in an ever-deepening reciprocity of astonished recognition and adventure. Only a churlish, mad soul would refuse love because it spoke with the passionate insistence of the one thing necessary.

"And where have you been, my love? Isn't it good to find one another?" said the wise woman, the lilt of her song honeying her words.

The face of the island

There is no person without a face. The face of the living island had a long, flowing body that shimmered and moved with the grace of a porpoise at play in blue waters. Yet her physical presence remained lightly rooted to the land, as though she had powers that were sometimes attributed to holy men like Padre Pio — the capacity to bilocate, for instance. This enabled her to serve tea to a friend in the stone cottage at the edge of the island, whilst simultaneously she watched over the large sea otters barking amidst the rocks offshore.

Sky admired greatly the chameleon fabric of her flesh, which was also double, somehow naked and yet dressed with a living light of chromatic bliss that conveyed song, emotion, and wit. She could tell a joke by altering the dorsal light from aqua to peach and turn her gamine eyes upon one with daring enough to provoke a blush gentled by a sudden flourish of soft, velvety mirth that invited one to share in the moody fantasia of her sinuous kindness. *I know you*, thought Sky. *You are different, yet the same.*

"I know you, too," said Lady Winterbourne.

Davita's gift

The spiritual body is free. Resurrection is initiation into its creative capacities. The eschaton of the kingdom founds infinite stories. One is not reborn as a different person, for the person is unique; it is intrinsic for a person to be unrepeatable and irreplaceable. Sky began to understand that Lady Winterbourne shaped her body to the needs of the world she inhabited, and there might be many worlds... Nonetheless, it was nothing arbitrary. No one else could give her kiss. *We flourish, dear one, in ever greater creation. Within the Plenitude of Eternal Joy, we live a never-ending discovery, where ever greater love manifests as ever more ardent flesh.*

Though these words teased Sky with a promise that enchanted, it was too much for her understanding. She walked the island with gratitude, slowly coming into herself. She breathed in air redolent with the salt tang of the sea, softened by the fragrance of flowering shrubs with diminutive white petals. And it was then that she saw the loveliest monkey imaginable; even those who think the simian countenance is a displeasing caricature of the human face could not find fault with her. Davita, adorned in golden brocade, was waiting for Sky as if they had long planned the meeting. Sky laughed with simple pleasure to see her, the guardian of grapes.

The monkey approached the girl then with formal steps, a ceremony of austere beauty. She carried the Virgin's command, the red flower. And then Davita insisted that Sky take the precious gift.

"For you, it was given," said Davita.

There was something in the crimson flesh, the fabric of flame; Sky felt both honored and afraid. Yet Davita's kindness, the elegance of her manner, it would be utterly boorish to refuse or even to hint at reticence. When Sky reached for the blood bloom, her eyes widened. She was no longer standing on an island. A living cathedral of incomprehensible fecundity surrounded Sky, for the many dimensions of the cosmos arise from within the flower.

Davita danced with joy. "You are, you are the girl with the hazel-nut!" she said.

Maybe you begin to understand

"Maybe you begin to understand," said Lady Winterbourne, who was young now as Rachel Moon. "That is what I tried to let him know, my man. It was when our love took root that I became, What do you call it?" She looked at Benedicta and waved her hand in the direction of the canopy of tall trees above them that stood like pillars in a gothic nave.

"Yes," said Benedicta.

"My heart grew bold," said Rachel. "There was nothing it would not draw into love."

"And that is why," said Shadrael, "that nearly everyone is wrong about the Threshing."

"Why is everyone wrong then?" said Sky.

"Because they think it is something on the outside, a kind of terrible invasion of privacy where one is shoved naked before hostile eyes and tortured. It's because that is what . . . "

"What we would do," said Vanaya.

"Have done," said Benedicta. "They think that it is like being forced to make confession, to read out a list of all you've done, down to the last tittle."

"Yes, it might seem like that," said Rachel.

"Only, it isn't," said Benedicta, "not really."

"No, not really," agreed Rachel.

"Why not really?" said Sky, feeling like the dullard who tries to hide on the back row of the class.

"First, because it is a relief," said Benedicta. "Once one has tired of lies, grown weary with running, once the little drop of oil touches the forehead and weeping takes over, the dry pump has to be primed," she said.

"Then it is like a lovely bath where the grime and sores and all sorts of horrors drop off."

"Not that it doesn't hurt," added Benedicta with a sad smile.

"Oh, yes, it's death," said Lady Winterbourne, who now appeared as the mistress of Regency Park. "There are those who despair. Try to escape anguish. They hurt themselves by trying to get away."

"You can't get away," said Shadrael.

"Not that way."

"You still come to the Threshing," said Benedicta.

"We come together. And that is what is so often missed."

"Yes, entirely," said Lady Winterbourne. She looked at Sky with tenderness, as if she wanted to hold her as a mother grasping a long-lost child.

"We're unique, but not separate. We respond before we act, and so . . ."

"And so, when one of us fails, we all fail," concluded Benedicta.

"We fail a lot," said Sky. "There's an awful lot of horror, an awful lot of wasted lives. All that love wasted. The mamas feeding the children, and the papas breaking their backs, and it comes to nothing; worse than nothing."

"Yes," sighed Shadrael. "It's hell."

"And that is why he screamed like that," said the friend who anointed his feet.

In a mirror darkling

Before her was Uhraine. The ancient crone smiled a crooked smile. "Dear one," she said, "home at last." And Sky shuddered. "You seem uneasy," said Uhraine. "Do not be. I have always been with you. I am your first and last truth. I am the shriek as the plane goes down, though do not scream, dear. It's so unbecoming."

Sky understood that she herself was Uhraine, that Uhraine was the story she kept telling herself, the story everyone told, nature. This image, this river, the dark waters, they ought to have finished her. Uhraine knew that look, that resignation, the acceptance of annihilation, reentry into the nothingness. She cooed softly, to bring the girl in easy.

Except it didn't. Something else, something unexpected, bringing astonishment, and then perplexity. What had happened?

"Water shall become flame, the darkness is light," said Sky, not with a shout, but sweetly, gently — and Uhraine shook.

And then, the girl leapt with joy, that, too, was all wrong, such a girl, the little one, the one the Father loves, when everyone forgets, the little one laughs, because she knows the House, she knows the House she belongs to. She rose up just like that, like a maiden greeting the sun peeking through the morning curtain, and the girl placed before Uhraine a gift.

It was some little gift like the girl, something small, she might have picked it in some meadow while at play, it was a little flower like the girl, that maiden, something she just picked along the way, only it wasn't, it was something she'd carried, some strange parasol, the small monkey had insisted, that little Davita had made her promise, so she'd carried it, even when it seemed ridiculous, only nothing was ever quite ridiculous, because even a little red flower, it might bloom in a desert, far from everyone, but still, it was loved, because it too, had its angel.

The mother of consent

The red flower, too, was a message, so she gave the message, she said the red flower, and Uhraine shook; she didn't know what to make of it, she was surprised, this flower surprised her, she was going to say something, she was going to speak, and then she did speak, and she still spoke of home, only now Sky saw her clearly. After all, that red flower was given to Davita in the first place so that Sky might know the Lady well.

And now Sky turns to you. Yes, *you*, don't look behind as if it might be a mistake, might be another; her words sought out the one who is before these words, the universal reader.

"Her face was the most exquisite beauty I had ever seen, her eyes as sweet and sensitive as a young doe. She was more innocent and fresher than any babe you have ever met. The Lady looked upon me, and I felt in her gaze compassion and gravity and something else, endeavor, I think — as if she could hardly yet understand me.

It was as if a shadow of some kind still lay over me, and she could not easily discern my visage. She continued to peer into me, and nothing has ever made me so happy. They are wrong who say it is a misery to be judged, not by such as she. I saw her bite slightly on her lower lip, like a child girding itself for a difficult task. She held me gently until, at last, she beamed with delight. 'Ah, it is Claire,' she said with a girlish laugh, and I couldn't help laughing back."

"Yes, yes, it's me," I said.

The beauty surprised her

Claire was dead. The petty irritabilities, the fear of humiliation, the stab of unrequited desire, the enervating pain of boredom — all had left her. And then the strangest gift: she returned and walked incognito amongst her own. She was not remembering. It was not the past bathed in nostalgia. Claire walked in the living moment of all her times. A gentle laughter and a soft smile filled her heart. What had happened?

She saw her canary, Petey, whom she had chosen from a dozen others. "Ach," said her aunt, "the ugliest one." Petey had a goiter. Yet Petey would fly to her when she came into the room and give kisses, drinking drops of water balanced on her lips. And there was Uncle Teeter, a dirty old man who had pull with the coppers. He once got her out of a speeding ticket. Then she was walking along a beach, and it was covered in black rocks, and people were playing and yelling, and some were nice and some not so nice, and many of them were too fat and looked silly in their straw hats and multicolored bathing suits. A young man was throwing a Frisbee, and his dog was catching it and running back with the prize so it could be thrown again.

She even discovered herself, awkward and gangly, she thought, wishing to get away from them all. And what she saw was their vulnerability and the transience of their clock time, and how some were earnest and others very foolish, but all of them were a surprise, a beauty called out from nothing. The beauty surprised her.

Aufer a nobis, quæsumus, Dómine, iniquitátes nostras: ut ad Sancta sanctórum puris mereámur méntibus introíre. Per Christum Dóminum nostrum. Amen.

Claire began to cry for the love of them, for the goodness of it all that had surrounded her, but which, in her insecurity and the blind need of her mortal body, she could not see but for a rare, fugitive glimpse.

Sancta sanctorum — she laughed at how dim she was! How could she not know the Hoolie Hoolies?

I know how to take him. If my grace is insidious, clever as a thief/And like a man hunting a fox./I know how to take him. It's my business. And this liberty itself is my creation. For the Blue Hunter had tricked them. He had entered into all their paths, into all their monstrous ways and sorrows, the long and the short of it, and mapped them in his flesh. Into all their weakness and contemptible hate, he had brought the inexhaustible wellspring, sprinkling the earth with the wine of immortality.

Godwit on an Elder-tree

"Sing, now, Taliessin, sing of how it was," said Hal.

"Sing, now, Taliessin, sing of how it will be," said Ewa.

"Sing, now, Taliessin, sing of how it is," they said.

"I've been a sow, I've been a buck,
I've been a sage, I've been a ploughshare,
I've been a piglet, I've been a boar.
I've been the tumult of the storm,
I've been a spreading flood,
I've been a wave in a gale,
I've been the disperser of ruin.
I've been a lynx on three trees,
I've been a godwit on an Elder-tree,
I've been a crane looking to eat its fill."

—Fragment of "The Wild Horse is Broken" from the *Llyvyr Taliessin*

Ape-men of the abyss

In their hapless wandering, the anguish that dominated hardly had a name. *This couldn't possibly end well* was the repeating mantra that echoed Joss's frustration and the building feeling of futility. So it is ironic, or fortuitous perhaps, depending on one's inclination, that just then the Morweni occurred.

Joss ignored the sudden anxiety of the shadow creature, who hopped about his shoulders with unusual, manic energy. "Pipe down," he said, though the child only spoke in gestures of distress. It was only when it was too late and the path was blocked, and they were surrounded by Morweni that he inferred the meaning of its actions.

From their speech and the ponderous affectations of ritual and moral dispute, Joss gathered the Morweni were an ancient tribe following elaborate and well-established precedent. They were insistent on a certain order in the grouping of those who led and those who followed them into the rough ground surrounded by rocks and fallen slag, where they again fell into a lengthy conversation amongst themselves before turning to Joss and the vile one, as they referred to the shadow child.

Joss tried to guess from various bits of colorful cloth or talismans hung about the neck which of them was the voice of authority, but the logic of their deliberations was so interior to an insular and complex mythology that he was unable to focus his attention upon a single figure.

The typical Morweni was certainly imposing, standing seven to eight feet tall, hominids, yet with heavy mandibles and thick frontal ridges that resembled primates somewhat removed from *Homo sapiens*, those unwise wise. They might be the giants of mythic lore. Joss wondered why they did not simply drag the offending creature off to do with as they willed. Joss was certainly no physical deterrent to their desires. Then he thought some taboo refused this easy solution, and later, he suspected there was something about his presence that forbade such action.

Eventually, two of the Morweni spoke before the assembled crowd. The first may have been an elder or medicine man. He spoke an archaic tongue that induced hushed silence in the Morweni. The second speaker was younger. He surprised Joss by managing a reasonable approximation of modern English. He raised himself upon a makeshift dais and said grave words. He said the repulsive was despicable and vile, and it was that. He appealed to Joss to return the Nocturne to the darkness from whence it came. The creature had chosen. The darkness, after all, was its desire.

Besides, the Nocturne was a completed thing, a finished story, to which nothing more could be added. Joss understood them. He wanted to repel the wretched thing away as much as any of them. But the maiden had commanded, and in that command, there was something that registered, just barely. So, Joss said to them what he did not understand yet felt because of her.

"I'm sorry to upset you," he said. "I know it doesn't make sense. She needs this one. She can't be herself without it. None of us can."

When it became clear that Joss would not be persuaded, the Morweni began to fidget. The imposed decorum broke down, and soon they were jumping up and down in a state of angry agitation. Joss expected violence to follow, but for a half minute of shrill demonstration, nothing more happened. The Morweni almost seemed to have forgotten the reason for their wrath and simply vented moral outrage.

The shadow child clung desperately about Joss' neck, almost itself a talisman of some unspecified nature. Seeing no other resolution but painful attack and physical extinction, Joss turned and ran past the incoherent mass of Morweni towards a broken path that ended in a steep decline. Whether a Morweni could make that leap, Joss did not know, but they had shown trepidation at the sight of it.

At the last moment, Joss threw himself over on a wing and a prayer. The angels answered. Somehow, he made it, rolling on his side in agony. The reckless hurdle over the abyss, the tumble amidst the rocks, had knocked the breath from Joss. He raised himself, sprawled on all fours, and then darted a briefly panicked look to see if the creature had survived the tumult. The child grasped his shoulder with the slender insistence of a pet spider-monkey.

Apparently it had strengthened in their journey, gained a measure of substantiality, almost taken from Joss himself. There was little time to congratulate themselves. First small rocks, and then more serious boulders, were hurled at them from the Morweni side, accompanied by howls of protest. Stumbling forward, they hastened without regard for destination, so long as it was far from impending missiles. When they were finally free of it, Joss spoke in a laconic humor.

"That was well-observed," he said. "If you should descry another such worthy comment, feel free to point it out." And shortly, he felt the even suspiration of the infant's sleep beating against his neck.

The truth about Jane

Afterwards, the shadow child began to jump down and walk alongside him. He'd reach up his hand and grab Joss's arm with a friendly, proprietary air, rather like Cheetah's affection for Tarzan. Every few steps, it would look up at its caretaker with a shy glance, as if it wanted to communicate some special word that might seal their bond with enduring sincerity. The transformation of the eyes was rather unnerving, and though Joss did not believe them and found the repeated, silent request in their liquid solicitation somewhat irritating, it was quite impossible to ignore.

"What is it?" he said at last, stopping with a sigh and shouting just short of a roar.

The child was seemingly bereft of language, so it was a hopeless ask. When they resumed walking, however, a polite, somewhat baffled voice was whispering in his thoughts.

"Isn't it rather self-serving, after all?" it said. "All this concern about survival. Rather petty and neurotic. Hardly worthy of a mature spirituality." Cheetah, of course, would have said something much more endearing, such as "Jane only loves you for bananas."

"Who says we're going to survive?" said Joss out loud.

The tone of violent indifference, if not disdain for the proclivities of the ego, was so pronounced that the shadow child stopped looking up and soon crawled back onto the perch of Joss' shoulder, where it could sulk without being observed.

You start the way you came

It was after this that Josh made a discovery. The closer they came to her, the nearer to the maiden, the more the orb ring began to glow. Joss began to descry the way by attending to its light. How long they wandered is hard to say. Duration for the soul is not measured by standard chronometers. It began to end, however, when they came to a land of lakes and lush green fields, which for some reason were dotted with emus.

An imperious young woman stared down from the top of a crenellated tower, which was decorated with intricate gingerbread. The way she looked at them, you'd think she never saw humans before. She seemed to consider leaving them to whatever business they thought they were about, but at the last moment she shouted down that they should come up to her.

"Everyone thinks the front door is on their level, but you start the way you came," said Aurora.

By this obscure provocation, she seemed to imply they ought to float up and join her. I'm afraid there was no elaborate arboreal passage to allow entry into her realm. They tried the front door in spite of Aurora, because it was there and nothing else seemed possible. Politeness lasted long enough to wonder if anyone would answer. Then a muffled voice said, "Come in, come in," with mild exasperation. But she was right. When they went through the door, they found themselves in the tower.

Aurora was focusing the lens of her telescope on a stellar birth. "It happened a long time ago," she advised. "Only they've just now got around to the christening. I said that Ugmat was not entirely euphonious, but cultural differences don't always translate."

The wandering plant

She was really a strange girl. She said the wildest things. Aurora explained that human beings were mirrors of plants. The roots of the vegetal world reach deep into the earth. They pull up the nutrients, bringing forth green leaves and flowering branches. But a plant lacks organs; the sun and the stars, the earth and sea are the larger body that acts on behalf of the being sprung up from the earth. The roots of mankind are otherwise, reaching into the heavens.

The mind of human beings manifests by sensory organs, and the brain draws sustenance from the realm of subtle bodies where forms are discovered as ideas, but the entire body is the cosmos as flesh. Man is the wandering plant. When Joss asked about the fruit bearing element of the analogy, where the flowers were, Aurora answered without blushing, she didn't think of him as a boy: it was the organs devoted to lovemaking.

It's hard to say where the conversation would have gone next. Aurora had unconventional notions regarding the elliptical of retrograde planetary objects surrounding a binary dwarf star. She'd been aching for someone sufficiently not her family to tell them all about it, but unfortunately, a door flopped open in the middle of the floor and Diana appeared, the golden penumbra of a hurricane lamp raised above her like the torch of the Statue of Liberty.

"Oh," she said. "I did not know we had visitors."

"They are not visitors," said Aurora. "I am talking to a dressing dummy and a sheet because I wanted something intelligent to speak with."

"Well, when you are done with them, send them down."

"Very well, you can have them now," said Aurora. "Only Deco wants a new suit. Don't give any biscuits to the sheet. It's recently come from the Shuddering realm. If you do, it will retch and spit up monsters."

What they said on the way down

"It is you who are the sheet," said Joss rather crossly.

"Very well, that makes you the dummy," said the shadow child.

Ambiguities of the house of man

It must be admitted that Diana was rather severely tempted to ask Cook for a plate of biscuits. Fortunately, she had just enough respect for her sister's arcane knowledge to avoid mischance. They were ushered into an exquisite sitting room, the sort where intimate confessions and revelations of character were apt to occur if one were so inclined.

The shadow child behaved rather badly, acting as if even the soft cushions were made of sackcloth, breaking into extended fits of bawling and so forth. Joss nearly lost his temper, but Diana had such composure and natural beauty that he attempted to match her patience. Courtesy prevailed when the dark infant fell into one of its frequent naps. Joss thought about explaining their presence, why he was encumbered with a creature from the Expanse. He did not quite know how to begin. Diana resorted to discussing the weather and asked if Joss enjoyed the countryside.

"One always imagines Arcadian retreat as idyllic happiness," he said. "It is a picture of peace and loveliness one carries about as a kind of talisman against the hectic impositions of the city. But to be honest, I don't think most folk believe it. I have often been told by rural folk that it is actually deadly dull."

"Ah, but those were country folk in the city. They might have been traitors. Most likely, we sent them to spread rumors, so the mob would stay away."

Joss smiled at that. Diana charmed without trying. Next, the subject of marriage was broached. Diana waxed eloquent upon the mixed motives of many such alliances, the political element that always intruded, especially for wealthy families or those with noble lineage. Joss conceded that the institution was hardly immune to venal calculation, but refused to disavow the small domestic intimacies that have traditionally been held the particular reserve of married friendship.

"I cannot speak from experience," said Diana. "Of what I have seen, such beauties are an endangered species. Our authors present such lively narratives, we are drawn towards a picture one rarely encounters in life."

Joss barely suppressed a sigh. The shadow child awoke and started to crawl under the divan.

"I was asked to bring it," said Joss in exasperation. "The maiden wanted it; the Lord knows why."

At this, Diana became curious. She quizzed him in a manner polite, yet with surgical precision. A man knows nothing of this form of questioning. Diana had a notion of who the maiden was, and soon, she had concluded that Joss was Sky's secret. Once his guard was up, however, Joss resorted to evasive banalities.

"In spite of cruelties and betrayal, there is something venerable in family," said Diana, as if they were continuing an unbroken conversation. "It's something to begin to perceive a narrative across generations. I often think the story of life must be meaningless orphaned from the broader tale."

Joss shrugged. A sour dejection threatened to overtake him. He could not quite account for the ill mood that had come upon him. "Who can tell that story? The farther back you go, the easier to fib."

"So you think everyone is simply proud of a lie?" asked Diana. She was suddenly angry. "I cannot think that everything we love should be so cynically cast aside."

"Forgive me," said Joss, truly abashed. Fortunately, a fat Pekingese named Smoogs popped out from beneath the divan and began to make a show of assaulting the child burden with yippy growls and kisses. The shadow was most embarrassed by this ferocious display of affection, and then everyone laughed, even the burden.

Forbidden topic

Diana flushed, and touched upon the subject of Sky Odyssey with delicacy. Deco had word of her arrest, but nothing more. Silence was often the end of such affairs. Joss hardly knew what to make of this information. Diana was sure she was right about him, but the name was evidently wrong. She dropped it with a frown and observed that she was distressed to bring up another topic avoided by polite society. "But we are not quite that," she said with that charming fire in her eyes.

She then asked his opinion on religion. "So many nowadays prefer to claim no connection of that kind," she said. "Instead, they assert spirituality, though I find that word is nearly always a vague gesture that means indifference towards truth and indulgence for certain feelings that are cultivated at little or no cost to the individual."

"I'm not sure if I'm qualified to speak on that," said Joss.

"Oh, surely you are wrong," she said. "You love someone, or you would not be here, Mr. Wherryweather. And love is not nebulous, nor possible without the acceptance of suffering."

"Are you saying you cannot love without faith?" he asked.

"I think perhaps love is faith, or that faith is an action of love. I'm afraid I can't be clear on these things." Diana stared at the shadow child. "It's a pity my brother is not here. Deco is so much more clever than I."

"I doubt that greatly," said Joss, who felt indeed the paucity of his own generation. How many could even think her thoughts?

The Unicorn

Narina gazed upon Joss with open curiosity. He'd discovered her surrounded by deer and carrying a rooster that clearly was accustomed to the cosseting of the goddess upon the green.

"Well, you're not bad, I suppose," she said.

She was thinking of Deco. The shadow child she mentioned not at all. The story she told, however, was a strange one about Sky. "No one else knows," she said. "I wasn't to say anything, unless her fella shows up. You're the fella."

And then Narina related the day of the hunt for the white hart. It was not too hard to follow even if Joss knew none of the principals, though by this time he had guessed the identity of the person who went by Sky Odyssey in this world. As this sudden equation began to suggest itself to him, Joss felt tears coming into his eyes, but Narina seemed oblivious to this private drama. It was as if she'd been keeping the story like a delicious, profound treasure and now could hardly help racing to set it free.

Sky was fascinated by Phylida; at first, she'd been irritated by the transparent ploy to get them away from danger, to go somewhere else, anywhere else, where danger was far, far away, though she ought to have known, that was the way of it, that precisely this would call the danger. As the most plaintive suppliants imaginable, just by running, they were calling, invoking, and bringing down upon themselves the nameless unknown, that terror causing the hounds to bay in the human, keening manner. It was certain to find them, and it did.

And perhaps she did know, expected it, because her horse was bristling with expectation, and she rose a bit in the saddle, bracing for it. But on the surface, oddly, she was amused. It made her giggle, and then she shouted like lightning into the open air. Phylida was too scared and too relieved to have gotten away to notice, utterly obtuse to the spiritual tectonics bound to irony.

Sky found herself watching the movement of the perfect little lips, and the expressive widening of the eyes. How lovely, this artifact, telling her something that was nothing except, we are safe, safe, temporarily thrown away from herself so that Phylida was not even unconsciously performing, even if you might suggest it was so ingrained she could no longer help it, still, what a lovely creature, it was surprising they weren't all in love with her, even Deco.

Narina paused here and looked intently at Joss, but he could make nothing of her meaning, so she returned to the story. And then . . . Then Phylida's eyes widened even more if that were possible, and she gasped and Sky was laughing with a kind of zealous hilarity and her horse was charging, and she was riding the equine wave, and she might have screamed, charging with the horse into a darkness of nearby trees, tall, thick, twisted by years. The woods embraced her, and Phylida's cry, so different, shock and dismay, became a distant speck along a far horizon.

For now her horse burst into gallop, sure like an arrow shot with perfect knowledge, and propelled Sky forward until she came to the white hart, and all sound seemed to stop and motion, too. There they stood in timeless, tranquil joy, or better, a different time, a time that moves, but does not pass.

Then without taking her eyes from the hart that met her with sweet and gentle patience, Sky heard words, words that might have seemed violent and jarring next to the courtesy and kindness of the hart's gaze, but there was no discontinuity but the strange convergence of reverence and passion invading her, no, responding to a request, and the request was her own, rising up from within, as if it had always been there, waiting, yet something new, so that words that abided in the silence were now heard, and the words were shouted across waters, she had that sense, they were words crossing a river, words spiced by desert air, words crossing a river, and it was a voice ardent, and she heard it say "Come" and she heard herself say "Come," and all around her the very trees and the earth, the birds and everything that moves upon land and sea said "Come."

And she heard, as if from a distance, a voice that cried, "Daughter of time, he is coming, he who is and shall be, he who was before me. Here at the river, the Jordan of time. It is the day he revealed himself to the universe, though hardly anyone noticed."

And she knew the voice from the deep, the friend of the portal. It was the Angel Man. Then there was a darkening of the sky and perhaps a rushing of the wind, a portent and a fear, though nothing contravened the serenity of the hart, and so nothing disturbed Sky, only she was aware of the signs.

Sky heard the long echoes of the hounds and the consternation of hunters, but only echoes, and she saw the river in the woods, it was a river, though she did not recall it, this river in Prince Raveh's woods, and the river was full, had taken upon itself, had taken into itself, from hidden sources, she knew this, all the words that were ever spoken or ever would be spoken, the words that were sharp and broken, and the soft murmurs, the words with no need of grammar, the words of curse and imprecation, the chatter, coarse banality, dullness, everything turgid, insipid, the cruel, the vulgar, the addled, and also words of blessing, of kindness, insight tongue embodied, everything, everything, this river, this water, covering the earth, and then she saw him, the reason for the cries, for the anguish of the hounds, more terrible than death. "They are a pair," she said.

Only then did Sky begin to know the boldness in the humility of the hart matched by this purity, which was not at all timid or icily sacrosanct, not a moral scrupulosity, nor a thing of rules, perhaps not even a power, though powerful beyond calculation, this radiant, kingly perfection, that granted the incomprehensible wholeness of the kingdom.

How he could be both, no, it was more than that, perfect, stunning precisely within the shattering, you couldn't stand to look, were it not utterly beautiful, this bearing of every disfigurement, all that was horror and aimless, foul cruelty, some fearful, unimaginable bearing of all things disparate into a harmony not at all tranquil, but dancing, infinitely charged, integral.

And then her horse knelt, or had been kneeling. You couldn't see any of this otherwise, and she knew herself joined to his reverent action, the horse bowed its head, and fell down to its knees. The beasts of the field and forest, the rabbit and the fox, the oxen and the long-suffering mule, and somehow the eagle high above, and the creatures of the slumbering depths bowed, and all saw the unicorn come to the waters.

Men, however, did not know. Sky discerned shepherds and hunters and scholars, artisans, and all manner of men walking away, they showed only their backs, none heeded, so that Sky alone stood with human eyes to take part, to join in the creature's cosmic liturgy, to ponder that endless river where the unicorn lowered his kingly head.

And the king's horn parted the waters, punctured the waters, the king's horn rivened the waters, chastened the waters, and this piercing was also a sword foretold by Simeon, and perhaps also a lance in the hand of a Roman soldier.

Then Sky saw the Man, heard a human voice regal, winsome, creative, and he said to her, "I am the house of Mnemosyn."

Fire rushed into her heart as a river of living water, and the whole earth radiated the blaze of Uncreated light, for his flesh embraced all and all were like a sea of glass mingled with fire so that she must no longer have lived.

At the end of the telling, tears flowed down Narina's face. Sky had explained some sense of the meaning of it, but Narina did not comprehend it. She knew the words, however, and gave them to the boy who was not Deco.

Though everyone thought that time was gravity moving relentlessly towards a mortal end, that life came first and ended in sorrow, the king was not bound, he was the Lord of times. It was death that came first, it was the end that contained the fullness of aeons, the beginning of new speech. What was old, tired, or condemned to failure was not etched in stone, but wildly open to an infinite horizon. Every bitter curse and howl of misery, every cry of hopeless anguish, every silence from the ice of Outer Darkness was unable to stand apart, to resist, to claim sham liberty, because even that had become fire.

When she came out of the woods, where Phylida and Deco, Prince Raveh and the others were waiting for her, she could tell them nothing — to preserve the world, it was kept hidden.

Orientation of the heart

The Hebrew scriptures redact various oral traditions. The original four rivers are given as the Pishon, the Gichon, Chidekel, and Perat. The last two we still know as the Tigris and the Euphrates. The first two are less clear and subject to speculation.

Rashi identified the Pishon with the Nile. Josephus suggested the Indus, while others have plumped for the Ganges. These latter take Havilah, the land encompassed by the Pishon for a corruption of the Himalayas, discerning evident roots of certain biblical names with Sanskrit originals. Putting aside the lack of consensus, the majority opinion tends to identify the land of Cush associated with the river Gichon as Ethiopia, though there are dissenters.

Taken as a heuristic, assume for the moment that the Pishon and Gichon are most likely the Blue and White Nile. If these are the four rivers that flow forth from the waters of Eden, their identification should give a clue as to the whereabouts of the Garden. The problem is there is no central location from whence all four flow. The Euphrates and Tigris are in the Northeast, and the two Nile rivers are in the Southwest. Lacking any point of convergence, the place of Beginnings eludes into the mists before time.

Four seasons, four directions, four primordial elements, four cardinal virtues, not to mention apocalyptic horseman, and ecclesiastically condoned gospels, one can multiply the list of four sufficient to prove the ancients, and certainly the medievals, saw in four a symbol of completeness, sometimes cyclic in nature. If one recognizes the index of affection in the Adamic compass, something of interest may be suggested.

The East is elemental air, announcing the newborn sun, grace the deepest truth of nature. And Sky searched that path. The West is gravity and sadness, the bane tree — and this struggle with the darkness of earth marks the wrestling of Soren. The North is water and ice, the liquefaction of desire into infinite image, asking one to climb, nay, to fly into the heights. And this is Rachel. The South is instinct, a roil of blooded passions, but also language, the quest for flame that would illuminate free from false fire. How to love and defeat the curse? Joss seeks the answer.

And now consider our story, the paths they take. The northeast, the Tigris and Euphrates, the feminine, Rachel and Sky thrown together, see how that works; the southeast, the masculine, the Elder in the spectrum of his incarnation, Joss perplexed, but ardent, loving in loss. If you object this is counter to the tradition, that woman is the earth and the sky is kingly, remember that desire is drawn by completing opposites, and perplexity may cure itself.

The Hebrew word Eden means delight, pleasure. Think not of sensation, a passing moment; that river flows from the unseen, the Uncreated, it is a name of God. From God's delight comes all that pleases. And yet, the rivers do not meet. What weaving can bring them together, tell the story right?

We come to the sea

There was marshland nearby. You skirted that a bit. The rain had been light, and it was possible to pick your way to the shore. When they arrived, the sea had rolled back at low tide. The burden was just getting up from a nap. It yawned widely, and then began to point at various shells glittering in the sun that were somehow appealing. Joss picked a few of these up to satisfy its sudden, imperious desire for shiny objects, though this quickly became insufferable.

Apparently all the shells were fascinating and worthy of serious study, which is fine unless one is tasked with bringing each one of them to a demanding infant persistently attached to one's shoulder. Joss opined that a parrot would do just as well and be far less annoying. Then they walked along the shoreline. The silence of this world embraced the hushed murmuring waves. No sign of wharves or huts of reeds inveighed against the solitude.

Childhood seemed to come in from the sea, a glimmer from the shadows. *Dream and memory came woven together, without trauma, the pierced wound of historical existence escaped us, and we lived in the waking sleep of the ancestors.*

The coracle

The coracle was loosely tied. The current took the vessel, and it would meander as if it might sneak into the flow before the line grew taut and pulled it back. Joss got in and let slip the craft. The shadow child made a piteous display of sincere misgiving, and then huddled beneath the plank seat and engaged in miserable spasms of retching.

At first, Joss laughed at the melodramatic excess. The seas were calm, and the skies were fair. Yet the caprice of nature paid him back. It was not long before the waves grew large beneath surly clouds. Joss could not navigate against the storm, and soon his face mirrored the burden of gloom. There was nothing for it but to ride it out. The winds would take them where they pleased.

Once the wind relented, their little craft becalmed. All that could be seen was the unbroken monotony of more and more sea. Then the shadow child uncorked a heretofore unsuspected talent for swearing. Joss was a moron of gigantic fat headedness. The Outer Darkness at least did not torture one with unending nausea. Whatever reason did a dithering landlubber have, casting himself and an innocent infant into harm's way without the least semblance of a plan? (This, of course, is the expurgated version.)

Joss fought off the urge to toss the imp into the sea. He endured hours of remorse. It was unpleasant to admit he'd acted foolishly. Joss could not bring himself to explain that a feeling of inspiration attached to a dreaming vision of his girl had propelled the insouciance of his act. At the day's end, as the sun was sinking below the horizon, they came to the island. The coracle almost seemed alive, the way it skipped into the wide bay and settled beneath a jutting dock.

Relief was so great, Joss did not bother about whether he had been vindicated or not.

Saying of the wise woman

The Green Man is the Angel Man who sees now, making the path straight in the desert. We are the crooked men and crooked women. Can you look with innocent eye? The open maw of the nestling does not imagine want. The cruelty of the earth is beyond its ken. Shall we leave it to nature's whim?

The Green Man looks with posthumous eyes, and having died, there is no worry for pride, survival, or the regnant glory of petty mortals. What he brings to the crooked eye is innocence. It was always there, before your ambition and your sorrow, before every attempted essay upon the world, and every strife of war. You'd miss it, not looking, blind, weeping, grasping; you'd never see the fierce mild; it seems like wrath in mother's milk, but it's not. It's the spirit, the surprise of life. Holy, holy, holy.

The cottage

The light on that island was milky, with an incandescence that melted from a hint of lapis lazuli to amber and soft ivory. A quiet tranquility appeared immune to the vicissitudes of weather. Lush green turf, pristine, grew right up to the single stone cottage with no indication of a footpath. The cottage was a simple square, windowless, with a high thatched roof of long reeds and a door of rustic timber.

When Joss knocked upon the door, a woman's voice with a musical lilt and the slightest touch of laughter beckoned them to enter. Her straight back was to them, attending the fire, so that when she turned, Joss was startled by the thick veil that covered her face.

"Welcome," she said, pulling out a cane rocking chair for Joss to rest his weary bones.

"I see you have a wee old one with you," she added with a sharp, spry tone that caused the burden to grimace. It put as much distance as it could between itself and the woman without coming close to the fire.

"It's peculiar how the nose and the ears keep growing with the years, whilst everything else shrinks," observed Joss.

"Wait long enough, and you'll have a miniature elephant," said the woman.

The amen

The island mother fixed a small bowl of porridge for the shadow child and poured a little islet of maple syrup onto its surface, saying, "I see that the bairn clutches to the nether pendant. It is his stubborn 'no' of which he is so proud."

"I cannot make him take it off," said Joss. "I fear he is such a fragile tissue, and it has grown so embedded. To pull it from him would surely cause what small coherence he possesses to fall apart."

"That is not so," said the veiled woman. "He mistakes that foolishness for brave show."

She turned then to the shadow, and golden eyes blazed through the gauze of her veil. "The most courageous decision was also the most humble, the most attentive, the least remarked; it is the very heart of human time. All things prepared for that moment, and all creatures flow from it. Everything else is a lie."

"What is this decision?" asked Joss, almost breathless.

"Why, all creatures awaited and yearned for that moment. It is the decisive instant when humanity chose the cross of God's love. It was the Virgin who did it, saying 'yes, yes, always yes.' It is the amen on the lips of mankind."

The wee one's lament

I tell you we were lucky to escape that witch who so easily beguiled the great lummox. I says to him, "why does she wear that veil? Does she think she is a bride on her wedding night?" Even the dim can guess she is a horror behind that thick curtain wound like a shroud. I would leave this monumental brute but for pity that he is an imbecile the only sort the girl could find to do her bidding yes I know this catastrophe is her little try at revenge though nothing will come of it I have the secret no they will not beguile me I see through them only it was so quiet, so quiet, nearly peaceful in the dark except they are never leaving us alone they pry the nagging kind it's what comes of trying to help a woman I was always soft that way.

The land cries out

And whose image marks the coin? Render unto Caesar the things that are Caesar's.

Know ye not that the idol is scrupulous to attain fair value? That it is the privilege of the moneychanger to approve equity, this much death to atone for such and such grave offense. An image to barter, to negotiate and to set value — *that* is what the dead take for wise. It cannot bring justice, for it knows nothing of life.

And Iscariot despaired, throwing down the silver coins of betrayal. He hung himself in Akel Dama, the field of Blood. The rebel son burst, his innards sinking into the ground. Abel cries out from the land, and so, indeed, does Judas.

And this, too: Joss began to labor. Though the child shadow remained as it was, something so insubstantial one could almost be prepared to forget it, the further they progressed, the more undeniable it became. Irony provocative and acute skewered his tendons and muscles with searing pain. Mockery grew with each step, so that Joss was first astonished, and then thrust to the edge of desperation at the immense weight of the miserable infant.

The discomfort of the archons

The archons watched carefully. Something stirred in their faux, ever greedy, ersatz bellies; a desperation came upon them remarkably like an ague. They knew, as their populace did not, that in the midst of this obscurity, at this odd time, in the reign of the stolid Tiberius, that brutal and dutiful soldier, in the Syrian Provence, in that desert city of irritating priests and barbarian nomads, those who thought every image an idol, something stirred, a tug upon an invisible line that said, "Now." The Beginning was not then, in the putative past, but Now, Now, Now —

The apocalyptic mode

So, the literal is what they think of as the real. Anything else is something imposed, something subjective, by which they intend an illusion. Only it isn't so simple. The literal is not mere matter or the momentum of the dead past or anything at all apart from spirit, for the flesh is the register of being where meaning shows itself.

And then, those many dimensions vaguely alluded to by categories allegorical, anagogic, and so on, ranging from the felt interior of the proposed self to the edge of the cosmos, well, they are also implied by the literal, and thus not contradictory or smuggled in against the protests of reasonable intellect.

When the Anointed One carried the Cross, it was indeed a burden of torturous wood. It was a device to torture, to raise up in ridicule and ignominy to crown a public, humiliating death, yet it was also everything embraced in the rich woven symbolic suggestiveness, such as the manner in which the temporal stretches horizontally from the still living past into the original future, and vertically from an eternal song taken up by the angelic chorus and echoed in time's musical, counting response.

The apocalyptic mode is the proper translation, whereby ordinary historical time is suddenly apprehended and pressed into service, just as Simon the Cyrene was asked to bear the Cross. The typically hyperbolic imagery that results suggests something of its bizarre quality, whereby one must negotiate a temporal being in the world that cannot be contained by the world. Prosaic certitudes emerge as genuine fantasy, the dim prisons of what William Blake termed "mind-forg'd manacles."

Calix sanguine

The binding of the Christ is never passive, neither the constraints of the powers of empire, nor the machinations of political priests, but the raising of the Cup. The elevation of the *calix sanguine* initiates from the middle of the story the foundation of all the acts.

Etymology is slippery, almost as flexibly amenable as statistics, nonetheless, *religio* as a binding aptly suggests the same root as the word for ligament, the securing of muscle or organ so that the body might leap and run, plant and harvest, sing the mysterious flourishing that is true liberty. As the vates David Jones explains, "the binding makes possible the freedom." When the soldier's lance pierced the side of the Anointed, water and blood came forth, the last of the wine poured forth.

The thirsty earth burdened with the dead lapped up the offering. After that, there were rumblings. The elixir gave a flash of surprise. The quickening of Sophia, it was said folks woke up in their shrouds. You might write that off as legend and miss the larger implication. Strange sweetness, that sour wine given as the *hallel*: the chalice is the cosmos.

In the Cenacle

In the Cenacle, the arrangement was not at table. It was not the way DaVinci painted it. Folks reclined themselves in such a manner that you could lean back into the bosom of the near companion.

And so, the most ardent of them, the warrior of the heart, the one who in exile would bring forth visions, who would take into his home the Woman, the flesh of the universe, they shared together the secret gnosis — it was not an esoteric message about Mary Magdalene.

The fierce youth of thunder leaned back and rested his head upon the chest of the loyal brother, the solitary king made slave to every mad whim of amok humanity. And all throughout that strange meal, initiatic, comforting darkness that did not comfort, while the others were talking, gossiping, worrying, wondering about Judas, the friend of charity was listening.

You think it was just the usual thing, the muted, regular beat of the cardiac muscle? It was not. While he was listening, the beloved did not heed concerns — his own or, strangely, even those of the Anointed. Something was being enacted; later, he recognized that he was more aware than he imagined. He corrected others' memory, placed the order in a way that illumined events for the Wise.

Yet in the Cenacle, the sheltering breast of Love carried the sound of an eternal ocean. John abandoned himself completely to the vibrations of the primordial music by which all things were summoned from unthinkable nothing to the joy of eternal dawn.

Failure to ask

Parsifal is guilty of not asking the question, which was not only the matter of ritual strangeness at the court of the Fisher-king, but more deeply, the question of woundedness, of pain, and the apparent despair of healing. Earlier, he had thoughtlessly killed Ither, whose playful kindness the youth was too ignorant to recognize. Entangled in immature egotism, Parsifal has left behind the child's effortless, nearly spontaneous cosmic familiarity, which is nonetheless full of wonder and discovery. He is caught in a perhaps unavoidable adolescent narcissism, lacking the wisdom of compassion.

Not yet purged of disordered desires, his spirit fails to rise to a renewed, more reflective awareness of his own nature, which is not separate from relation to other created beings. And something of this narrowness prevented him from entering into his own existence properly, which would have alerted him to the way desire ultimately always aims at generous unity beyond merely individual achievement.

Know that all creation is granted a boon. For each child, each man, each woman, every creature given to death brings forth its radiant night, comes back to the Father bathed in abyssal light. The creature had to give up its memories, gently, and without regret, as the beasts, without tears, even as the tree is felled by the axe, or otherwise, as with most of us. All had to give up their memories — not in order to consign them to oblivion, but so that they might be received back purged of horror, rendered supple, and shared.

Plump fruit of the devious lie

Finite minds cannot grasp how Life can be full and still adventure, still go out into discovery, that there is flourishing act without a trace of potential, and yet event where something that appears like addition occurs. Unaware and deceived, we took the gift and began to try our hand. Unwise and ignorant that being and love are one, we made the false worlds in a mist of death, the monstrous inanity. And the God had to answer for all that. Love had to rid us of the void flowering in our hearts. And that is what we call hell, the facts of our history torn away from the truth of love.

Lady Winterbourne says, "To love a being is to give credit, to be attached to them at least as much for who they will be as for what they are." This is how love is creative, and so judgment is always overcoming death. The vates, Octavio Paz, says "the beloved is . . . both *terra incognita a*nd the house where we were born, what is unknown and what is recognized."

And there was Robinson Peacock, who thought he had nothing to offer. And then he saw her, huddled into herself, abashed and hopeless, and he remembered that moment, it was still alive in his heart. *I have seen past the idols,* he said. I have seen *you,* standing with the child in you looking out, and your face was beautiful. He said this to the wife of Vorhaas.

The madness of the Mobracht

The endless innovation and discovery of love is faith, a dark knowledge. And yet, Arthur's court knew that "devoid of questing, the happy man becomes deadly dull." While Parsifal may appear to have blithely forgotten his beloved in search of adventure, it may be that his action was always a romance, the way of prolonging and deepening love. The Triune is nothing men can measure. The imagination cannot aspire to what can only be revealed, for the trace in creatures is limited to suggestion that pales before the ever greater difference of the Unknown and Incomprehensible.

And yet, perhaps more strangely, it turns out this is not quite true. There is unexpected congruity, the answering thirst of the creature that finds itself somehow fit for amatory delight, capable after all of hearing the message.

And now we must try to explain the consternation of the Mobracht. It is really quite simple. Though theologians have scrunched their brows over Bulgakov, he is not wrong to recognize in the dyadic action of the Logos and the Spirit a nuptial enterprise. The human image of the divine requires the fruitful tension of the sexes. (And incidentally, this means when the sexes are blurred, denied, or treated as mere playthings of our willful ambitions, the whisper of the divine is necessarily lost in the maelstrom of vapid ideology.)

There is an archetypal husband in the king, the richness of the brooding feminine in Spirit. None of this reduces to the concrete image, but the relation is not adventitious. When Ravaisson intuited habit as graced action, as the knowing body that transcends mere reason and intellect isolated from feeling and the art of motion, he found himself overwhelmed by his discovery. He thought that he had discerned the mystery of nature which is a palpable longing for the Good. What he did not guess was that feeling is Sophianic.

What the Wise means is that the Infinite Light of the Father that can only ever be encountered as Invisible Darkness is never for Love a lucid comprehension of detached Intelligence. One is never quite quenched by Thought thinking Itself, as Aristotle imagined. On the contrary, the Father knows himself as a "feeling" for the Infinite Good. Divine gnosis is amatory adventure, play where the truth is never a proposition and always Event.

Prayer is not extrinsic to the Divine nature, for before any thought of creation, eternal Life beckons as Beauty and responds as self-sacrificing Love. The subtle revelation bestows reverent wonder. This begins to be suspected by creatures through the long pedagogy of timely flesh. The angel, too, must risk the courtesy of love, learn its finesse. In short, the gnosis of creative love is inescapably a faithful trust leaping across abysses because it is synonymous with the delightful manner in which the Father comprehends, and the Triune Life reveals.

The aesthetic flesh

Why is it that the human creature is so naked, so lacking in fur, scale, or feathers, so scantily covered in hair that the gloss of luxurious locks fascinates as the crowning glory of some exotic plant? Why is there no rutting season? Man and woman full of desire, always susceptible to appeal. It is excessive, beyond need. Skin is more than a protection. It is an aesthetic flesh.

The infant gurgling at the mother's breast, lover's kiss, limbs pressed, body yearning, lusting to break through the barrier, to enter into the other so that intimacy crosses over. The bitter brine of salt water, the velvet down of peach, sun in morning gentling, in blaze of noon torturous, caress, slap, playful nudge — the membrane between self and world registers difference in the porous borderland.

Before ever there is a notion that you are you, or I am I, elemental feeling, the flesh bathed, the skin held and touched, some ineffable communion without words, these first energies, yes without reflection, before care and perplexity, before the daggers of distrust. It is still thick time before the unraveling, before velocity and thin certitudes, dull, rapid, fading into nothing.

The ones they took for sage, trapped in their own agony, could only see the mark of time as recrimination. Scheming, grasping, and worried, when they saw the wounds of the Anointed, they thought they were there as a means to extort, to rub their noses in it. What was not understood was how, in the new flesh, the wounds do not persist as accusation. For the artist, there is a necessity to what is fitting, but at the opposite end of the spectrum from any sort of blunt coercion, of the loss of freedom.

Glim of recognition

In the ambit of the sun's recent declivity, along the trail of wooded hills covered in soft, purple flowers, the dreams of sea anemone, they made their passage to the Cenacle of Times. Joss and the shadow were feeling music most twined, full of lambent emotion. In the heart of one was yearning; the image of the other was wrought in despair, a weight of hopeless ignominy. And yet the bond of the journey made for spiritual entanglement, as if the desire of one were joined to the anguish of the other.

A dove flew over their heads, swooning low unto the meet and proper place. In the green threshold of that traveler's end, the maiden stood, enchanting Demeter's daughter in the bridal gown of love.

You are where you have always been

Joss could not remember reading about a servant girl. He'd always imagined the disciples alone in the room with the Christ, so it was rather a surprise. She was, indeed, radiant with a purity and beauty you could hardly imagine. Her gown glowed with the blush of a thousand autumn trees. The Grail-bearing maiden led him into the chamber. Her smile gave warmth that touched his entire body.

There wasn't need, perhaps, for introductions, but she seemed to introduce herself all the same. At least, that's how he took it, though what she said was rather not the thing a servant girl would normally say. "I made play in this world of dust, with the sons of Adam for my play-fellows," she said.

As for the other fella, Joss surmised she could not see him. It was hard to tell. He was hiding in the shadows. Or perhaps he was the shadow. It was very, very quiet. But then she said, "So you have come." It was declarative, solemn, and sad.

"Yes," said the shadow.

They were silent together. She watched the sun filter through the small, high windows. A fine dust seemed to float in the solar glance.

"There wasn't any point to it," he said. "I wasn't even there. I don't know where I am."

"You are where you have always been," she said. "Nestled in my Father's hand."

The shadow sighed, as if a great burden had dropped from its umbratile shoulders. It began to look faintly like a child.

"You think, like Cain, that you have ruined yourself, that pain is branded upon your forehead, so that forever and a day you must remember what everyone sees, that you have broken the innocent land with wounds that cannot be healed. You think that once the gift is missed, it cannot be received, that you are a dead letter destined for loneliness."

And as she was speaking, telling the way of it, Joss saw that the Cup bearer was familiar, loveliness lost *and* found. He understood that her words were perhaps meant for the fella he had brought, but mainly, they were meant for him. He had thought the task onerous, and it was, but only so he could learn the lesson that forgiveness is the beginning of vision.

Thus, one comes to know reality. Every one of us — the child that died of disease, the woman that grew old with no one to care, the man who murdered his friend — all are borne into desolation by the Lord of Hosts. He has dispossessed us of our idols that promised us protection from harm. He has carried us through the death that we might receive again the deep down freshness, the love that does not quit.

It was the renewal of their love. *It is seeing her here, now, that I see her for the first time.* Claire blazed like the sun, and his heart cried out, "*She was, she is, she will be!*" And the aroma of sweet bread filled his nostrils.

The We Are

"Are you ready?" she asked.

The creature from the Expanse nodded. It was the best it could do. Its voice was frozen, the tongue cleaving in dryness to the top of its anxious mouth.

"I make myself large," said Claire.

And then she pulled away the pendant. Instantly, it crumbled into dust, it was so much a nothing. Mordred was dead, had never been. All he was, the dust of idols.

"You see?" said Claire. "No need to grieve. Here, at the beginning, all our names restored."

In the Origin, compactly, all dimensions await unfurling. You don't know all that you are. The love of others calls forth tacit dimensions. And so Joss discovered that he was also a gypsy king. Deco stretched and yawned like a child awakening from a long midday nap.

And then we saw the brilliant fire, the unguessed beauties, the gorgeous multi-flamed plenitude, the mysterious us, and we all cried out, "Holy, holy, holy," and the very seraphim trembled.

A different kind of war

David Jones, ruminating upon the matter of Arthur, recalls the sober beauty of Malory, the long twilight in the wake of betrayal, and the wreckage of the Court at Camelot which concludes with the death of four knights who travail to liberate Jerusalem.

No need to decry febrile generations industrious in their scholastic peace eager to castigate, the blithe unifiers of the Inquisition and Crusades. Even secular clerics have their orthodoxy and the history it tells. Consider, however, what god hails in such ready condemnation. It may not bear much scrutiny.

Yet there is beauty discerned in Malory's lapidary dismissal of the heroes. Jones says the war ponies were released from chivalrous effort; they took to the forests, grew shaggy and perhaps magical, touching upon liminal states; that the Company of Arthur, those that remained, retreat into hermetic isolation and from this a lush vigor of asceticism enters into the world; saints bold, uncompromising, imbued with a curious care for the land. The beasts are dear, the wilds are not wild as they might be to city folk.

Jones tells of a meeting amidst the Irish Sea between St. Brendan the navigator "leading a wondrous life on a marine animal" and the Irish abbot, St. Finbar of Cork, returning from pilgrimage to the Tomb of the Apostles by way of the community of St. David's in South Wales. Finbar, the tale says, left upon David's terrestrial horse, which, upon the occasion of need, transformed itself into a seahorse in order to carry the Irish prelate across the waters.

Rather than derision and incredulity, Jones exhibits admiration. "God is wonderful in his masters of illusion, in the transmogrifications, in the heroes who sustain the folk and the land." Continuing the momentum of change, the tragic shadows of Arthur's demise, the end of "the fabulous lord of the world" hidden in the mists of fable bequeaths a different battle — Celtic saints and monks marching into mundane lands to extend frontiers into "the other side of time."

The story I tell

The story I tell, says God, is always prayer. The Anointed did not seek the desert as a form of isolation, a desire to keep things private. The God is utterly open, perfectly vulnerable, the mysterious omnipotence of the unprotected. The distance of relation is the refusal to absorb the other, to marionette them, to predetermine what they will say.

The love that is always patient and kind, the index of flourishing you take from St. Paul as onerous impossibility, a virtue of saints to smugly show up your failures, it isn't an agenda to prove your weakness. It is the way of the God. God knows very well what and who you are. On both accounts, yourself and the God, *you* may be deluded.

And so what may seem like blank indifference or the dull machining of an accidental, impersonal universe where all your pain is a curious byproduct of chance occurrence is actually quite different. Incomprehensible to you is guileless suffering limitless in endurance that puts up with all your errant nonsense, thievery, cursing, self-tormenting failure after failure, sinking into madness and apparently irrecoverable doom marked by the incessant wounding of the beloved.

The sustaining love of the Father, the gift that makes you possible, *that* is the hidden.

Hidden glory

In the old days, on Easter night, the Russian peasants used to carry the blest fire home from Church. The light would scatter and travel in all directions through the darkness, and the desolation of the night would be pierced and dispelled as lamps came on in the windows of the farmhouses one by one. Even so the glory of God sleeps everywhere . . . .

— Thomas Merton, *The New Man*

Humility

God is the tree in the forests that allows itself to die and will not defend itself in front of those with the ax, not wanting to cause them shame. And God is the earth that will allow itself to be deformed by man's tools, but He cries; yes, God cries, but only in front of His closest ones. And a beautiful animal is being beaten to death, but nothing can make God break His silence to the masses and say, 'Stop, please stop, why are you doing this to Me?' How humble is God? Kabir wept when I knew.

— Kabir, *How Humble is God*

The labour of the God

I know nothing deeper in him than love – nay, that there can be anything deeper than love. The being of God is love, therefore creation. I imagine that from all eternity he has been creating. And he saw that it was not good for man to be alone, so has he never been alone himself; — from all eternity the Father has had the Son, and the never-begun existence of that Son I imagine an easy outgoing of the Father's nature; while to make other beings — beings like us, I imagine the labour of a God, an eternal labour.

— George MacDonald, *Unspoken Sermons*, "Life"

Forecourt

You are my guests and my children who come into my temple.
   You are my guests and my children who come into my night.

On the threshold of my temple, on the threshold of my night,
wipe your feet and don't let's mention it again.
— Charles Péguy, *The Mystery of the Holy Innocents*

Friend of God

When they say "friend of God," that is just a way of trying to name an ineffable relation. Aquinas, Ghazali, the secret passion of thousands of poor, apparently simple folk who live out the ordinary mysticism of longing, tears, and hidden ecstasy, whatever they intended, touches upon that which no concept can capture, call it the living eternity.

That is the mystery or the absurdity of the human heart: fallible, finite, prone to strife and misery, yet always, always, even in its unhappiness, nay, precisely in its unhappiness, crying out for the plenitude of the Unbound. And what might that sound like? The anguish of Thérèse of Lisieux in that night of childhood ardor: "Ah! my Jesus, pardon me if I am unreasonable in wishing to express my desires and longings which reach even into infinity . . . To satisfy me I need *all*."

Too many require less, seek to abort the headlong leap into the unknown that is the mystery of yearning. Though do not be tempted to anticipate, as if one could count this all; it is not a sum, not even the whole of everything, "my *little childish* desires" that reach out to that which is "*greater* than the universe." More than thought, thought grown radiant with audacious bliss, it is the prayer of fire.

Gift

And so we came to the sheer face of that cliff; there was no way up. All that effort, for what? You can't imagine an answer that isn't there. When you're stuck, you're stuck.

And then there was someone. From here, no one can say for sure who it was, but I have a feeling it might have been a little servant girl, someone from the Near East, a poor, ignorant, dusky girl dressed in dusty clothes, hardly above the rags of beggars, someone like that; her life was drudgery, hardly seemed worth living, there are lots like that.

Though it may have been someone else, say, a retired factory worker, the kind who didn't know what to do with themselves, read mystery novels and puttered about in the basement doing a bit of woodwork, a fella who was angry all the time and didn't know he was depressed; or perhaps it was someone born with handicaps, the kind folks try to ignore, and look away from. Someone forgotten, dispensable.

It was not understood that the divine uniqueness is gifted to every singularity, that even the most obscure has some privileged gnosis, some secret of the Father given to him or her alone. And one of these lost ones, the unloved, remembered something, a seed sewn, waiting for just this, the moment of revelation.

Flight

Even in the groaning, the gift. Sewn amidst tears, it's coming; it's here; it was always here, arriving from the nothing. In the desert, in the silence, the song of the garden.

Then we held our breath in wonder at the divine child born laughing, then we ourselves laughing, putting aside our foibles, our monstrous fables, the lost time that faded into darkness, that was not, for the life spoken is the life sung, our earth and ashes now the shimmer of light, it's dancing across the clouds, everywhere, it's what was yearned for, the blood, the instinct tangled and warped, yet always driven, the thirst for something more.

And the minerals said amen, and the most familiar was sacred, radiated light more splendid than any mundane diamond, though still homely, gentle, approachable, nearly common, still what was known, but filled with glory unknown, speaking a *logoi*, an act unique, for being is always that way, flowing over from an invisible well, telling jokes, and winking at everyone's surprise.

And the wild grass, the flowering trees and the mighty, sentinel woods shook off their slumber. They wove patterns, waltzed ornate, mirthful, entish joy; and creatures of sea and river swam and leapt, from the quicksilver schools to the strange beings that bear their own luminescence, the sun paints them in secret, and the moon says hush; in the abyss, from the gliding rays to the giants of the depths that had waited the long aeons and kept faith, calling in the ancient manner the eerie, enthralling remembrance, the felt amity, the kenotic bonding; and the beasts that had long journeyed with the enigmatic, dangerous, yet nurturing stargazers, the treacherous mystery, the dog and the bovine, the goats and wooly sheep, the laconic camel, the feline majesty, all cried out, "yes, it is here!"

And the wild ones, some despised and reviled for vermin, the poisonous, the repellant, unseen as holy, and the lovely, endowed with strength, speed, and beauty, the gazelle leaping, the lion watchful, the bison thundering, all knew in mute certitude that *this* was what was hoped for, that elusive justice that is not on the map. The whence that calls, why friendship was offered, and the crown was descending, the holy oil was streaming down the beard, the wine was flowing past the chalice brim, the happening, the naming, the endless discovery and delight, the four-fold ineffable, the Father's joy, and the human thing said, "It is good," and the divine papa said, "What shall we do?"

And the human thing looked about and saw yet the seed of history, an awkward, friendly, doomed little bird, the subject of rapine and ridicule, and then there stirred a reverence for the gift, for the sweet offering, for the gift that would not be lost, never, and the dodo waddled, poignant and beautiful, and then, you could almost hear it . . . Flight.

Chapter Seven

Envoi

Rhodion-el and the Man

The wilderness was cool in the morning. The plain was filled with low, oblong rocks, suggesting loaves of bread or perhaps the skulls of many beasts called forth from the abyss. Alone, sitting upon a nest of these stones, built up into a kind of ironic throne, the Man. Come from Dare Wicket or from infinity, time and flesh were such perplexities, the angel pondered the figure before him.

Clearly, the Man was all in. His shoulders slumped, and his head stared forward, almost scowling. He was weary, yet defiant. A pale ghost of a fire seemed to catch in his eyes. As Rhodion-el approached, he began to wonder what he would say. He was not exactly shy or embarrassed, but a tinge of diffidence crept into him like a stealthy creature at the approach of dawn, seeking its abode in the darkening earth.

And then he was upon the Man and the words came, almost unbidden, with a twist of teasing he had not intended or expected from his mouth. "So, Man, you have wrestled with the Nothing. You have kept your Court with the Wild. You have kept counsel with the Mystery of the Flesh."

To this, the Man said not a word. He looked at Rhodion-el with blank exhaustion. The angel was full of awe. This was a new thing, something unexpected. Of course, to discover the unfathomable was part of an angel's function. Rhodion-el knew the Unfolding, an Unveiling, well, the angels had many names for it; still, this was really new.

He was dumbfounded. All at once, a wave of tenderness washed over him. He at first thought it was pity for the Man. Then he realized it was coming from the solitary figure in the desert. His own heart echoed with the great passion of the human heart. It was a fierce, thirsty tenderness — so fierce in its intense refusal to be brooked. No creature stood outside this love. All were welcomed into Life, raised into love by the Divine Blood, the Holy Spirit.

He was afraid of this tenderness. He wanted to flee from it. "Do you know this place?" he asked at last. He did not know how long he had been silent. Then the Man smiled, the most innocent, fresh, pure smile. A child's smile. "What is this place?" asked the angel.

The Man answered, his voice hoarse and dry: *Care. Time. Sorrow. Earth.*

The Hallow Ways

First, there was the rush of waters, it was velocity, the sound of it, you were not part of it, but near, and then a kind of jump, into silence, no, music, sweet, heartrending, a violin crying, and then you were back, only now part of it, the surge of waves, rolling upon the endless vastness of ocean, a world of ocean, roaming yet with a sense of unison, Poseidon's horses, and then another leap or perhaps descending, the waters falling headlong over the unseen precipice, and there are people about, hushed chatter, a priest at your shoulder, no higher, above one, you are kneeling, from behind you hear him praying, and your head is bent, the paid Frenchman raises the beheading blade, and swoosh, you are swinging from limb to limb in the Zanzibar palm, laughing with the other children, the sun is glinting, it's cold and windy, the Nazis have carried off the priest, already he is roaming with the dead, the suitcase with his life's work, typed, amended by hand, crossed out, decades of ascent towards the joyful mystery, lies in a ditch, the pages scattered beyond recall, one of them drifts into a misty bog, and the young man hears the echo of unread words, softly they imprint his spirit, a word of compassion, he brings the butcher's slops in that part of the city where the hyenas gather to wait like pleading dogs, and you turn the corner to slowly mount the spiraling stairs, at the top, the maestro is putting music to vespers, he is saying that the wounds of the Savior are the open do orways, then asks if you remembered the donuts.

I stumbled when I saw

The Elder leaned back into the tall, richly brocaded chair that clearly longed for the palace it had once adorned — or perhaps, was still adorning. He sighed for the weariness in his bones, but also rejoiced. Sky watched him in happy silence. He returned her admiration with an expression of bemused irony. "I stumbled, when I saw." And to her understandable confusion, he added, "Gloucester in Lear. He only learns vision when he is blind. Milton, Tiresias, some of us are like that."

Sky dawdled, playing with the things on the Elder's mantle, searching for their knowing winks, for the voices few seemed to hear. There was a long, brightly colored ribbon of paper, though there was no need to decipher its message. It was written in a clear, flowing hand. *"Between silence and speech, my love for you."*

And then there was a sculpted miniature she had often wished to question. It was a thin, raggedy knight astride a thin shadow of a horse. "And who is this?" she asked, holding it playfully in her hand, but her heart was suddenly beating wildly.

After a pause, he answered, "That, Claire Bright, is the fool, Henry Ellwood."

Bread

That morning, Mrs. Wherryweather was ripe in her emotions. She felt the long history of her sorrows and the strange, unaccountable joy that had begun to rise in her breast. The little satin sack suddenly would not wait. "Now," it said.

Had she been a poet, she would have written a stab of lyric to voice the strange gift she had borne. Not being such an artist, she gathered together yeast and flour and herbs. She kneaded, and she sang, and she baked the mystery of bread. It was a good bread, sweet and dark, redolent with a tang of the mountains and the whispers of men and beast. A wave of euphoria washed over Mrs. Wherryweather, followed by sobbing. She was glad there was no one there to see her.

She looked about at her kitchen, at the honest wooden table, and at the earthenware, glazed and blazoned with the colors of the rainbow. The chairs were empty. There should be somebody to enjoy the bread. It was wrong that no one should taste its goodness. The twins were nowhere in sight. The dog was not interested.

"What should I do, Jewels?"

Then it came to her. She would break the bread and offer a parcel to that great fellow in the pond. Solomon would be waiting. Like a child, she rushed out to the bridge, and stopped short. Julian rushed on ahead, barking with glee. There, on the bridge, a lanky, flaxen-haired figure with a long coat stood leaning out over the water, doubtless talking to the king.

Mrs. Wherryweather began to cry. The young man on the bridge turned to her then. "Hi, mum," said Joss. "I'm home."

By way of explanation

"In the sight of God," said the Lady Julian, "all man is one man and one man is all."

As one can guess, this is all a deep, interior process. As Nick Cave suggests, "Your imagination, it seems to me, is mostly an accidental dance between collected memory and influence, and is not intrinsic to you, rather it is a construction that awaits spiritual ignition." So there is no private property involved; we all plumb the common depths. Yet insight is personal, the inflection point of spirit. And here, if it's any good, one finds the unexpected, discovers what could not be planned or known beforehand.

To a nihilist, every attempt to discover meaning rather than imposing it on neutral brute facts is akin to a crazy conspiracy theorist making illusory connections and finding unjustified coherence. Much of the contempt is driven by a failure to understand the robust nature of causality. What is needed is recognition of forgiveness as the fruit of vatic imagination. The vibrancy of fiction is eschatological — the gleam in the Father's eye from which the vates proclaim true destiny.

And thus, none of this should be taken as a kind of preordained, rigid allegory. I forgot all about the four rivers and the dance of the compass, whilst listening for the story. It was afterwards; only after the actions of the characters had revealed something of their hidden mystery did I go back to discern what living gold might be found.

The mercy seat

Tragedy is exile. Some think that the most profound lives are necessarily sad. Yet joy is by far the graver vision, bliss the holiest profundity. Lady Winterbourne was strolling along the beach, and the Elder knew his love. The closer she came, the more he saw the beautiful one in all her many dimensions. When she approached near enough for the kiss of breath, Soren said, "I am the stone."

Then Rachel Moon laughed and, lifting up a glistening conch that sang the song of dreams, sprinkled him with water, saying, "And I am the shell."

Acknowledgments and Quotation References

Acknowledgments

Many moons ago, this story began as a rambling, ambitious, and quite naive attempt at a screenplay provoked by the insistence of my friend, Wayne Bryant. Years later, Wayne gifted me a printout of our mutual efforts, which has long since disappeared amidst the inevitable losses incurred as a result of various moves. Before the new millennium, my pal had entered into the mystery of that journey that awaits us all. I like to think there is a perfected library in the eschaton where this story may greet him in some form as the strange flower of that original seed.

There is a twenty page bibliography that could gesture after the many sources that contributed to this tale, which grew according to its own providential rhythms over the course of decades. Some are mentioned explicitly in the reference notes. One's dear are personal, and yet to begin a recital risks the failure to mention someone. The beloved know who they are. I would mention a work of scholarship encountered first as a dissertation somewhat late in the process of writing this narrative. Richard J. Barry's *Jewish Temple Theology and the Mystery of the Cross: Atonement and the Two Goats of Yom Kippur* is a work of insight and care I am happy to recall here.

Quotation References

p. 6: Job 28: 9 – 11 NKJV cited in Sworder, Roger. Mining Metallurgy and the Meaning of Life: A Book of Stories. San Rafael, CA: Sophia Perennis, 2008.

p. 50: The lyric passage is original for the most part, however, the end line "my blood and yours, the tide that beats below the skin" is a quote from "Posidonius and the Druid" by Rowan Williams found in Williams, Rowan. The Poems of Rowan Williams. Oxford: The Perpetua Press, 2002.

p. 55: The Elder's reply line about the star-gazing planet is a quote from "Sobieski's Shield" by Geoffrey Hill found in Hill, Geoffrey. Broken Hierarchies: Poems 1952 – 2012. Ed. Kenneth Haynes. Oxford: Oxford Univ. Press, 2013.

p. 73: The lines between Mar Isaac and the Mobracht about despair are quoted from Isaac of Nineveh.The Ascetical Homilies of Saint Isaac the Syrian, Rev. 2nd edition. Trans. The Holy

Transfiguration Monastery. Boston, MA: Holy Transfiguration Monastery, 2011.

p. 78: The line about the region of tears, as well as the one about the birth of the spiritual infant, are from the same source. Ibid.

pp. 84 – 85: The various disquisitions on light and the epistemology of angels and demons also are quotations taken from The Ascetical Homilies. Ibid.

p. 99: Song of Songs 6: 1- 2 is from Falk, Marcia. The Song of Songs: A New Translation and Interpretation. San Francisco:HarperSanFrancisco, 1990.

p. 100: The quotes from Song of Songs 4:1, 5 are from The Jerusalem Bible. Garden City, New York: Doubleday & Company, Inc., 1966.

p. 106: The few brief Latin quotes are from St. Anselm's Proslogion. They are discovered along with intriguing discussion that informs the story in Borella, Jean. The Crisis of Religious Symbolism and Symbolism & Reality. Trans. G. John Champoux. Kettering, OH: Angelico Press, 2016.

pp. 107 – 108 : "I know how to take him" poetic lines from Péguy,Charles. The Mystery of the Holy Innocents and Other Poems. Trans. PansyPakenham. Eugene, Oregon: Wipf & Stock, 2017. 108: The story about St. Seraphim and the quoted last sentence are from Florensky, Pavel. The Pillar and Ground of the Truth: An Essay in Orthodox Theodicy in Twelve Letters. Trans. Boris Jakim. Princeton: Princeton Univ. Press, 1997.

p. 112 The Bachelard quote contains an embedded quote from Valery. Both are found in Bachelard, Gaston. Air and Dreams: An

Essay On the Imagination of Movement. Trans. Edith R. Farrell and C. Frederick Farrell. Dallas: The Dallas Institute Publications, 1988.

p. 115: The Péguy quote as indicated in Péguy, Charles. Temporal and Eternal. Trans. Alexander Dru. Indianapolis, IN: Liberty Fund, 2001.

p. 126 - 27: The George Steiner quotes are from Steiner, George. The Poetry of Thought: From Hellenism to Celan. New York: New Directions Publishing Corp., 2011.

p. 133: The quote from Evagrius of Pontus is from Clément, Olivier. The Roots of Christian Mysticism: Text and commentary. Trans. Theodore Berkeley and Jeremy Hummerstone. Hyde Park, NY: New City Press, 1995.

p. 137 - 138: The Péguy quote is from Péguy, Charles. Notes on Bergson and Descartes. Trans. Bruce K. Ward. Eugene, Oregon: Cascade Books, 2019.

pp. 172 – 173: Quotation is from Hillesum, Etty. An Interrupted Life and Letters from Westerbork. Trans. Arnold J. Pomerans. New York: Henry Holt and Company, 1996.

p. 176: The lines about Thérèse are from "Gwen John in Paris" by Rowan Williams in Williams, Rowan. The Poems of Rowan Williams. Oxford: The Perpetua Press, 2002.

p. 189: Strayed from among the nine and ninety Aurignacian beatiis quote is from Jones, David. David Jones's The Grail Mass and Other Works. Ed. Thomas Goldpaugh and Jamie Callison. London: Bloomsbury Academic, 2019.

p. 200: The R. A. Lafferty quote as indicated is from Lafferty, R .A. Arrive at Easterwine: the Autobiography of a Kristec Machine. New York: Ballantine Books, 1971.

p. 200 - 201: The Czeslaw Milosz essay quote is from Milosz, Czeslaw. To Begin Where I Am: Selected Essays. Ed. Bogdana Carpenter and Madeline G. Levine. New York: Farrar Straus Giroux, 2001.

p. 208: The lines beginning with the address "Human creature" are from Hildegard of Bingen.Selected Writings. Trans. Mark Atherton. London: Penguin Books, 2001.

p. 212: The lines about listening in fear and wonder and the fate of others following us into our dreams are by Eugen Rosenstock-Huessy (exact source unknown.)

p. 226: The quote is from Rosenstock-Huessy, Eugen. The Fruit of Lips or Why Four Gospels. Ed. Marion Davis Battles.Eugene, Oregon: Pickwick Publications, 1978.

pp. 234 - 235: Song of Songs 8: 6- 7 quote is from the Marcia Falk translation. Ibid.

p. 240: Lamentations 3: 7 – 9 quote is from The Jerusalem Bible. Ibid.

p. 242: The quote from the Ramayana is from Egenes, Linda and Kumuda Reddy. The Ramayana: A New Retelling of Valmiki's Ancient Epic – Complete and Comprehensive. New York: TarcherPerigree, 2016.

p. 242: The Bulgakov quote is from Bulgakov, Sergius. The Lamb of God. Trans. Boris Jakim. Grand Rapids, MI: William B. Eerdmans Publishing Co, 2008.

p. 242 – 243: The Péguy quote is from Péguy, Charles. The Mystery of the Charity of Joan of Arc. Trans. Julian Green. Providence, R.I.: Cluny Media, 2019.

p. 248: Psalms 17: 10 -12, 17 translation from the Latin Vulgate comes from Merton, Thomas. The New Man. New York: Farrar Straus Giroux, 1986.

p. 248: The Rumi quote is from Rumi. Thief of Sleep: 180 Quatrains from the Persian. Trans. Shahram Shiva. Prescott, AZ: Hohm Press, 2000.

pp. 249: The Jean-Louis Chretien quote which also provides the quotes from Kierkegaard is from Chrétien, Jean-Louis. The Unforgettable and the Unhoped For. Trans. Jeffrey Bloechl. New York: Fordham University Press, 2002.

p. 250: The quote from Pseudo-Dionysius is from Pseudo-Dionysius.The Complete Works. Trans. Colm Luibheid. New York: Paulist Press, 1987.

p. 282: The quote is from the Latin Mass.

p. 282: "I know how to take him" poetic lines from Péguy,Charles. The Mystery of the Holy Innocents and Other Poems. Trans. PansyPakenham. Eugene, Oregon: Wipf & Stock, 2017.

pp. 283: Verses are from "The Wild Horse is Broken" in Lewis, Gwyneth and Rowan Williams. The Book of Taliesin: Poems of Warfare and Praise in Enchanted Britain. Trans. Gwyneth Lewis and Rowan Williams. UK: Penguin Classics, 2020.

p. 309: David Jones quote is from Jones, David. Epoch and Artist. London: Faber & Faber, 1959.

p. 312: The Lady Winterbourne quote is from Marcel, Gabriel. Music and Philosophy. Trans. Stephen Maddux and Robert E. Wood. Milwaukee: Marquette University Press, 2005.

p. 312: The Octavio Paz quote is from Paz, Octavio. The Double Flame: Love and Eroticism. Trans. Helen Lane. New York: Harcourt, Inc., 1995.

p. 320: The David Jones lines are from Epoch and Artist. Ibid.

p. 321: Thomas Merton quote is from The New Man. Ibid.

p. 322: Kabir quote is from Ladinsky, Daniel. Love Poems from God: Twelve Sacred Voices from the East and West. New York: Penguin Books, 2002.

p. 322: Quote is from MacDonald, George. Unspoken Sermons: First, Second, and Third Series. Whitehorn, CA: Johannesen, 1997.

p. 322 - 323: Verse quoted is from Péguy, Charles. The Mystery of the Holy Innocents and Other Poems. Trans. Pansy Pakenham. Eugene, Oregon: Wipf & Stock, 2017.

p. 323: Thérèse of Lisieux quote is from Thérèse of Lisieux. The Story of a Soul: The Autobiography of St. Therese of Lisieux. Ed. Mother Agnes of Jesus. Trans. Michael Day. Charlotte, NC: TAN Books, 2010.

p. 332: The quote from Lady Julian is from Williams, Charles. The Forgiveness of Sins. Grand Rapids, MI: William B. Eerdmans Publishing Co., 1984.

p. 332: The Nick Cave quote is cited in Popova, Maria. "Nick Cave on Creativity, the Myth of Originality, and How to Find

Your Voice." The Marginalian. 20 January 2022, https://www.the marginalian.org/2022/01/20/nick-cave-creativity/.

The Labyrinth of Dreams Quartet
by Brian Christopher Moore

Wonder Stories for the Fierce and Childlike

City in Exile

Arcana of the Twisted Diadem

The Hallow Ways

Available in paperback, hardcover, and Kindle editions from Amazon

Follow Brian's blog "Christ the Symphonic Adventure" at http://bcmoore2.substack.com/

Brian's novel *Beneath the Silent Heavens* –a reimagining of the story of the Flood and the Ark—is available in paperback and hardcover from Amazon.

www.ingramcontent.com/pod-product-compliance
Lightning Source LLC
Chambersburg PA
CBHW051329250626
47155CB00007B/2512